Protecting NICOLE

USA TODAY BESTSELLING AUTHOR
SHANDI BOYES

PROTECTING NICOLE
A BODYGUARD/POP STAR ROMANCE

SHANDI BOYES

COPYRIGHT

Copyright © 2023 by Shandi Boyes

All rights reserved.

No part of this book may be reproduced in any form or by any electronic or mechanical means, including information storage and retrieval systems, without written permission from the author, except for the use of brief quotations in a book review.

Editor: Crossbones Editing

Editor: Courtney Umphress

Proofreading: Lindsi La Bar

Cover Design: SSB Covers & Design

Photographer: Cadwallader Photography

DEDICATION

*To all the readers who remember Nicole from the Saving Noah days.
You guys rock!*

WANT TO STAY IN TOUCH?

Facebook: facebook.com/authorshandi
Instagram: instagram.com/authorshandi
Email: authorshandi@gmail.com
Reader's Group: bit.ly/ShandiBookBabes
Website: authorshandi.com
Newsletter: https://www.subscribepage.com/AuthorShandi

ALSO BY SHANDI BOYES

* Denotes Standalone Books

Perception Series

Saving Noah *

Fighting Jacob*

Taming Nick*

Redeeming Slater*

Saving Emily

Wrapped Up with Rise Up

Protecting Nicole *

Enigma

Enigma

Unraveling an Enigma

Enigma The Mystery Unmasked

Enigma: The Final Chapter

Beneath The Secrets

Beneath The Sheets

Spy Thy Neighbor *

The Opposite Effect *

I Married a Mob Boss *

Second Shot *

The Way We Are

The Way We Were

Sugar and Spice *

Lady In Waiting

Man in Queue

Couple on Hold

Enigma: The Wedding

Silent Vigilante

Hushed Guardian

Quiet Protector

Enigma: An Isaac Retelling

Twisted Lies *

Bound Series

Chains

Links

Bound

Restrain

The Misfits *

Nanny Dispute *

Russian Mob Chronicles

Nikolai: A Mafia Prince Romance

Nikolai: Taking Back What's Mine

Nikolai: What's Left of Me

Nikolai: Mine to Protect

Asher: My Russian Revenge *

Nikolai: Through the Devil's Eyes

Trey *

The Italian Cartel

Dimitri

Roxanne

Reign

Mafia Ties (Novella)

Maddox

Demi

Ox

Rocco *

Clover *

Smith *

RomCom Standalones

Just Playin' *

Ain't Happenin' *

The Drop Zone *

Very Unlikely *

False Start *

Short Stories - Newsletter Downloads

Christmas Trio *

Falling For A Stranger *

One Night Only Series

Hotshot Boss *

Hotshot Neighbor *

The Bobrov Bratva Series

Wicked Intentions *

Sinful Intentions *

Devious Intentions *

Deadly Intentions *

Coming Soon

Maksim Ivanov

CONTENTS

1.
- **LAKEN** 1
- **NICOLE** 8
- **LAKEN** 14
- **NICOLE** 26
- **NICOLE** 32
- **LAKEN** 49
- **NICOLE** 54
- **NICOLE** 62
- **LAKEN** 71
- **NICOLE** 87
- **LAKEN** 97
- **NICOLE** 104
- **LAKEN** 109
- **NICOLE** 116
- **LAKEN** 122
- **NICOLE** 127
- **LAKEN** 131
- **NICOLE** 138
- **LAKEN** 146
- **NICOLE** 159
- **LAKEN** 170
- **NICOLE** 173
- **NICOLE** 185
- **LAKEN** 196
- **NICOLE** 204
- **LAKEN** 209
- **NICOLE** 217
- **LAKEN** 221
- **LAKEN** 235
- **NICOLE** 243
- **NICOLE** 252
- **LAKEN** 259
- **NICOLE** 265
- **LAKEN** 271
- **NICOLE** 274

EPILOGUE 283
ALSO BY SHANDI BOYES 290

2.
3.
4.
5.
6.
7.
8.
9.
10.
11.
12.
13.
14.
15.
16.
17.
18.
19.
20.
21.
22.
23.
24.
25.
26.
27.
28.
29.
30.
31.
32.
33.
34.
35.

1
LAKEN

"Sign here."

A clear plastic zip-pressed bag slides to the side of the counter before a pen follows its fumble. Inside the bag are possessions I haven't seen for over nine years. A watch with a sentimental worth that will forever exceed its value, a money clip with a few crinkled bills, and a wallet that appears flatter than it did years ago.

I discover why when the officer preparing me for release says, "Your driver's license expired during incarceration, so they will organize a new one through the BOP system."

"BOP?" I ask, a little overwhelmed.

My release from federal prison is occurring as swiftly as my incarceration. The past month has been a blur of release prep meetings, two in-depth parole hearings, and multiple one-on-one prayer sessions with the prison chaplain.

I'm not a preaching man. I was merely willing to do *anything* necessary for a reduced sentence. Three years might not seem like much to the average man, but to me, it is more than I could have hoped for.

Not looking up, the officer replies, "Board of parole. You have a meeting with your parole officer tomorrow morning. Details are in here." He slides a second baggie across the counter dividing us. It is thicker than the first and full of paperwork. "If you don't want to return here by the p.m., don't be late for your first check-in." Finally, he looks up. "I don't want to see you back here."

Nothing but honesty rings true in my tone when I gabber out, "I have no interest in returning."

He *pffts* me like he hears that line every day, before nudging his salt-and-pepper afro to my release form that states what items were in my possession when I handed myself in to authorities. "Unless something is missing, you're free to go once that's signed."

"It all appears in order," I mumble, more to myself than the prison officer with "Riley" marked on his uniform.

After scribbling my name across the slip I've been working toward for the past nine years, I stuff my wallet into the back pocket of my jeans and my bill clip in the front before securing my watch on my wrist. Its fit is as snug as my jeans since I've spent almost a decade working out and have gained significant muscle in my calves and thighs.

I had nothing else to occupy my time, so I kept my head as low as my percentage of body fat. Being incarcerated with mass murderers, rapists, pedophiles, and drug lords meant even if I didn't want to play the part of a criminal, I had to look it, or I would have left prison in a body bag instead of the ride arranged by the parole office board when they granted my early release.

"Eleven a.m., Howell," Officer Riley reminds me in a snide tone as I make my way to the double exit doors. "Don't be late."

"I won't."

Hot, sticky heat hits me in the face when I push through the paned glass doors. Summer ended a few weeks back, but Florida never seems to get the memo.

After relishing the warmth of the late afternoon sun on my face, I drop my chin and scan the guarded grounds. The officers walking the jail's external walls are armed like the ones manning the yard from above, but since I'm wearing jeans and a ripped white T-shirt instead of a federally issued jumpsuit, they don't pay me any attention.

Well, that is until my name is shouted across the grounds in an egotistical jock-running-onto-the-field way.

"Laaaa-keeen Hooowwwelll."

Even with a low-hanging cap hiding his eyes, and his stubble the thickest I've seen it, there's no mistaking the face of the man catcalling my name. His visits were sporadic over the past twelve months, and his care packages nonexistent six months prior, but before a possibility of early probation was sniffed at, his visits were bi-monthly.

Noting the surprise on my face, Knox slaps his hand into mine before using his sweaty grip to pull me in for a man hug. "Did you seriously think I'd let the parole board reintroduce you to society?" With his free hand, he whacks my back until the nerves in my stomach rattle free. "How the fuck have you been, Laken? Feels like forever since we've caught up."

As I inch back, my brows furrow while I stray my eyes to the massive brick-and-steel establishment next to us. It stands out like Captain Fucking Obvious.

"Oh shit, man. My bad." Knox barks out with a breathy chuckle. He glues his hip to mine, his arm not dropping from my shoulders. "I figured it was best to stay away while they were discussing early parole." He scrubs under his nose with his free hand, the diamond-encrusted family crest ring on his pinkie finger dancing in the low-hanging sun. "I'm not the best character witness."

He isn't lying. He was removed from the courtroom twice during my hearing and found in contempt three times. My lawyer believes he was the catalyst of my harsh sentencing. Pleading no contest to the charges brought against me when I handed myself in should have seen me serving an eighteen-month sentence with the possibility of parole in six months.

I received twelve years with no stipulation of an early release.

"But you'll forgive me when you see what I've got up my sleeve." When we reach a blacked-out top-of-the-line SUV, Knox's arm drops from my shoulders before he grips the back passenger door handle so hard his knuckles go deathly white.

His pause to build the suspense is nothing out of the ordinary. He was the captain of our high school's football, basketball, and lacrosse teams because if there was a chance it would secure him attention, he demanded a front-row seat.

When we met, we were the equivalent of chalk and cheese, but since Knox refused to let his family's wealth and stature wedge a gap between us, we became joined at the hip. We've been friends since the sixth grade and have each other's backs no matter what.

The past nine years of hell have been a testament to this.

My heart rate kicks up when Knox grins before announcing, "He refused to get a haircut, but no amount of unkempt locks can taint the Howell genes."

Aware he has me on tenterhooks, he kicks at my tennis-shoe-covered foot with his designer polished black boot before pulling open the tinted door of his pricy ride with dramatic flair.

When River's eyes jerk up from the tablet playing a current episode of *Love Connection*, his pupils widen before his mouth gapes.

"Laken?" he queries, like I've aged a hundred years in the past nine, so he no longer recognizes me.

My reasoning is plausible. I didn't want him to see me in a prison jumpsuit while surrounded by men who'd yell at him if he attempted to hug me, so I asked Knox to tell him I was housed in an interstate prison that didn't allow visitors.

River has an affectionate soul, and he refuses to contemplate anyone's dislike of hugging. If denied the possibility of greeting me with a hug, he would have a meltdown, so I did what was needed to ensure his happiness wasn't impacted by my decision to plead guilty.

"Laken," River murmurs again when the hint of an orange tinge in my cropped beard and the fond twinkle in my eye can't be denied.

After tossing his tablet onto the seat next to him and clambering out of the car the best he can without crinkling his freshly pressed suit, he throws himself into my arms, almost knocking me over.

With an extra chromosome hindering his physical growth, his head slots below my chin, but there's a lot of oomph to his tiny stature.

He was of average weight and length at birth but fell behind his peers during his schooling years. His short stature has never affected his attitude, though. He's been a menace to society since he was born, and although his care is technically still under our mother's guardianship, he's been on my watch full time since I was eleven.

Our mother was only nineteen when she had River. She was already struggling to make ends meet with two children under four, but River's Down syndrome diagnosis was the straw that broke the camel's back.

She couldn't afford to take him to the specialists who'd help him reach the milestones in development and growth, let alone purchase the formula needed for a baby with severe colic, so her care disintegrated quickly during his first two years of life.

The more our mother stepped back from the role of parent in the four years following, the more responsibility I had to take on.

I should resent River since most of my childhood was spent raising him, but he's taught me more about compassion, understanding, and love than our mother ever could have. He is my reason to breathe. Though, at the moment, his body-crushing hug isn't allowing much air to reach my lungs.

"He said we were getting something to eat," River announces in my ear, still grasping me to death. "I should have known he was up to something when he made me wear a suit." He holds on tight for a few more seconds before he eventually lets go so he can issue Knox a death stare that cuts worse than a knife. "I would have agreed to a haircut if you said it was for Laken."

I grin when Knox rolls his eyes before messing up River's almost shoulder-length locks. "The number of lies he's told the past nine years hasn't made him a better liar. He's still the worst."

"Am not," River denies, his tone too high for someone telling the truth. His almond-shaped eyes tilt a little higher when teasing morphs his face. "I told you last week that the girl you brought home was hot, and you believed me." Knox scoffs at him as if insulted before briskly walking around the SUV and sliding into the driver's seat. "She looked like a shovel hit her in the face, and that's coming from someone with flat facial features."

River often uses his diagnosis for joke material. The school psychologist I questioned about it said it's a standard coping mechanism for those with DS, and unless I believe it is causing him mental harm, I shouldn't discourage him from using humor to diffuse a situation.

"You can't exactly pick on someone by using their punchlines against them," the psychologist said.

I wanted to deck him that day, but after watching River take down a schoolyard bully in the exact manner he mentioned only minutes after our appointment, I realized he was right.

The bully had nothing to come back with because River had used all the suitable material. Not even the "don't be mad that the girls want me for the extra chromosome you can't give them" could be retorted.

River also has the Howells' looks and charm. He simply rocks an extra chromosome that saw him gaining as much attention as Knox and me when we attended after-school events.

Sometimes he even stole the limelight.

It pissed Knox off more than it did me. Though he'd never admit that if it would risk him losing the world's best wingman.

River is a lady magnet, even more so when it is announced he was raised by his brother, who is only three and a half years older than him. It has everyone looking at me like I'm a big softie—another reason I denied my little bro's many requests to visit me in prison.

I needed more than a "touch my brother and die" vibe to survive a maximum security penitentiary. I had to become the title my name will forever be associated with.

Murderer.

2
NICOLE

"It's one night. What's the worst thing that could happen?" says Jenni, a daredevil mother of two wrapped in a humble-looking package.

Emily, the more subdued of the duo even with our first meeting occurring while she was so heavily intoxicated she could barely stand, backs her campaign. "And this will be the last time we'll see you in person for weeks."

Since freshman year, I assisted my older sister Petra with a designated driver program that offered safe, alternative rides home to intoxicated partygoers in our hometown. Emily and Jenni were our first clients. They were attending a frat party similar to the one our eldest sister, Colette, attended the week before her eighteenth birthday.

It was the event that saw "Forever seventeen" engraved on her headstone.

I shake off the negative thoughts entering my head when I realize Emily and Jenni are awaiting my reply. They've subdued a lot from the raucous fifteen-year-olds I assisted up the stairs of Jenni's stately family home.

Love does that to you. It can change you in a way you'd never imagine.

It can even alter lyrics.

With Noah, Emily's now husband, writing a majority of Rise Up's—the world-famous band Jenni's husband, Nick, plays lead guitar for—lyrics, they went from a grunge metal group to a pop-rock, indie soul sensation in under two years.

Emily's inclusion in Noah's life immensely improved his songwriting abilities, but that isn't something I can capitalize off as well. I signed with a label not responsible for Rise Up's almost five-year reign at the top of the charts because I don't want to be accused of coattail riding on their success more than I have been.

The task is mammoth since one of their own discovered me.

I've tinkered with songwriting for years, often carrying a notepad with me to jot down compositions that come to me at random times, but I gave no true thought to singing the lyrics until Marcus requested assistance during an impromptu recording session.

Although Rise Up is signed with Destiny Records, Marcus produces most of their albums. He has talent by the bucket loads, and his musical abilities are far more reaching than the bassist position their fans believe is his sole talent.

When he asked me to check the acoustics of a recording studio contractors built in the basement of Emily and Noah's home, I was clueless about what he required. I thought he wanted me to speak the lines on the music sheet before me, so you can picture my shock when he asked me to sing the lyrics instead.

I wanted to die a thousand deaths when the opening of a now chart-topping hit came out super squeaky, but after a handful of encouraging words and a shimmy of my shoulders to loosen up the nerves, the following few lines were more polished.

"I knew it," Marcus murmured that humid summer morning after a handful more lines. "I could feel it in my bones like when I bumped into Noah at a music store." He joined me in the sound booth, his grin brighter than the stage-inspired lights above us. "Why are you hiding such talent?"

"Are we really having this conversation?" I asked, well aware I wasn't the only one keeping secrets.

Marcus and I had met a couple of years earlier. We were the only singles left in the group of friends, so naturally everyone thought we were a match made in heaven.

They couldn't have been more wrong.

Don't misconstrue what I'm saying. Marcus is a great guy who is also incredibly handsome. There's just no spark between us. We were instant friends, but it will never amount to more than that. Marcus knows it, and so do I.

We can talk for hours about everything and anything, though, and it was during one of those conversations Marcus let slip that he is an all-rounder. He encouraged me to consider more than a career as a songwriter by forcing himself to do the same. He co-produced Rise Up's second album while assisting me in creating a demo EP.

Nothing came from his dedication until around a year ago. Somehow, my demo CD landed on the desk of an up-and-coming music executive. He liked what he heard, scheduled an interview, and the rest of the story is my slow and scary claim for fame.

The route wouldn't be as painful if I'd take Marcus up on his numerous offers of a personal introduction with Rise Up's manager, Cormack McGregor, but I'm already slandered in the media for my friendship with Emily, Jenni, and Marcus. I don't need more campaigns smearing my family name.

The paps continually make out it is impossible to be single, happy, and friendly. Almost every article starts with the same headline: "Watch Your Men, Ladies. The Single Friend Is in Town."

Thankfully, Emily and Jenni know the gossip is nothing more than manufactured lies to sell magazines. They encourage my friendship with the Rise Up band members, and although they voice caution about my wish to find my own path to success—since they've seen firsthand the bad side of show business their first two years in the industry—they also understand it.

They've been endeavoring to do the same even while paired with rock star partners. Jenni is making a name for herself in the fashion industry with world-class designs, and Emily is being scouted by agencies across the globe who want her to be the publicist for their superstar clients.

Their knowledge of the entertainment industry has been invaluable over the past five-plus years, but since I don't want my career handed to me via association instead of hard work, I pulled back on public engagements with the band, slapped an alias onto any feelers I sent out, then continued writing songs while finalizing my studies.

With the royalties of a handful of the songs I co-wrote with Noah still earning even now, I can't say I'm a struggling artist, but it will be nice once the endless hours I've put in the past twelve months pay off.

I've been working nonstop on an album due to be released at the end of this month, and the press junket Knox Records organized will squeeze every available minute I have over the next three weeks.

I'm exhausted just thinking about my upcoming schedule, and it has me looking at my bed as if it is four in the morning instead of the afternoon.

"Knox said I should spend the evening resting."

Jenni rolls her eyes before drifting them to me. "Because he can't be here to watch your every move." When my lips twitch, she arches a strawberry-blonde brow. "Don't look at me like that. I've been around enough the past week to notice how possessive he is of you. He gives Isaac a run for his money." Isaac is her brother-in-law who takes her personal security so seriously that even when she isn't clinging to the side of her famous husband, a bodyguard shadows her every move. "And he's the most possessive man I know."

She doesn't seem icked by her statement.

She's more flustered than turned off.

After screwing the end of a lip gloss container into its lid, Jenni spins to face me. "Are you sure he hasn't hinted at wanting more?"

"Who? Isaac?" I couldn't sound more shocked if I tried. I've performed at Isaac's clubs a handful of times while endeavoring to get my stage name out there, but he's never presented as anything more than friendly. He is also head over heels obsessed with his wife, who gains as many admirers as him when they enter a room.

"Not Isaac." An expression I can't quite work out crosses her face. "Knox." She props her hip onto the edge of the vanity mirror she's spent the last hour hogging while Emily and I rummaged through her latest collection of dresses—we get first dibs on her creations before the leftovers are mass marketed for well-known clothing chains—then asks, "His possessiveness screams more ownership than concern for your safety."

I sling my head to Emily when she joins our conversation. "I might have agreed with you if I hadn't overheard his conversation on his way out." She pops a loaded spoon of chocolate ice cream into her mouth before talking around the calories she's gobbling down like she isn't concerned about weight gain. I understand why. Even four months pregnant, she is still waif thin. "He was signing up a new security detail to the label." My mouth gapes more when she announces, "He starts tomorrow."

Upon noticing my shocked expression, Jenni asks, "Did you not know about this?"

"No." When I think back on the many conversations I've had with Knox over the past month, I renege on my lie. "He did mention something about increased security for the upcoming press junket, but I thought he meant at the venues we were attending, not for me personally." I look up at Jenni. "No offense, but I'm not sure how I will handle having a shadow twenty-four-seven."

"It can be a little annoying." Jenni locks eyes with Hawke, her long-term live-in bodyguard, who's standing outside the presidential suite's primary room, looking bored. "Especially if they don't know boundaries." Hawke shrugs, unfazed by her gripe. "But you eventually get used to it." Her smile is teasing. "I sometimes forget he's in the room with us until he whines about needing soap to wash the filth from his eyes."

Hawke tries to hide his laughter, but the jutted movements of his chest give him away.

"Then jealousy comes into play." Hawke's chest stills when Jenni leans in and whispers, "My sex life has never been so good."

Her statement is lost on me until she nudges her head to Hawke standing frozen in the hallway. He is easily six foot three. His shoulders are wider than the doorframe, and although his haircut hasn't strayed from the military-inspired crewcut most recruits don, his face could make any woman's panties combust. Having a guy like Hawke following a man's wife around all day would make any man jealous, so Nick's extra compensation in the bedroom isn't surprising. Hawke is sexy as hell... but also taken.

Even Marcus is moving on from the "single" title we shared when Rise Up's claim to fame commenced. I'm the only one desperate and dateless, and the reminder has me throwing caution to the wind.

"One drink." I hold my finger in the air to amplify my statement. "One."

Silently squealing, Jenni curls her arm around my shoulders and guides me out. "Then I guess we're in luck that it's Friday."

"Punch bowl margarita Fridays at Mavericks!" Emily shouts, following us out like her steps don't already characterize the duck waddle most pregnant ladies get.

3
LAKEN

A wolf whistle sounds from my lips when Knox pulls the SUV under the awning of a fancy hotel in the middle of Ravenshoe. I've spent the last hour of our trip with my mouth unhinged and my eyes bugged. Ravenshoe grew at a mammoth rate before I left one of its distant cousins for a prolonged stint of absence, but this is beyond anything I could have comprehended. The downtown district is ginormous, and almost every street has glass-and-steel structures stretching past the skyline.

"If you think this is impressive, wait until you see the presidential suite." River hugs me like I'm not following him inside before he uses the SUV's wide floorspace to slip out of the now-stationary vehicle before me.

After watching how he tips the valet with a fist bump and a man hug, I join him and Knox in front of the elaborate hotel foyer steps. "I thought we were heading to your place?"

Not looking up from his phone, Knox replies, "This hotel is closer to the airport." When my brows furrow in confusion, he bumps me with his shoulder. "I'll explain everything in the morning." He stores away his phone before replacing it with his wallet. "Until then, how about we get you settled in, showered, and dressed in jeans that don't look like you painted them on?"

Knox comes from old money, so the generosity of his tip to the valet shouldn't shock me. But it does. He's always believed you don't get rich by giving it away, so a hundred-dollar tip for opening the door of the hotel-owned SUV is a little extravagant.

When we enter the elevator that is so spacious, even with us riding with a dozen guests, it doesn't feel cramped, Knox says, "I had planned for you to stay with us in the presidential suite, but I figured you'd prefer your own room." He flashes me a grin before speaking loud enough for the elegantly dressed lady beside me to move away. "After being locked up for almost a decade, the only people you should be sharing a mattress with are A-class hookers."

The disgruntled patron jabs her finger into the elevator open button even with the panel showing she is floors from her desired exit point.

Knox's chuckles fill my ears as she leaves the elevator car in a huff. "What?" he asks when I glare at him. "Her perfume reeked like a low-end hooker, so I thought I'd give her an in with a high-class client."

"She was close to sixty," I scoff out.

"More like eighty," River butts in, his expression humored.

"And?" Knox asks, still laughing, his eyes bouncing between us. "This isn't high school anymore. You've got to do more than let your little bro tag along to pick up the ladies." I'm more annoyed by his statement than River is. He looks pleased until Knox curls his arm around his neck and noogies his head for the second time tonight. "This chick magnet has become a hog. You must have forgotten to teach him how to share."

"Did not." River pushes him off with more oomph than needed before straightening his suit jacket. Once he has himself right, he locks his eyes with the stranger not endeavoring to hide his snooping, and says, "It's the extra chromosome. The chicks dig it. I'd offer you one, but then I wouldn't be more special than the average Joe, and no one wants that."

With the ding of the elevator timed to perfection, he winks at the elderly gent before strolling out of the car with his head held high.

"Your unmanageable ego didn't deflate his in the slightest."

"I told you it wouldn't," Knox agrees while gesturing for me to exit first. "That's why I was the prime pick to look after him while you were away." His words are like a knife to the chest, but he seems oblivious. He's too busy barking out orders like he can't wait to get rid of me. "Your suite is paid for in full. Order anything you want off the room service menu, and this will help with any restlessness you might stumble into later tonight."

Outside a room, he grabs my hand, flips it over, then slaps several hundred-dollar bills into my palm, along with a string of condoms.

After shoving the condoms into my jeans pocket, which is too tight to fit more than one strip of three, I attempt to tell him I can't take his money, but he shuts me up with a promise. "This is just the beginning, Laken." His eyes drop to the bills as River and I enter my room. "There will be plenty more where that came from."

I'm stopped from replying for a second time by his ringing cell phone.

"When?" Knox asks a second after squashing his phone to his ear, not bothering to issue a greeting. "For fuck's sake. I knew leaving her with them was a bad idea."

"Everything okay?" I ask when he scrubs at the back of his neck, a telltale sign he's stressed.

He jerks up his chin before shifting his focus to River, who's checking out the minibar in the suite. "Will you be all right here for a couple of hours?"

"Of course he will be. I'm his fucking brother," I answer on River's behalf.

This isn't the first time I've taken offense to Knox stepping into the role I was born to fulfill.

I doubt it will be the last.

Mistaking the annoyance in my tone as something more, Knox stuffs another three Benjamin Franklins into my pocket housing the condoms before saying, "He was up at ass-crack o'clock this morning, so I doubt he'll make it past ten." An amused twinkle darts through his eyes. "But if you can't hold out that long, the concierge announced the suites on this floor are always available for *professional* house calls."

With a roll of my eyes, I barge him out of my suite while striving not to relish in his laugh. I haven't seen a woman's naked breast for over nine years, but it's been just as long since I've spent one-on-one time with the brother I raised from infancy, so sex is the last thing on my mind.

Well, it would have been if River didn't pike halfway through the second movie on what was meant to be an eight-hour movie marathon. It's barely eight, and I have far too much sugar running through my veins to contemplate sleeping.

My routine has also been structured over the past nine years. Lights out at half past ten. Not an hour before or an hour later.

I couldn't crash now even if I wanted to.

As I scrub a hand over my hair, which is more maintained than River's, I move to the window in the corner of the ample space. My cell was a four-by-four concrete box I shared with an inmate who smelled like stale cigarettes.

This suite is bigger than the rec room at prison. Its window has no bars, so I face no issues peering at the street below.

All walks of life fill the sidewalk at the front of the hotel. They're the size of ants and have no distinguishable features, but not even the high floor count of my stalk grants me access to the stars. They're hindered by the skyscrapers bordering the hotel.

My heart rate increases when I spot the shadow of my building in the glass structure across from me. This building is taller than those surrounding it, meaning its rooftop would be the perfect vantage point to see the stars I haven't stared at in over nine years.

My cell didn't have a window. I was housed in J block, an octagon-shaped windowless structure. The last time I stargazed was the night my life was upended. It's been far too long, but I'm not given the chance to rectify the injustice when a phone on the bedside table commences hollering.

It is loud and obnoxious, on par with the man who tosses a pillow at the noisy contraption before rolling onto his opposite hip with a grumble.

River doesn't budge when the pillow lands on his head for a second before I squash the phone to my ear. He's out cold again.

"Hello…"

I assume my caller is Knox since he is the only person who knows I'm here, so you can picture my shock when a deep elderly voice asks, "Mr. Howell?"

"That's the name I was lumped with at birth."

He waits like he has all day before announcing, "It is James from the concierge. I have a special *package* here for you to collect."

"Oh…" I peer down at my skintight jeans before slinging my eyes to the empty closet at my left. Knox alluded to a new wardrobe, but I only found extra pillows in the closet. "Can someone bring it up?"

"Unfortunately, I am the only concierge undertaking such requests at this time." Suspicion runs rampant when he adds, "I also think it would be best for you to collect the *packages* yourself. I wasn't given much to go off, so I can't be confident in my selections."

Packages? That escalated quickly.

"All right." Don't ask me why I scan the room for the second time. I have no clue what I am seeking. I'm just telling you how it is. "I'll be right down."

James sounds pleased. "Wonderful. See you shortly."

After hanging up, I scribble a note to River to let him know where I am, toss on the only other article of clothing I left prison with—a bulky jacket rarely used in this climate—and then exit my suite with more spring in my step than usual.

I curse my stupidity to hell when I enter the elevator. It only goes one way when you don't scan your key. To the lobby. Since Knox only handed me cash and condoms, I'll have to visit the check-in counter for a key before I can return to my floor.

When I approach the concierge desk, a man with platinum-blond hair and a huge grin greets me with a head bob.

"James?" I ask, shocked. He looks heaps younger than his voice.

"James is outside... *assisting* a guest with a special order." A red hue hits the stranger's cheeks. "Is there anything I can help you with?"

Straightening up, I reply, "He called saying I had a package to collect."

While scrolling a finger down a thick wad of papers, the concierge asks, "Floor number?"

"Thirty-seven," I reply after quickly pausing to recall the markings outside the elevator doors.

His hue deepens, stretching to his ears, before he stops scrolling the list of guest names and returns his eyes to mine. "Yes, well, they shouldn't be too much longer." He arches over his podium-like desk before whispering in a sneering tone, "Most gents wait in their room fortheir *package* to arrive."

"James asked me to come down because he wasn't confident with his selections."

His shock is as elevated as mine was only minutes ago. "*Selections?*" I swear this man's face is the color of a tomato. "As in more than one?"

I lift my chin before nudging my head to multiple glossy bags on a counter behind him. "Are you sure they're not the *packages* I'm meant to collect?" I say "packages" with the same high squawk everyone else has used tonight.

The concierge coughs, scoffs, then reluctantly checks the tags on the designer-looking bags when my arched brow announces I'm not accepting a scoff as an answer.

"Oh..." His eyes are back on me in an instant. They're full of silent apologies. "Laken Howell?"

His flustered expression reminds me of the giggled greetings I received whenever I attended parties during my final year of high school. It gives me a boost in confidence I haven't experienced in almost a decade. "The one and only."

"I'm so sorry, sir," he gabbers out while pulling the packages down and rounding the counter at the speed of light. "When you asked for James and said you had *a* package to collect, I misunderstood." He hands me the glossy bags that are heavier than they look. "I profusely apologize for the confusion."

"It's fine. Truly." Once the bags are distributed evenly between both hands, I say, "Though I'd appreciate your assistance in getting me back to my room. I left my key on the nightstand."

That's a lie, but the concierge is clueless. "Certainly."

As his promise leaves his mouth, a commotion outside the hotel silences the lobby. A woman is shouting, and although her voice is cultured and smooth, the language she uses to express herself isn't.

She swears like a sailor on shore leave.

"I'll just… Ah…" The concierge is flustered again, but this time, it is directed outside instead of at me. "Lesley is a whizz at room key consignments." He waves his hand at the check-in counter. "If you wouldn't mind…" He issues his gratitude with a smile when I move toward the short queue before all his plea can leave his mouth.

"Good evening. How can I help you?" asks the stunning brunette operating the counter a short time later.

I wait for Lesley's eyes to reach my face before announcing, "I locked myself out of my room." When I realize I didn't catch the concierge's name, I murmur, "*James* said you could assist me."

I don't know if her blush is because I busted her staring at my crotch or from me bringing James into the conversation again.

His name alone brings out an array of emotions from his colleagues.

Lesley's embarrassment switches her attitude from friendly to professional in less than two seconds. "Certainly. What is your room number?"

"Umm." Her suspicion increases the longer I delay answering. "I'm not sure, but it's on the thirty-seventh floor."

She smiles. It isn't as genuine as the needy gawk she hit me with when I approached the desk. "What name is the booking under?"

"Laken Howell," I reply, confident that's the name Knox used since James mentioned me by name when he called to advise I had packages to collect.

A keyboard being clicked is the only noise between us before Lesley says in a professional tone, "Thank you for choosing to stay with us, Mr. Howell. I can organize a replacement keycard once I'm supplied with some identification."

Naturally, I dig my wallet out of my pocket before my fingers veer for the slot that houses my driver's license.

I stand frozen for a few seconds when I notice the empty compartment, and the truth smacks into me.

"My license expired a few weeks back, and I haven't gotten a new one yet."

Lesley doesn't sound a smidge apologetic while asking, "Do you have any other form of ID?"

When I shake my head, she purses her red-painted lips and peers down her nose at me, her temperament suddenly icy.

"You can call the room. My brother is in there. He'll vouch for me."

"I'm sorry, I can't do that. Your room has a do not disturb request on it."

"It's my room, so how could you disturb me by calling it?"

She shushes me, and I deserve it. I'm being a nuisance. I am just not accustomed to being shot down so quickly. It stings my ego and has me wondering if paying for services is in fact the only way I'll be able to loosen the tension that's been binding up my shoulders for the past ten years.

"Sorry." You'd swear my short temper got the best of me again when she glares at me for endeavoring to find another way to access my room. "What about Knox Samson's room? Does it have a do not disturb order?"

She only clicks her keyboard a handful of times before saying, "We do not have a guest of that name staying at our hotel."

"He's here. He dropped me off earlier. He's staying in the presidential suite."

Barely two keystrokes sound in my ears before another abrupt headshake. "That is *not* the guest's name on that booking."

As I scrub my hand down my face, too tired for more theatrics, Lesley signals for the next guest to step forward.

Pissed at being disregarded so rudely, I hold up my hand, stopping the gent's approach before shifting my focus back to Lesley. "What do I need to get back into my room?"

"Identification," she answers matter-of-factly, her tone as snappy as mine.

As she impatiently taps her fingers on the glossy counter, I place my bank cards on the ledge separating us. They're all expired but in my name.

"*Photo* identification," she clarifies after taking in the cards for barely a second, her tone unapologetic.

"I don't have any photo ID on me right now, but James—"

"Then I'm sorry, *sir*." She spits out the last word in a snarl. "I cannot grant you access to your room." She slides a complimentary drink voucher my way, her tone not as aggressive as earlier. "The bar is open until two. Perhaps you can wait there until your brother can grant you access to your room."

Mindful arguments rarely end in my favor, I stuff the complimentary drink voucher into my pocket, thank her for her help, then trudge to the bar.

Partway there, I'm mesmerized by a vision even a man surrounded by topless beauty queens would stop to admire. I can only describe the redhead entering the revolving glass doors of the hotel one way. Perfection. Her piercing green eyes and voluptuous red locks starkly contrast her almost translucent skin. And her body... *fuck*. My skintight jeans were already uncomfortable, but now they're downright painful.

As she crosses the foyer, gaining attention with every step, her emerald-green dress swishes against her milky-white thighs, which bounce in rhythm to the generous swell of her uncontained breasts.

She isn't wearing a bra. I'd place money on my assumption. That's how confident I am that her erect nipples are strained directly against her silky dress.

I am not ashamed to admit I'm hard. Even if I hadn't had a prolonged absence from sex, my body's response would be the same.

She could make any red-blooded man forget the world existed. They'd see nothing but her... *and perhaps the brute tailing her.*

The giant stands a foot taller than her and has bulging, steroid-inspired biceps and enough arrogance that any unwanted interests considering approaching the unnamed beauty wouldn't. They'd stare from a distance with their mouths as unhinged as mine.

I watch with interest when the redhead cruises past the concierge desk with a shy grin and a wave before she accepts a recently encrypted hotel room keycard from Lesley without handing over a single form of ID.

Just before she reaches the guest elevator, she stops her shadow's follow by fanning her hand across his chest.

My clipped nails dig into my palm better than the heavy bags' woven handles when she peers up at him, blinking and with hued cheeks. They appear friendly.

"I've got this," she assures him, her voice as sugary sweet as her ageless face.

I've never been good at guessing ages, but I'm confident she would have been in junior high when I was incarcerated. That makes her only a couple of years younger than me since I was charged my senior year. The difference in our age seems like more since you age two years for every one behind bars.

The brute denies her assurance by folding his chunky arms over his chest and briskly shaking his head. "I'd rather make sure you arrive in one piece."

A vein in the man's forehead presents as fast as my confusion when she replies, "And run the risk of losing the girls' tail?" She looks past him, her expression hard to read. "They're probably already halfway to Hopeton by now."

My brows stitch together. Hopeton will never hold the stigma of sex and intrigue like Ravenshoe. It's somewhat like my hometown, Johnston Bay, the equivalent of Ravenshoe's seedy half-brother. It is expensive and upcoming, but its services are more for hire than long-term investment.

It is usually the town men visit when wanting the services of a prostitute.

I take a startled step back when a theory trickles into my woozy head. Knox said the concierge keeps the room next to mine empty for professional services, and every time my floor number was mentioned tonight, someone's face turned the color of beets.

Could that be the reason for the beauty's visit?

Is she here to work?

It makes sense that the hotel staff know her. She didn't give Lesley anything but a smile to gain access to the guest-only elevators. She breezed in like she owned the place—a common trait for the women Knox was notorious for associating with my first year of incarceration.

My focus shifts back to the redhead when her promise that she can take care of herself causes hesitation to harden her shadower's features. He contemplates for half a second before an engine revving outside the hotel sees him issuing a stern warning. "Straight to your room."

The redhead's salute is adorable and condescending at the same time. "Yes, sir."

"I'm not joking, Nicole," he snaps back, as distrusting of her answer as I am.

She couldn't lie straight in bed if paid to do so, and playfulness is all over her face.

It truly appears as if her night is only just getting started.

When tires shrieking add to the commotion outside, the brute mutters under his breath, "I don't get paid enough for this shit," before he hotfoots it out of the hotel, leaving Nicole alone and me with a chance.

25

4
NICOLE

As my thumb jabs the door close button, a muscular, tattooed-to-the-elbow arm shoots between the almost-shut doors, halting their closure with only a second to spare.

"That was a close call," murmurs a dark-haired man with a cropped beard, bulky jacket, and jeans that leave *nothing* to the imagination.

Although I shouldn't be looking, even a nun would be tempted to drink in the outline of the beast in his pants. The bulge is ginormous, and it dries my mouth in an instant.

When I snap my eyes to the side, mortified I'm acting like the harlot I'd tried to portray earlier tonight, the unnamed gent I'm eyeballing like dessert enters the generously spaced car. The span of his step is impressive, but it has nothing on the smell radiating off his ruggedly handsome outer shell.

He smells like freshly laundered sheets and another scent I can't quite work out.

Too curious for my own good, I lick my lips to soothe their dryness before dragging my eyes from the elevator wall to the stranger's face.

The beat of my heart grows even wilder.

His rugged yet polished features are as captivating as his scent. His jaw is tight and covered by a few days of scruff. His light-brown, almost transcalent eyes put my head in a tizzy. Although his sense of fashion is a little off for this decade, not even a full-blown clown suit could detract from his sexiness—and that's saying something because I can't look at a clown without wanting to pee my pants.

He is gorgeous, and his panty-wetting voice makes the heat in the elevator car even more noticeable when he thanks me for the opportunity to ogle everything he has on offer. "Thanks for waiting for me."

When he mimics my silent stare, waiting for a reply, I stammer, "Y-you're welcome."

My nostrils flare when I step toward the elevator panel so I can tap my room key over the security scanner. His smell is too intoxicating to ignore. It is a much sought-after scent after the night I've had.

I love Ravenshoe. It will always be my hometown, but Mavericks has seen better days. Ever since Maggie left to run the bed-and-breakfast the band purchased her as thanks for the years she dedicated to their success, it hasn't been the same. The patrons are loud and obnoxious, and if it weren't for Rise Up making an impromptu appearance like they do anytime they're home, one hundred percent of them would have reeked of BO.

It was one disastrous pickup line after another, which is sad. Tonight is my last night of freedom for weeks, and Jenni and Emily made out it is easy to secure a noncommittal night of lust with no strings attached.

Tonight's duds are what I get for accepting advice from taken women. They haven't been single in years, and it showed earlier when they tried to steer me through the horrifying maze of single life.

Don't misunderstand. I love being single. I just miss the connection you can't achieve when you go it alone.

After a second lick of lips to loosen up my words, I ask the stranger, "What floor do you require?"

"Ah…"

He spins to face the unlit panel, wafting up more of his delicious scent, before he attempts to select floor thirty-seven. I say attempt because if you don't scan your hotel room card across the security box, you can't access any floor in this hotel except the lobby.

When I announce that to the mystery stranger, he murmurs, "Oh... ah... I left my keycard in my room." Something must cross my face that I didn't mean to show as he quickly attempts to settle my worry. "It's cool, though. My brother is asleep in my room, so he'll let me in."

"That could occur if we were traveling to the same floor."

He sounds more relieved than annoyed when asking, "You're not going to the thirty-seventh floor?"

Strands of red locks swish my shoulders when I shake my head. "No, I'm not."

My heart beats for an entirely different reason when I remember Knox warning me to stay away from men seeking the thirty-seventh floor.

They're not standard hotel guests.

Most rarely stay longer than an hour.

"Are you an overnight guest at this hotel? Or can you book rooms on the thirty-seventh floor by the hour as well?"

I'm not usually so bold, but something about this man has me acting how I usually would when interacting with a friend. It could be that I spent the past several hours surrounded by people I've known for years, but it seems more than that.

He appears oblivious to who I am, which is more endearing than frustrating.

The stranger's pupils dilate before he stammers, "I'm not staying in any of *those* rooms."

His flabbergasted response is cute, and it has me eager to continue to rile him.

He deserves to be on the back foot as much as I am since his gorgeous face and panty-wetting body swiped my smarts out from beneath me in under a second.

When I arch a brow like I don't believe him, he crosses his heart while pledging, "I swear on my brother's life *that* isn't why I'm here."

He grins shyly. *My god.* I didn't think he could get more handsome, but his dimples have made me a liar. They're not as deep as Noah's, but just as attractive.

After shifting his bags from one hand to the next, he murmurs, "Though I'd be lying if I said I wouldn't contemplate going down that route if I learn that's why you're here."

I don't know whether his insinuation should shock or intrigue me. My ginger locks, pasty-white skin, and innocent facial features have me accused of being the preacher's daughter more often than a pop star, so you can be assured this is the first time anyone has mistaken me for a sex worker.

My high tone reveals I'm more playful than annoyed when I ask, "You think I'm a prostitute?"

"No. I just..." My heart whacks my ribcage three times before he hooks his thumb to the elevator doors still clamped shut despite the car not moving, as neither of us selected a floor. "That guy was your pimp, right?"

"Who?" My eyes bulge when the truth smacks into me. Then humor takes over. "Hawke is a bodyguard," I gabber out through a fit of laughter.

My giggles halt when the stranger stares at me with shock blazing through his captivating eyes. I hate that the daftness his presence caused may have blown my cover. "Not *my* bodyguard. He works for a friend of mine."

I fold my arms over my chest, hoisting my moderately sized bosom higher before attempting a serious expression. It is no easy feat. I've always been described as cute with a reserved personality, so for someone to believe I exude enough confidence to be a sex worker is rather intriguing.

"A friend asked *her* bodyguard to walk me inside to ensure I didn't have any run-ins with men from the thirty-seventh floor."

There's no pussyfooting around with this man. He's onto my underhanded claim he purchased a prostitute for dessert the second it leaves my mouth. "I swear to God, that isn't why I'm here."

"Then why do you have condoms in your pocket?"

I nudge my head to the evident circle disc imprints embedded in the rigid material of his jeans pocket. They're just to the left of the massive bulge I'm once again staring at.

Did he stuff a banana down his trunks after squeezing into them? What other explanation is there for him needing to hire a prostitute other than a cock-stuffing incident?

After the past few months I've had, the honesty in his tone is refreshing. "They were given to me by a friend." His tug on the crotch of his pants doesn't give him an ounce of leverage before he confesses, "Who most likely booked me a room on the thirty-seventh floor on purpose." When I scoff, faking repulsion, he murmurs, "Should I go?" He doesn't give me the chance to reply. "I'll go." The elevator doors pop open a second after he stabs the open-door button with his index finger. "I hope you have a pleasant night, Nicole."

He freezes partway out when my curiosity speaks before my disappointment. "How do you know my name?"

A hundred scenarios run through my head except the one he gives. "I was eavesdropping on your conversation with your..."—he almost stumbles—*"friend's* bodyguard." After quickly evaluating my response to his near miss and gifting me a grin that makes me dizzy, he says, "He called you Nicole."

I don't know this man, but I believe him. My trust is as sturdy as my regret that our brief exchange of banter is already ending. The heaviness on my shoulders will never entirely shift, but it didn't feel as heavy during our discussion.

"I hope you have a pleasant night too...?" I leave my question open for him to answer how he sees fit.

I can't help the smile that hooks my mouth to one side when he replies, "Laken. Laken Howell." It's a groovy name that matches his relaxed, calm demeanor.

Laken waits a moment for me to work his name through my head a trillion times before he issues a final pledge. "And I swear to whatever mythical being you believe in that I'm not planning to do *anything* but sleep on the thirty-seventh floor. They just refused me access because I'm not carrying any ID."

The elevator doors shut before I can offer a solution.

5
NICOLE

*J*ust as quickly as the elevator doors close, they open on the floor of the presential suite. I don't recall scanning the hotel room keycard Knox organized for me after I called him panicked I'd forgotten to take my keycard with me, but the reason for my magic trick comes to light when I step into the hallway.

Knox is waiting in the entryway, his expression furious.

"Hawke was with us the entire time." With my purse stuffed under my arm, I kick off my stilettos and pick them up before slowly trudging down the elaborate space filled with priceless paintings and restored antiques. "And I only had two drinks."

"Two drinks in a smoke-plumed bar. You may as well sign up for a laryngectomy." He scoops my pumps from my hand, dumps them next to his boots in the entryway, and then guides me toward the main suite.

The presidential suite has four rooms, each with private ensuites. Though you wouldn't know that with how many of Knox's hair products are spread across the vanity in my bathroom. He swears the lighting in my bathroom is better than his, but I know he's hiding his pricy products from River, his little brother who only wants to emulate him, not frustrate him.

"We're offering for you to sing live at each event," Knox says, his grip around my waist tightening. "If vocals aren't strong, they'll tear you to shreds, baby cakes."

"They're strong. They are untainted. I've been resting my voice all week."

I wish that were a lie. Knox is so paranoid that I'll strain my voice before a live performance, I was placed on voice rest for a week.

My wrist hurts more from scribbling down notes to him than writing song lyrics—regretfully.

"Untainted before you ruined a week of rest by clogging it with dangerous fumes and voice-hindering chemicals." Sighing, he enters the bathroom, switches on the faucet full blast, and then spins to face me. "You've possibly undone twelve months of hard work in less than two hours."

I *pfft* him, confident he's not being serious. "It isn't that bad. Singers across the globe get their starts in pubs and clubs."

"And most retire before they're thirty."

With his mood teetering more and more toward negative, when he instructs me to breathe in the steam fogging the mirror he hogs every morning, I follow his order to a T. I'm not exactly an argumentative person, but I'm not a lapdog either. I assess the situation and implement an attitude that will ensure the best outcome.

Sounds like a lapdog to me.

As my sigh adds to the mugginess of the room, Knox says, "We have four years max, Nik. Two if you don't start taking my advice." My heart slips to my feet when he murmurs to himself, "I don't know if that will be enough time to see through my plans."

"I'm sorry, Knox. I don't know what I was thinking. It won't happen again."

He lets me off quicker than expected. "I only want what's best for you, poppet." He strays his eyes to my closed bedroom door. "And him. It has *always* been about him."

With the week draining on all of us, Knox leaves me to my own devices only twenty minutes after marching me into the bathroom. He'd usually hang out in my suite with me until I crashed, but his focus seemed elsewhere today.

I want to say I use my freedom well, but that would be a lie. After flicking through the reruns of the late-night shows Knox Records is endeavoring to get me featured on, I wash my hair while analyzing my exchange with Laken in the elevator.

It was a fun and flirty encounter that has had my head filling with lyrics the prior twenty minutes, but I can barely hear them over the questions that won't quit circling through my head.

Has Laken made it back to his room yet?

And did he arrive there alone?

Doing my best to ignore the jealousy my final question hits me with, I snatch up my beloved notebook from the bedside table, plop my backside onto my bed, then open it to an untouched page.

Like multiple times over the past several months, the nib of my pen butts against the notepad designed for both songwriting and musical composition, but unlike the times I was left brokenhearted, a handful of lyrics soon grace the page.

Feel your scruff on my neck.

Be your biggest regret.

> We don't even need to go slow.
> Not when we already know how this will go...

After a handful more lines, I try to make sense of the jumbled mess in front of me.

If there's a song amongst the chaos, it isn't close to production ready, but it is far better than the blank song sheets I've stared at over the past three months.

It could become something. *Eventually.*

"Just a little more. Please," I plead when the string of words tumbling in my head are drowned out by the faint purr of the mini refrigerator in my room.

The refrigerator keeping my cans of Pepsi cold isn't loud. It's just hard to utilize a muse for an entire song when he only stood across from me for a minute.

When my frustration reaches the breaking point, I dump my pen onto my notebook, then stretch leisurely, hopeful unkinking my muscles will also unknot my writer's block.

As I stretch my neck muscles, my eyes lock with the secondary entrance of my room. The concierge said the hotel owner included a second entrance so future presidential mistresses could "entertain" the president and bypass the first lady and his secret service staff.

When I learned the hotel owner's identity, I realized his decision had nothing to do with future presidential visits and everything to do with the quickest and most accessible way to reach his wife no matter where she sleeps.

Isaac hasn't designed a single structure in the past six years without Isabelle influencing its accessibility scale. Whether here or in Tahiti, every room she could stay in has an easy-access point for Isaac.

The remembrance has me curious if there's a helipad on the hotel's rooftop like the many other hotels Isaac owns across the globe. Rooftops with uninterrupted views are prime spots to soothe unwanted throat spasms, and they're also wondrous for creativity.

While praying I've found a solution for my wailing inspiration, I regather my songbook and pen, drag the bedding off the hotel mattress like its thread count isn't in the millions, then head for the secret corridor hidden halfway in the massive walk-in closet.

As suspected, at the end of a weaving corridor, I stumble onto a second hallway with stairs at the end. The presidential suite is on the top floor, which can only mean one thing.

This hotel has an accessible rooftop.

Yes!

Careful not to trip on the bedding tracing my every step, I climb the concrete stairs with reflective tape coating each edge before pushing open the heavily weighted door.

Wow.

That is the only word that enters my head when invigorating salty air hits my lungs while my wide eyes drink in the view. I've never seen Ravenshoe from this vantage point, but it isn't solely the art-inspiring visual stretching from Bronte's Peak to Hopeton gaining my attention. The clawfoot tub and open shower to the side of a Zen-like bedroom also have my heart stuttering.

Isaac didn't design solely a quick entry point to the presidential suite. He brought its glam to the rooftop. The airy outside "room" just left of a helipad has a king-size bed canopied by a bulky wooden frame and breezy mosquito netting. A sexy yet stiff-looking sectional sofa hogs the outer wall of the hotel, and a gas-lit fireplace next to a fur rug reminds me of the glamping trip my parents took for their twenty-fifth wedding anniversary.

It is spectacular… *though not as stunning as that.*

A rigid, muscular back and tall, athletic frame showcase a backside that doesn't need to be paraded naked to ooze desirability. The sight gives my eyes the workout of their life.

I'm so mesmerized by the view I trip over the bedding huddled at my feet, more falling into the rooftop "room" instead of graciously entering it with the sophistication its high-end design deserves.

The clap of the emergency exit stairwell door slamming shut behind me announces my arrival. It breaks through the sound barrier at the speed of light and sees the man I was admiring spinning to face me.

My heart thuds in my ears when not even the hint of ginger in his beard highlighted by the moon's rays can conceal the familiarity of his features. I only drank them in for mere minutes, but they've held my thoughts captive for the past thirty.

After hooking his lips to the side, Laken drags his eyes down my body. His slow, heated gawk has me forgetting I'm wearing a slip of satin as a dress until his stare puckers my nipples into firm buds.

My breasts become heavy with need as a slickness dampens between my legs, but try as I may, I can't cover up. I like the way he looks at me. It stirs something profound inside me and makes me feel as wild and carefree as the laugh that rips from my lips when he locks his eyes with mine and asks, "Are you stalking me?"

When a snort joins my laughter, I clamp my mouth shut with my hand before replying through the cracks of my fingers. "I was about to ask you the same thing." I encroach a little more, my footing not as graceful as I'm hoping when the mangled bedding makes itself a nuisance for the second time in the past minute. "Are you alone? I'm not interrupting anything, am I?"

After narrowing my eyes at him in suspicion, I sweep them right and left. I know he's alone. I scanned every inch of the rooftop penthouse. I'm simply teasing him as rigorously as the delicious rumble of his voice teases me when he asks, "What could you possibly be interrupting?"

A playful twinkle in his eyes douses the nerves bubbling in my stomach. Not a lot, but enough for me to say with a serious expression, "I thought perhaps you'd brought your... *date* up here. A starry night can be a great opener." I wave my hand at the massive bed to my right. "Let alone a four-poster bed."

"*Date*?" Laken asks, his brow arched like his jaw didn't spasm when he followed my hand's veer to the romp-inspired furniture. "I don't see anyone here but you, Nicole." I envy his teeth when they're dragged across his lower lip. "So I guess I should ask if it's working?" Confusion barely crosses my face for half a second before he aims to end it. "The starry sky? You said it could be a great opener for a date."

He doesn't bring up the bed. He doesn't need to. His devilish grin announces how wickedly deviant his thoughts are.

I look at nothing but his playful grin while answering, "This isn't a date, so my opinion doesn't matter."

"It could," Laken replies, his smile widening. "If you stopped seeking the prostitutes you're forever expecting to be glued to my hip."

"It isn't your hip I'm imagining them glued to."

Eyes wide, I slap my hand over my mouth for the second time.

"I didn't mean to say that out loud."

While laughing like he finds my bitchy side endearing, Laken darts past the leather sofa and sidesteps the fireplace before he removes my bedding and songbook from my hands, places them on the edge of the bed, then slowly inches me toward the railing he was leaning against when I arrived.

His unhurried pace, constant eye contact, and non-sweaty grip are the only things stopping me from fleeing.

Don't look at me like that. I said rooftops are great for creativity.

I never said anything about them curing my fear of heights.

"Wow," I murmur, purposely out loud this time.

Since this hotel is the tallest building in Ravenshoe, the view is even more spectacular from the vantage point on its roof.

"You can—" we say at the same time.

"You go," I offer.

Laken shakes his head, which sends the dark spikes on top bouncing side to side. "That wouldn't be very *date*-ish of me."

"There you go with that word again," I say with a huff, my annoyance faked.

His breathy laughter tickles the baby hairs that have sprung free from my damp mop. "I'm reasonably sure you brought it up first. I am merely—"

"Milking it for all it's worth?" I nudge him in the ribs with my elbow like we're long-life friends before finishing the sentence we started together. "You can see the stairs that lead to Bronte's Peak." I highlight the dancing lights in the middle of what should be an endless sea of blackness if it weren't the locals' favorite hookup spot. "Seeing it during the day is mesmerizing, but there is something even more spectacular about witnessing its beauty at night." I crank my neck back to peer up at Laken, startling when I notice the only view he's drinking in is me. "Have you ever been to Bronte's Peak?"

"A handful of times." He smirks at my miffed expression before shifting his eyes to the dazzling skyline. "But it was nothing but a swampy wasteland the times I visited."

His reply hints that he's a local who hasn't been home for some time. Before Holt Enterprises put Ravenshoe on the map, Bronte's Peak was a swampy, hill-less location filled with alligators and sea creatures.

With the vision of an Italian coastal community like the one Isaac's grandmother was raised in, a construction crew commenced building a manmade marvel they hoped would attract millions of visitors each year.

My father and many other residents of the area rallied against Isaac's proposal for months.

They ate their vicious words only a year later. House prices skyrocketed soon after the development was finalized, and businesses on the verge of foreclosure blossomed into mighty empires.

A lot of money was poured into this town, but with the wealth came responsibilities youths at the time couldn't grasp. They were living the high life, unaware of how quickly it could crumble beneath their feet.

Before my past can sour my mood, Laken says, "From your response, I assume you've been to Bronte's Peak before?" When I nod, his brows dip low on his handsome face. "To visit the caves?"

My insides tap dance, loving that the jealousy I experienced earlier is no longer one-sided.

"I've explored the caves and had barbecues along the shoreline…" I pause to build the suspense. "And made out a handful of times in the back seat of my boyfriend's Pontiac." When he groans, I laugh. "What? It's a Ravenshoe right. If you haven't made out in that unlit lot by age thirty, there's no hope for you."

I feel he's closer to thirty than I am when his second groan rolls through my chest before clustering between my legs.

After spinning to face him, the move no easy feat with how close he is standing, I let him off the hook. "There are a handful of exceptions, but you'd have to undergo a rigorous interrogation to be granted one."

"Hit me." His following words are whispers almost too soft for me to hear. "Doubt it could be worse than any I've faced previously."

Most guys balk when you ask them how old they are, so I'm a little stumped about where to start since he's given me free rein.

After a beat, I ask, "Has the timeline lapsed, or do we still have a shot?"

My brow shoots as high as Laken's when he clarifies, "*We?*"

"*You.* I meant to say *you.*"

Will someone please find me a hose? It may be the only way to cool the heat on my cheeks when his breathy laugh adds to the mess between my legs.

"*We...*"—he takes a moment to relish my pink face—"have a couple of years at *our* disposal." I'm unable to speak, much less calculate anything above two plus two, so Laken finalizes the calculations on my behalf. "I'm twenty-seven." He checks his watch. "Almost twenty-eight."

"Is it your birthday tomorrow?" I ask, assuming he's counting down the hours until midnight.

His husky chuckles are back and more vital than ever. "No."

He shows me a watch that displays it is barely ten. Even though it's as outdated as his fashion sense, it still appears pricey. It's one of those old-school watches that doesn't just announce the time. It shows the date, month, and year as well.

"It's been a while since I've seen a watch like that. Most people just use their phones these days."

My sassy attitude dips below my belt when he murmurs, "It was my father's." He shifts nervously from foot to foot. "He wasn't around much, and when I found it in the back of a bathroom drawer, my mother said it was probably the only thing I'd ever get from him of any value, so I may as well have it." My heart breaks for him when he whispers, "She left not long after that."

"I'm sorry," I apologize, hating that our conversation has veered to the negative. My parents have been together since high school, so I often forget over fifty percent of marriages end in divorce.

"For?" Laken asks after stuffing his hand into his pocket, his tone not the slightest bit sarcastic.

After twisting my lips, I shrug. "For bringing up a sore point so soon into our…"

When I can't find the right words to explain our immediate kinship, Laken brings humor back into our exchange. "Date?" he suggests, his brows waggling.

I pop my elbow into his ribs for the second time. It switches the unease on his face to joy in under a second and has me confident if I don't place distance between us soon, I'll forget we're strangers.

"This isn't a date," I murmur when no number of screams from my brain have my legs following its command. My body enjoys being cocooned by Laken's warmth, and not even remembering that I know nothing about him, bar his name and age, have my feet budging.

Laken hums like he disagrees with me before shifting his focus to the vast skyline stretched to Hopeton.

I suck down an unhealthy whiff of his scent before following the direction of his gaze. It is surreal that I'm so close to the edge but not breaking out in hives. I feel free, almost weightless.

If it wouldn't make me look like an imbecile, I'd be tempted to thrust out my arms and do a corny rendition of the famous *Titanic* scene.

A couple of seconds later, I crank my neck back to Laken. His laugh is soundless, but since my body is scrutinizing every minute move he makes, I know laughter is rumbling in his chest.

"What's so funny?"

"Nothing." His one word is chopped up by a chuckle he can't hold back. "It's just that you're humming the lyrics from the 'I'm flying, Jack' scene"—he mimics Rose's voice—"but also gripping the railing so tight your knuckles are white."

"Because I'm scared. A fear of heights is nothing to be laughed at."

His eyes widen as his smile is wiped from his face. "You're afraid of heights?"

"Yes!"

"Then why the hell are you standing here? Looking down at that." My head grows woozy when he thrusts his hand at the people too small to resemble ants. "Whoa. Careful." He bands his arms around my waist and draws me back until my backside squashes against his crotch, and his breaths tickle my ear.

Our closeness doubles my wooziness, but before I can force distance between us, he skyrockets my pants to gasped breaths. "Step onto the railing."

"Are you insane? I'm not doing that."

If his voice gets any hotter, I'll melt where I stand when he whispers in my ear, "Do you trust me?"

"No, I don't. I hardly know you."

Laken acts as if I never spoke. "Don't peek. Keep your eyes closed."

"That's not what he said," I gabber out as we inch closer to the edge of the railing. "Jack would have stopped the instant Rose said no."

"But then the magic would have never occurred, and we'd still believe *Casablanca* was the greatest romance movie of all time."

"At least until *The Notebook* came out," I argue, my words not as strangled by panic as they were only seconds ago. "Oh my god, I can't believe you're making me do this."

"I'm not making you do anything, Nicole. This is all you."

When I peer back at him, primed and ready to call him an idiot, my words lodge in my throat. Inches separate us—far more than my deviant head is happy about—and I suddenly feel hopeless.

"I can't—"

"Step onto the railing," Laken encourages before I chicken out.

"I—"

Another denial is cut short, but the cause of the interruption is nothing close to what I was expecting. It still follows the *Titanic* nature of our exchange but exposes I have a lot to learn about the man standing across from me.

Even with his facial expression teasing, Laken's voice is more polished than Leonardo DiCaprio's when he sings a line from "Come, Josephine, in my Flying Machine."

I assume he will stop at the one line everyone knows from the movie, so the fact he recites more shows his love of music is as strong as his love of classic films.

Only a true music buff memorizes lyrics to popular blockbuster jingles.

When Laken reaches the last line of the song, inspiration slaps back into me hard and fast. My run-in with him in the elevator already awarded me a handful of lines, but they're presenting more structurally now. They're almost entirely formed.

I stammer past Laken so haphazardly his swallow reveals he's certain I'm racing for the exit, much less his panicked mumble. "I'd never force you to do anything you're not comfortable with, Nicole. I just wanted you to see you as I—"

The panic on his face subsides along with his words when I snatch up my notepad, plonk my backside onto the edge of the mammoth bed, then commence scribbling down lyrics like a deranged woman.

Unlike every other man I've sat across from while penning lyrics, Laken doesn't interrupt me or try to tell me how to do it better.

He watches me with interest, but not a single word escapes his mouth until my pen shifts from scribbling to tapping out a beat to match the song I scored in under twenty minutes. "You make that look easy."

I laugh. It's either laugh out my relief or cry. I went for the one that wouldn't have Laken looking at me with anything but the awe he's hit me with the past twenty minutes.

"It isn't always like this. I've been struggling with writer's block for months." My heart beats in my ears when I peer up at him. "I'm not facing the same issue tonight. Inspiration hit like a bolt of lightning." *Kind of like your introduction to my life.*

He smiles sheepishly, aware of what budged the clog but unwilling to take credit for it.

My smile mimics his until he asks, "Do you mind if I take a look?"

"It's a mess."

My breath catches in my throat when he replies, "All songs are until you find the right melody to go with them."

He slots his backside next to mine before carefully prying my songbook out of my hand like he knows its sentimental value will forever exceed its bankability. It was the last gift I received from Colette, and I treasure it more than I do my heart.

After reading the scribbled lyrics three times, Laken holds out his hand palm-side up, silently requesting my pen.

I'm hesitant to hand it over. Not because I haven't memorized the words, but because this is usually when my creativity gets squashed like a bug.

I haven't penned a single lyric since Apollo, the producer Knox hired to produce my album, declared that country pop was dead, so he didn't think I should waste time on unmarketable songs.

I don't believe any genre dies, so I fought to keep some of the songs he'd discredited before giving them a shot.

Since Knox sided with Apollo, my bid was unsuccessful. Every song on my upcoming album is straight pop. Even the acoustic guitar riffs are played by the band Knox Records uses for all its artists.

I miss holding a guitar while standing before a microphone, but I've missed this even more. Songwriting is all I know, so going without it for so long felt like missing a limb.

After several painfully long minutes, Laken says, "This section will make a brilliant chorus." He highlights the verse I'd already picked for the chorus without the pen's tip touching the paper. "But I'd probably slot it in a little sooner than you have it." He moves the nib up to the top half of page one, two spots below the intro. "Just after—"

"The second verse?" I interrupt, speaking with him.

He nods, the praise on his face growing. "And I'm not sure what you're thinking…" I grin when he murmurs, "I'm not overly skilled at hooks, but the instrumental component you choose should be repeated throughout. It doesn't need to change, because the hook won't tell this story. It will—"

"Unfold it," we say simultaneously before I finalize our mutual thought. "Because the lyrics are the story."

"Exactly." After a few more minutes of silence, he taps the pen against his jeans-covered thigh. "What about something like this?"

The beat is similar to the one that played through my head while I'd waited for him to destroy my work. It's just a smidge slower than I've become accustomed to the past year.

"You're close." I love the vibe he's drifting toward, but Apollo would tear it apart. He'd say it's too country for the audience we're aiming for before drowning out the lyrics with a heap of remixed DJ samples. "It just needs… *more*."

I almost add "pop" to the end of my sentence, but before I can ruin lyrics too magical to be overwhelmed by electric guitars and drums, Laken gives the "more" I'm demanding by strumming his fingers across the knots in the wooden bedpost.

The acoustics are amazing. Even Apollo would have a hard time acting negatively toward them.

Within seconds, the words I recently jotted down flow from my mouth in a harmonizing melody that reminds me of when I started in this industry.

It is a Nicole Reed original instead of the mass-produced songs wannabe pop star Nikki J will perform on repeat starting three p.m. tomorrow afternoon.

"Yes," Laken praises, as in love with our impromptu performance as I am.

When his boots occasionally add a much-needed tempo to the soulful melody, he doesn't outshine me or drown out my voice that Apollo often complains is too soft. He rocks along to the beat with me, his sole focus on finding the perfect melody for a song that would rocket up the charts if I were a country-pop artist.

With my voice the key element of our performance, I give it my all. I sing with all my heart to ensure I gift Laken the performance of his life.

Even with only one man in the audience, it isn't disheartening when I reach the end of the final chorus. Laken's applause ruptures my eardrums more than any audience had before him.

He wolf whistles and catcalls before he slings his arm around my shoulders to hug me tight.

"Wow. That was…" He appears lost for words. "Fuck, Nicole. I've never experienced such brilliance. You have a gift. A genuine gift from God."

The pride flaring in his eyes when he peers down at me does wild things to my insides. It makes me nauseated and hot at the same time and has me acting so out of the ordinary that before I can contemplate the consequences of my actions, I lunge forward and plant my lips against his grinning mouth.

6
LAKEN

When Nicole's lips land on mine, I freeze like I haven't dreamed of her doing exactly this over the past thirty minutes.

I thought I'd blown the chance of us being more than friends when I cornily sang a line from one of River's top-ten favorite movies.

It shows how much things have changed in the dating world.

I would have never been so corny before my life was upended, and people once accused me of being cocky. It helped that I had just watched the scene half an hour before James called to say I had packages to collect. That's how I could quote some of the lines. I stuffed up a few, but give me a break. I'm more about melodies than lines from cliche romance movies.

I'll never admit that to River, though.

He loves the classics, and I love him enough not to give him hell about it.

My shock that I didn't royally fuck this up causes my frozen state, but Nicole mistakes it as disinterest. She pulls back as fast as she lunged forward before issuing an unwanted apology. "I'm so sorry. I don't know what I was thinking." She reneges on her lie before I can work out it isn't factual. "It's just been so long since *anything* has struck, much less something so cosmic, I dove headfirst before thinking. It won't happen aga—"

Before she can steal all my hope, I silence her with my mouth, freezing her as she did me. Then, after granting her a second to object, my tongue gets in on the action as well. I slide it into her mouth, moaning when its sweep steals the air trapped in her throat.

As we make out like the teens lighting up the lot at Bronte's Peak, I taste lime on her lips and a liquidy acid I haven't sampled in almost a decade.

The alcohol on her mouth isn't strong enough for me to be concerned she can't give consent, but I do wonder if it is why her limbs are so soft and transferrable.

Within minutes, she goes from being seated next to me to her knees hugging my hips.

I don't mind.

I can ravish her better this way, give her one-tenth of the performance she gave me, all the while using the same instrument she used to hold me captive.

My mouth.

My kiss is a caveman-type kiss, all macho and possessive but also nurturing and sweet. It's as contradictable as Nicole's personality and looks.

She has the personality of a saint but the sexiness of a devil.

Sweet as pie on the inside, but hot as hell on the outside.

After a while, Nicole takes the lead in our exchange, which I find as sexy as her fuckable body.

I rarely let go of the reins when I was a teen, but that had nothing to do with enjoyment. It was more based on who was the more experienced of the duo.

As much as this sucks to admit, it appears Nicole has me trumped this time around.

I'd been with a handful of girls before I was incarcerated.

By a handful, I mean no more than I can count on one hand.

Two went no further than third base, and the other three weren't overly memorable.

I don't see that being an issue this time around.

Our kiss is already setting my skin on fire, and it appears I'm not the only one heating up.

After pulling back with a moan, Nicole fans her heated neck with her hand.

She needs a minute to recover, but I don't heed her request.

After cupping her jaw, I nibble on the soft skin stretched from her chin to her ear. A shiver rockets down her spine when I tug on her earlobe, which showcases a simple gold hoop earring.

Her involuntary tremble when my lips drop to her collarbone wafts up her delicious scent. She smells divine, like soap and flowers, and her womanly scent increases when I drag my tongue across her neck to sample her no doubt delicious skin.

With a moan, Nicole's head lolls to the side as her nipples pucker against her silky nightgown. I want to cup her breast in my hand and roll her nipple between my thumb and forefinger, but I can't.

I can see the need in her eyes, smell it on her skin, but she's also panicked.

We're strangers, and no matter how much I wish I could go back to the youth I was cruelly stripped of in my prime, no number of lies will convince me that this is a frat party full of drunken teens. The linen under my ass is too silky to be from Walmart, and the woman putting my head in a tailspin is too cultured to think underage sex is cool.

I am also a grown-ass man... *who can't pull back no matter how hard he tries.*

Seriously, I give it my all. I try with all my might, but I barely get half an inch away before I suck Nicole's sexy bottom lip back between my lips, and we moan in sync.

Our connection is extraordinary.

Our moves perfectly synchronized.

We're even breathing in sync.

Only a fool would give this up.

That title has been associated with my name for too long. It is the *only* thing I should be giving up, so with my mind made up, I once again drag my tongue along the delicate skin on Nicole's neck before cupping her breast in my hand and rolling her nipple between my thumb and forefinger.

Her breast growing heavy in my palm makes me hard in an instant. My cock's head knocks at the zipper of my jeans, begging to be released as Nicole gropes at me.

Desperate and needy, her nails scratching my back, she thrusts her chest forward, encouraging my quest to devour her whole.

I can't get enough, so after tasting her skin until precum stains my boxer shorts, I return my lips to her mouth and kiss her with everything I have.

It was never like this before I went away.

Never so intense and fire sparking.

The heat is insane. *Intoxicating.*

I'm burning up everywhere, and Nicole melts against me.

She molds her body to mine so well I doubt I'll need to remove an article of clothing to get her off.

As her fingers weave through my hair, she grinds down on my erection, which sends a needy heat prickling over every inch of my skin.

"Good grief," I moan as my hands shoot down to her hips.

I'm reminded that she isn't as confident as the siren she has been exposing when her panicked eyes bounce between mine. They did the same multiple times during her goosebump-inducing performance, except this time, she voices the worry I see. "Did I do something wrong?"

"God, no."

I guide her pussy's descent down my cock this time around, moaning when the dampness of her panties can't be concealed even while clothed.

"I just don't want to make a fool out of myself." I lift and lock my eyes with her confused pair before confessing, "It's been a while." *Almost ten fucking years.* "And she didn't look like you." She can't take my compliment the wrong way. Just the need sparking from my eyes when I sweep them down her body announces how much I crave her, much less the pulse feeding my monster erection. "I'm about to blow in my fucking pants."

Nicole's hair is as red-hot as the confidence she rarely exposes when she murmurs, "Then I guess we better get you out of them."

7
NICOLE

*T*hose words did not come out of my mouth.

Surely not.

I don't have sex with strangers.

Don't get me wrong. I love the sparks you can't get when you go it alone, and the connection that tethers you to another for several blistering minutes, but I at least like to know someone for a couple of hours before I have sex with them. I don't open my legs for any random man.

What are you talking about? You haven't had sex in years, and even when you gave in to temptation, it wasn't anything to brag about.

I don't see that being an issue this time around, though. Laken's kiss alone has me on the verge of climax, and the way he's looking at me, like I have confidence by the bucketloads, makes me feel the most daring I've ever felt.

I can do this.

I *will* do this.

Even if it kills me.

"Nicole, we don't..."

The rest of Laken's words slip into a silent void when I push back on his shoulder, encouraging his back to become one with the bedding.

His teeth dig into his fleshly lip when I shuffle back far enough to expose the zipper in his jeans. He's hard. The lengthy girth in the crotch of his pants can't deny this, but it is even more telling by the small amount of wetness at the tip.

His cock is leaking pre-cum, and it inserts imaginary steel rods through my shaky hands.

I've only just gotten the button undone and am working on lowering the zipper when Laken's hand curls over mine, stopping my movements. "We don't need to do this." As his eyes bounce between mine, I'm shocked that they're filled more with respect than the disgust I am expecting. "I'm happy to wait." His hand swamps my face when he cups my jaw. "I'm sure you'll make the delay worthwhile."

His last word is a groan when I feed off the confidence his comment awards me. I suck his thumb into my mouth before curling my tongue around the tip.

His response would have you convinced his cock is between my lips, and I'm almost certain that needs to be the case when his reaction sends a pleasing zap over every inch of me.

I want him now more than I've wanted anything, and I will have him.

"I want this." I grunt and groan while endeavoring to remove his jeans. "I just need to get your jeans off first." Another handful of grunts makes my words breathless. "It would be easier if I had a paint scraper."

Sensing my struggle and unable to hide his smile about my witty comment, Laken raises his ass off the bed before tugging down his skintight jeans. He does it without the groans and grunts that emitted from my lips when I left dress rehearsal earlier today.

He's stripped as bare as me in no time, wearing nothing but boxer shorts and a shirt.

This is usually where I'd feel more clumsy than confident. It isn't an issue this time around. I feel daring, bold, and on the verge of having a stroke when my eyes lock on the bulge no longer taped to Laken's thigh with denim-colored duct tape.

"Umm..." I wet my lips, desperate for moisture somewhere else on my body other than between my legs. "I've never really... ah..."

Take it between your hands, Nicole.

Stop being such a wimp.

A terrifying dip slaughters my confidence when I follow the prompts of my deviant head. I grab—*choke?*—his cock as if it is a big, steely flashlight and there's a perp outside my bedroom window, almost crushing his manhood with my sturdy hold.

"Sorry... I'm not exactly confid—"

"Just. Like. That." Laken pumps the hand gripping him up and down his rigid shaft with each word he speaks. His tongue rolls between his teeth when my reformed grip has his cock throbbing in my palm. "Though I might need to encourage a little less eye contact."

Like a creep, I immediately lock my eyes with him.

I grow wetter when his moan rolls through me. "Fuck, siren. Maybe you're not as saintly as your heart wants you to be portrayed. Maybe your soul is blacker than Satan's." My cheeks burn the color of beets. "I guess there's only one way to find out."

In a maneuver too quick to describe, I'm on my back, and Laken is kneeling between my legs—*my splayed-open-for-the-world-to-see legs!*

"Oh, no." Laken's bottom lip is back between his teeth. He teasingly bites it as the hands he places high on my inner thighs keep my legs open. "Don't go acting shy on me now." Hot heat seers through me. "Not when you're so fucking sexy. The image of you splayed beneath me, flushed and needy, has me on the verge of blowing my load in my boxers." He palms his cock before dropping his other hand to my modest yet drenched-through panties. "I've never seen a more enticing sight." My knees tremble when he tracks the backs of his fingers down the drenched cotton maintaining some of my modesty. "And to know I caused this…" A moan ends his sentence before it starts a new one. "Fuck."

He toys with my clit through my panties until I'm on the cusp of begging.

Thankfully, he keeps talking before I can make a fool of myself. "I won't be able to hold back, Nicole. I won't be able to stop once this starts." He locks eyes with me over my thrusting chest. "So if you don't want this to go any further, you need to say the word now. Tell me to walk. I'll fucking do it. I'll leave right now." His eyes sling to his jeans hanging off the bed. "I'll never get my jeans back on, but this…" His hand is back on me. Teasing, punishing. Making me desperate. "You." His eyes burn into mine. "That kiss. Fuck…" A moan fills another slight pause. "It will keep me going for years. Easily a decade or three. I'll never forget it."

He's saying everything right.

Doing everything right.

So it shouldn't be shocking when I weave my fingers through his hair and pull him on top of me.

I want his lips on me, all over me, and I'm given a chance when the desperateness of our kiss sees Laken's lips falling to my neck for the second time tonight. He suckles on the silky skin, marking me with his mouth, before he drops even lower.

"Can I?" he asks, his eyes unmoving from the buds cresting the satin material of my nightwear. "Can I taste you here?"

Unable to speak from the need in his voice, I wait for his eyes to return to my face before bobbing my chin. "I need your words, Nicole. Crisp, unblemished words."

"Yes," I breathe out on a moan, my horniness too rampant to care how long we've known each other.

It is a night of fun.

A night off the clock.

It won't ruin anything.

"Except perhaps my panties," I mumble to myself when Laken's impatience gets the better of him.

He sucks my nipple into his mouth without lowering the straps of my nightie before cupping my lonely breast with his other hand.

His large hands make my breasts' cup size seem small. They're swamped by him.

Laken is more confident than me. More experienced. The way he has my back arching by doing something as simple as playing with my breasts exposes this, not to mention the temptingly slow pace he uses while making his way from the lace trim of my nightwear to its dainty hemline. He takes his time, savoring every inch of my skin until I'm about to combust, and then he once again seeks permission.

There are no words this time. No requests for me to tell him to stop. His eyes spear me in place with an indigent stare before his smile steals the words from my mouth better than my libido's ability to deny this man when he hooks his thumb into my panties and drags them to the side.

He kisses me right above my clit before flicking his tongue over the already hard and throbbing bud. When his tongue spears inside me, I buck against him as a moan I've never heard before leaves my mouth.

I have nothing to go off—not a single wayward lick or needy suckle—but I'm reasonably sure this is the best head I've been given.

It feels so good I can't hold back my praise when Laken devours me like I've never been consumed. "That feels so good. The best. I've never had better."

My words boost his confidence just as well as his attention skyrocketed mine. He eats me faster and licks me until my backside lifts off the mattress.

Then he adds fingers into the mix.

As he makes the world splinter around me, I dig my fingernails into the bedding and hold on for the ride.

It's intense.

Blistering.

I come undone in thirty seconds, but Laken doesn't stop. He continues devouring me while pumping his fingers in and out of me until I'm a blubbering, incoherent mess, pinned to the mattress with the heaviness of multiple orgasms.

I almost want to fight him off, the tension too much, but my hands never move further than his hair. I tug and pull on his spiky locks until some of his moans turn into groans.

I'm pulling too tight.

I am being cruel.

However, Laken can't get enough.

"Yes, siren. Take what you need. Mark me with your nails. Claim me as I plan to claim you."

His quick pace forces my eyes to close before they roll into the back of my head.

When I feel him rocking against the mattress as he brings me to ecstasy for the umpteenth time this evening, I wedge my foot between the bed and his cock, then use my foot's flexibility to drive him wild with desire.

When the pre-cum dripping from his cock soaks into the bedding along with my many climaxes, I should clam up. My embarrassment should be higher than my wish to come.

Stars are above us. We're in a public place. But nerves never present.

The only thing that steamrolls me is another orgasm.

It presents so hard and fast, before I can warn Laken of its imminent arrival, the stars floating in front of me erupt into beautiful fireworks.

I moan through my release, my limbs as jerking as Laken's movements when my "foot rub" forces our exchange to the very peak of ecstasy.

While strangling his erection through his boxer shorts, he snatches up his jeans from the floor, yanks out the strip of three condoms, then rips one open with his teeth.

Watching him prepping to get down to business is the most sensual image I've ever had the pleasure to witness, but it won't stop me from asking, "They're in date, right? You only just bought them for your…"

Even with his head in a lust cloud, Laken's smarts can't be denied. "For my date?"

After winking at me, he yanks his boxer shorts to his knees, then sheaths the monster I'm staring at with my mouth hanging open. Mercifully, he can multitask. He discovers the date on the packaging of the untouched metallic discs just as the condom reaches the base of his dick.

With the manufacturing date showing they were recently made, he says, "We're good to go."

"Maybe after a year of yoga classes." I gulp, my eyes unmoving from his crotch. "I don't think it's wise to place *that* in the hands of a novice. I don't think even a professional would come out of an exchange like this without crying. You might need to pay extra."

"I'll be sure to leave a bunch of bills on the nightstand."

Laken's laughter about my snarl sets free the butterflies in my stomach before his actions cause a mass resurgence. After removing his shirt the standard macho way, he curls my legs around his sticky waist before lining up the head of his cock with the entrance of my pussy.

He doesn't enter me with one powerful thrust or force tears to my eyes for any other reason than being overwhelmed by an all-encompassing orgasm. He waits until the lyrics my head hasn't been without our entire exchange are closer to love ballads before he alters them into masterpieces.

"If he doesn't make you happy, inspire you, or give you countless orgasms, he doesn't deserve to be a part of your life." As he watches me through hooded lids, he slowly enters. "So I guess I better make it three out of three."

8
NICOLE

The heavenly scent of coffee wakes me from a peaceful slumber.

I groggily wished for an IV of caffeine an hour into our exchange, but once Laken forced another set of body-quaking orgasms out of me, I could only utter, "Intermission. We need an intermission."

In all honesty, caffeine still isn't in the forefront of my mind. Not even the awkward routine we'll have to tiptoe through in the morning when I announce tonight is my last night in Ravenshoe for months.

I want to enjoy the moment. Cherish it for what it is.

A one-night stand without the sleaziness of a one-night stand.

Laken is attentive, sweet, and so determined to give me the performance of my life, he only came once for the endless number of climaxes he gifted me.

He's tipping the axis of my world so well that instead of dreading I fell asleep in his arms, wrapped in his warmth, I'm eager for another helping of all he has to offer.

"How long was I out?" I ask, my question cut short by a deliciously achy moan.

My muscles are stiffer than my greeter's snapped reply, "Since you're meant to be resting, let's hope a minimum of eight hours."

When I crack open an eye, the amused watch of my manager startles me more than the brightness of the early morning sun.

"Knox." While scanning my surroundings to ensure we're the only two people present on the rooftop, I scoop up the bedding until it sits under my chin, grateful that the high thread count sheets aren't the only material brushing against my chest.

I'm still wearing a nightie.

After assuring myself my encounter with Laken wasn't a dream—my body is too deliriously sore for it to have been fictional—I ask, "What are you doing here?"

Knox scrubs at the shadow on his jaw before slowly turning his eyes to me. "I could ask you the same thing."

He drops his eyes to the teasing curve of my cleavage before he stuffs his hands into his pockets and strolls to the ledge of the rooftop. I realize the coffee I was smelling must have been bounding out of his mouth when his distance returns the scent I was sucking in before I crashed.

The delicious fragrance of raunchy sex.

After a beat, Knox spins to face me. Suspicion is rife on his face, but he also appears amused. "Lesley mentioned there was a room up here, but I wasn't aware you overheard our conversation."

"The bellhop gave it away," I partially lie. He told me about the hidden entrance to the presidential suite but failed to mention that the rooftop had all the equipment needed for a steamy night between the sheets. "I thought it might be a good place for inspiration to strike."

My smile hurts when Knox asks, "Did it?"

While nodding as enthusiastically as he asked his question, I stretch for the bedside table Laken placed my songbook on when I kissed him.

I have so many lyrics swirling in my head, making me dizzy, it takes my hand slapping the varnished wood three times before I realize the table is empty.

What the?

"It has to be here somewhere." I slip out of bed before rummaging through the sheets. It could have fallen off the nightstand. We weren't exactly making love. The bed's feet are no longer indenting the rug under them. They're several inches over from their original starting point.

After searching the bed, the sectional sofa, and the bathroom I should have used before falling asleep to stop any nasties, I sling my panicked eyes to Knox. "Have you seen it? I left it right there." I thrust my hand at the bedside table, its tremor unmissable.

Dirty-blond locks fall across his eye when he shakes his head. "Maybe you left it in your room—"

"I didn't leave it in my room." I feel ill, physically sick. "I left it right there. Right next to..." My words trail off when I realize my songbook isn't the only thing missing. Laken's bags and the skintight jeans I had to peel off him are also gone.

Even the condoms we diminished from the stash in his pocket are nowhere to be seen.

He wouldn't have taken my songbook, surely. What benefit would he get taking a book filled with songs consumers will never hear since they're contracted to a label unwillingly to produce country-pop singles?

I freeze when a disturbing notion fills me.

The song I wrote last night isn't under contract. It can be sold and performed by anyone because the only witness to its copyright is the person who stole it.

Just the thought of Laken stealing from me makes me the angriest I've ever been, but it has nothing on the guilt that rains down on me when I remember the inscription inside the cover of my beloved gift.

I can't replace that. It is irreplaceable since the person who inscribed it is dead.

"Nik?" Knox murmurs, drawing my focus to him. "Are you okay? You're not coming down with something, are you? I plan to have you booked out until Christmas."

"I'm fine. I just…"—*feel like a complete and utter idiot*—"am excited about the upcoming tour." When my stomach gurgles, I mutter, "And maybe a little bit nervous." I step closer to him, my mind off my hurt and back onto the matter that had my songbook sitting empty for half a year. "Are you sure the pop angle is what we should be taking? The lyrics I—"

"I thought you trusted me?" he interrupts with his puppy-dog eyes on display for the world to see.

"I do. I just—"

He interrupts me this time by gathering my hands in his and gently squeezing them. "If it will ease your mind, we will discuss it more during our flight to LA, okay?"

I nod. "Thank you."

When he leans in to press a kiss to the edge of my mouth, I freeze. His overfriendly nature is nothing out of the ordinary. It is the fact I can smell sex and intrigue on my skin that has me clamming up.

Much to my relief, Knox acts oblivious to the intoxicating scent. After sucking in a big breath, he says, "But since you're adamant the world needs it to be Nikki J at rehearsal this afternoon, how about you put the facilities to good use before joining me downstairs for a quick breakfast? The jet is already on the runway."

"I can't shower here," I stammer out, like being screwed senseless in a wall-less room is far more acceptable than showering in one.

When Knox bows a suspicious brow, I make out the disgust in my tone isn't as potent as it is. "All my supplies are downstairs."

I gather up the bedding that didn't escape the deluge last night. Somewhere between peeling off his skintight jeans and screwing me unconscious, Laken transferred our make-out session to the rug in front of the fireplace.

Although my skin felt like it was on fire, he kept the blanket close in case we had unwanted visitors.

Apparently he didn't want anyone seeing my skin but him.

I'm such an idiot.

Determined not to be made a fool of twice in less than twenty-four hours, I say, "I'll be ready to leave in thirty. Ten if my detour pays dividends."

I need to get my songbook back from Laken because aside from its sentimental worth, the lyrics I penned last night could be the only stable foundation of my career.

Before Knox can get another word in or follow me out, I gallop down the secret entrance stairs of the rooftop room before throwing open the fire exit door next to the elevator and descending another two dozen levels.

I'm hot, sweaty, and moody when I reach the thirty-seventh floor.

No one will survive my wrath, not even a woman paid to take it.

"Excuse me," shouts a lady with bright-red hair and fishnet stockings. "I'm not expecting a client for another hour." I freeze halfway into the bathroom of her suite when she says, "So if you're looking for your husband, he isn't here."

"I'm not looking for my husband." I turn to face her. "Just a man who—"

Her sigh cuts me off.

Lucky, as I was lost for words.

"How much does he owe? If it's over fifteen hundred, Henry will cover it. If it's less, you're on your own. Henry only accepts debts his men will happily beat out of the johns who skip on their obligations."

I'm lost as to what she means until her eyes drop to my skimpy nightie.

"I'm not a…" I can't say prostitute while standing across from one. "I don't work in this… *industry*. I don't sell my body for money."

My last sentence is barely a whisper, but she hears it. "Then doesn't that make you silly?" My scoff doesn't bother her in the slightest. She moseys to the door, her hips swinging, opens it, and then gestures for me to leave with a head nudge. "You give it away and still get treated like trash. That makes you no better than me, baby cakes."

"He didn't… I didn't…"

I've got nothing.

Not a single comeback.

"I'm sorry for barging in on you. I'm just desperate to have something returned that can't be replaced."

Her huff bellows down the empty hallway. "You gave *that* away for nothing…"—her eyes rake my body for the second time when she says the word "that"—"*and* your virginity. What is wrong with girls these days?"

My eyes bulge. "I didn't give him my virginity." I try to hold back my grumbled comment, but it leaves my mouth before I can. "I wasted that on Tony Stepanova at the end of prom."

"Tony Stepanova? The balding man from Marcella's?"

With my heart in my throat, I nod.

I forget even sex workers have hometowns.

The redhead takes a step back. "He's at least double your age. How did you end up at prom with him?"

Her math doesn't add up. "I'm twenty-six—"

"And I'm the Virgin Mary."

This is usually when I'd dig out my ID, but since I am without my purse and an ounce of dignity, I reply, "Tony is only three years older than me. He got the balding gene from his father. There were more hairs than my womanly secretions on the back seat of his Pontiac after our three-minute wrangle."

I cringe at my poor choice of wording, but the beautiful specimen finds my disastrous dating life hilarious. I can barely hear her over her voracious laughter. "If you thought the shedding was bad back then, look at the sheets." Bile scorches my throat when she gestures her head to the unmade bed on my right. A noticeable sweat imprint shadows the bedding, and there's enough body hair to fix Tony's hideous combover. "The hair on his head now... nothing. Kaput." She shudders while saying, "But you can wax him on Monday and wake up to that Tuesday afternoon. The man has body hair for miles."

"And yet you called me silly."

She waves off my snarky comment with her hand before asking for the name of the man I'm seeking. "I have contacts who may be willing to share details if it'll stop you from walking in on them mid-deed."

I almost feel bad giving Laken's credentials away, but the guilt only lasts as long as it takes for me to remember he stole my most valued possession from me right under my nose. "Laken Howell."

"Howell." She tests his surname a handful more times before nodding. "I recall a booking under that name." I want to vomit until she murmurs, "He was a no-show," while flicking through her planner. "Room 37D." She checks the room number on the open door. "Third on the left."

"Thank you so much," I reply, racing for Laken's room.

"Anytime." My steps fumble when she says, "And if you ever want to take one of my prepaid clients again, reach out. I'll give you a cut of the profits."

"I'm good, thanks."

My denial of her offer is still rumbling down the hallway when I knock on the door of 37D.

When my bang goes unanswered, I flatten my ear to the door.

I startle when a heavily accented voice says, "No one there. Room clean. Checked out this morning."

"He's gone?"

I shouldn't be upset when a maid pulls open the door and nods, but I am. And not all my devastation resides with losing my songbook.

"Can you please let me in?"

"No, sorry." The maid backs away while clutching the master keycard on her lanyard. "I could lose my job."

"Please. There's something very important inside I need to get." When my begging tone doesn't get her over the line, I try another angle. "I can call Lesley and ask permission. She will say yes."

"No! Don't call Lesley." She looks desperate, almost petrified. "I'll look for you. What are you seeking?"

"A songbook." I recall how much I loved all its little quirks when Colette gifted it to me on my fourteenth birthday. "It has burnt-orange stitching, and my name is on the front in leather letters. It's about this big." I hold out my hands to show her the size. "And there's an inscription inside the front cover." Tears burn my eyes. "Words mean nothing—"

"Unless there is music behind them," the maid fills in, shocking me.

"Yes," I murmur, my voice a sob. "Have you seen it?"

She nods so fast she makes my head spin, before returning to her cleaning cart.

I send my thanks to God a hundred times when she pulls out my songbook from beneath bottles of shampoo and conditioner.

"I knew someone had to have left it by mistake."

"Thank you," I praise, my face no longer dry. "This means the world to me, and I'm so very grateful you didn't throw it out."

When I promise her a massive tip for her effort, she shakes her head. "No need. I'm glad to help." She places her hand over mine that's holding my songbook close to my heart. "The words in there are special. I can feel it." A fat, salty blob rolls down my cheek when she quotes part of my sister's favorite saying. "But they will be nothing without music behind them."

9
LAKEN

*A*s I cross the foyer of the hotel, my lengthened strides more a jog than a walk, I wink at Lesley. Nothing can dampen my mood. Not the disdained grumble of James when he recalls me sending away the "packages" he organized for me last night, or the grilling I got from my parole officer when I sprinted into his office two minutes past our agreed time.

Not even River's gripe when I asked him to man the entrance of the rooftop stairs for thirty minutes so I could attend my meeting before grabbing Nicole the caffeine fix she murmured about numerous times during our first intermission has drooped my smile.

I am on cloud fucking nine and dying to return to the rooftop responsible for the spring in my step.

I almost woke Nicole when the sun peeking through the canopy of the bed announced I had overslept. I was a shoulder shake away, but how do you explain to the woman who just rocked your world that if you didn't make it across town in under ten minutes for a meeting with your parole officer, you'd end up back in maximum security prison, serving out the remainder of a sentence most murderers get?

It's not a conversation I'm looking forward to, but it won't occur until I've had the chance to prove I'm not the man my conviction claims I am. So instead of waking Nicole, I yanked back my hands, jotted down a note in her songbook to tell her I'd be back with coffee ASAP, then sprinted like my life depended on it.

As disclosed above, the race was almost lost, but a quick adjustment of my watch while waiting to hear if Officer Barker would see me after the agreed time paid off. I argued that the battery in my watch had gone dead during my incarceration, so I'd missed a connection bus. Since I don't have money for a taxi, he believed my story.

He was still pissed, though. After demanding I get a cell to stay in contact, he handed me a cup and told me to use the bathroom in his office.

"If that comes back dirty, no number of lies will keep you out of lockup."

I'm not going to lie. I was worried I'd get more pee on my hands than in the cup when the lowering of the pants Knox had delivered to the hotel wafted up Nicole's womanly scent. Her decadent smell provoked an immediate response from my body.

I was hard in my parole officer's bathroom.

I didn't think matters could get worse.

Then a voice popped through the hole in the stall wall. "Can you spare some juice? My last lot came back positive." I assumed he meant for drugs until he added, "That's the last time I trust a bitch when she says she's on birth control." He stopped, made a noise I still can't describe, then murmured, "Never mind. You look busy." He rolled up a business card and slotted it through the hole his eye was peering through. "I get times are tough, brother, but you're not supposed to still go it alone once you've left prison."

When the card landed at my feet, it unrolled. The design matched the one I was handed last night when a prostitute promised she could assist me back to my room.

The redhead wouldn't take no for an answer, so I rode with her in the elevator to my floor before climbing the emergency exit stairwell to the top floor.

I stumbled onto the hidden stairwell by accident. I was seeking the vending machine River had mentioned while boasting about the perks of the presidential suite. It was just outside the main stairwell hidden by a maintenance door.

Its lock was broken, but I'm a curious guy who had nothing but time on his hands.

Thank fuck.

Just imagining how differently last night could have gone if I had gone back to my room halves the lengths of my stride.

I only just enter the elevator before the doors shut at the request of River's impatient thumb.

"What the hell, River? You're meant to be manning the stairs for me."

He scowls at me, disliking my language, before wrapping me up in a big, warm hug. He can't converse with anyone without hugging them first.

After squashing the muffins wedged between us, he inches back. "I was, but Knox said you didn't need me anymore."

"Knox?" I double-check, my chipper mood slipping.

River didn't stammer over his words. My blood is simply boiling too perversely to be sure I heard him right.

Even when we were teens, Knox saw me as his competition. He forever sniffed around the girls I was interested in hooking up with, seeking feelers on if they might pick him over me. It didn't bother me in high school. I was young and stupid. But now… now I feel like going on a rampage.

He's too late this time around. The verdict has already been decided, but since I'm not a man who kisses and tells, Knox doesn't know that. He could be trying to schmooze Nicole as we speak.

"Jabbing it won't make it go any faster," River says with a chuckle when I stab the highlighted presidential suite button over and over again. "It will only get us stuck in here." The reason for the annoyance in his tone makes sense when he says, "I left my tablet in my room, so you better quit pushing it. I don't want to look at your face and *only* your face for hours on end. I love you, Laken, and I missed you heaps, but a stud like me can only take in so much handsomeness in one day."

His reply reminds me of the words we exchanged when he raided the mini bar in my hotel room. "Your tablet is on the bedside table in *my* room. Remember? You spilled coke on it, so we cleaned it with the hotel towels before showering." I show him how the hairs on my arm are still sticky and standing on their ends.

"That's right," he replies, the relief on his face unconcealed. "Thanks for reminding me." He squeezes me tight for the second time, then selects the thirty-seventh floor. "I would have remembered if you hadn't woken me with the sparrows."

My words are scarcely heard through my chuckles. "It was ten a.m."

Extra spit arrives with his short reply. He always has an excess amount of slobber when he's being sassy. "Exactly." After exiting the elevator, he spins to face me. "Meet you up there?"

When he looks so far up I see only the whites of his eyes, I jerk up my chin. "Bring an appetite with you." I jiggle the bag of muffins in my hand. "I bought extra."

I only just witness his leap into the air before the doors close and the elevator continues its journey to the hotel's top floor. Thank fuck River was in the car when I entered. I don't know if my legs would have been up for another twenty-story climb. They almost collapsed on me multiple times last night, but I refused to give in to the exhaustion overwhelming me until Nicole was as riveted by me as I was by her voice.

My god, that woman can sing. She has the voice of an angel, but that's the only thing saintly about her. Her body is wickedly delicious, her face pure fucking ecstasy, and she sucks dick like she hasn't consumed a single calorie the entire day.

She's also witty, funny, and humble as fuck. She can't take a compliment if her life depends on it. She blushes before trying to push the praise onto anyone but her, and since that is usually done with sexual ambiguity, it kept the tension high until the wee hours of this morning.

We would have still been fooling around now if Nicole hadn't passed out.

The thought makes me grin like a smug prick, and it brings back the spring in my step when I exit the elevator outside of the presidential suite.

I manage two lengthy strides before my steps are halted by the man I am grateful as fuck isn't flirting with Nicole on the rooftop.

"Laken." Before I can pivot to face him, Knox requests me to join him in the foyer of the presidential suite. "We've got important shit to discuss."

"Can you give me a minute?"

I sound ungrateful and I hate it, but I'm more itching to get back to Nicole than to thank Knox for a generosity I earned.

He stares at me as if people not jumping to his every command isn't a common occurrence. "Come on, man. Stop messing. We're already meant to be on the road."

"Then what's another two minutes?"

Stealing his chance to deny me again, I sprint for the maintenance door, take the stairs two at a time, then burst through the door I glanced at a hundred times last night to make sure I was the only lucky bastard to see Nicole naked.

"Sorry, my errand took longer than expected. I had no idea how bad Ravenshoe's traffic had become until…" My words trail off when I notice the bed Nicole was resting on is empty and made. The bedsheets are pulled so taut I could bounce a nickel off them. "Nicole?" I query while pacing toward the bathroom. The shower walls are see-through, and a half wall hides the toilet, so I know she isn't using the facilities. I'm just hopeful she's close by. "Are you here?"

Heavy stomps gobble up the silence of an empty room. "The day I'm not chasing you is the day I'm dead." Knox looks winded while nudging his head to the door behind him. "Come on. We don't have time. If the private jet runs over, I get charged for every second it sits unused on the runway."

"Private jet?" I cough out, my shock too strong to ignore.

"Yeah. So will you get your fucking ass moving before you send me broke?"

When I remain frozen on the spot, Knox joins me in the middle of the rooftop "room." His wonderment isn't on par with mine when I stumbled onto this space last night. I was in complete awe, and the view improved tenfold with Nicole's unexpected arrival.

"Hey," I shout when Knox snatches up the breakfast I was planning to share with Nicole and River while introducing them, dumps it in the trash no longer housing used condoms, then guides me outside.

Where the fuck did the condoms go?
Did Nicole take them with her?

Shocked she'd do that, I follow Knox down the stairs and into the presidential suite. "You can eat on the plane. It'll be better than any shit you'll find around here." A reason for his clammy skin comes to light when he adds, "There's also someone I'm dying for you to meet. I had planned to introduce you last night, but things got hectic, and I ran out of time."

I don't know much about presidential suites, but I'm reasonably sure the one we're entering is the primary suite. It is massive. It has two walk-in closets, and the steam coming out of the door at our left exposes the water is piping hot and endless.

"A delay was probably for the best." He wiggles my shoulders. "Looks like you let off a heap of steam."

He isn't wrong. It just occurred in a way not even I had expected.

Knox squeezes my shoulder. "Was she good? I've heard great things about Candy."

"Candy?"

"The prostitute—"

The creak of a door opening cuts him off. Then a harmonic, cock-thickening voice has him acting like a choirboy. "If I stay in there a second longer, I'll become a prune."

Knox waggles his brows at me, slaps my back like a giddy kid on Christmas morning, and then greets the woman causing the hairs on the back of my neck to stand to attention before she fully exits the bathroom. "Sorry, baby cakes. I forgot I asked you to wait for me."

The reason for my body's response to the woman's voice is exposed when she breaks through the thick sheet of steam enough to reveal her gorgeous face and womanly curves.

I found you.

"Nikki, this is Laken," Knox introduces, pulling Nicole toward my frozen body in the middle of her room. She looked ravishing last night with a sweaty face and misted body, but there's something entirely different about seeing her drenched head to toe. It has me eager to push harder next time. To make her as saturated as she is now. "Laken, this is—"

"Nicole," I interrupt, too impatient to wait for a proper introduction.

Finding the rooftop room empty hit me harder than first believed. The relief of seeing her standing in front of me can't deny that.

"It's Nikki," Nicole corrects, her demeanor cool, almost icy. "And you are?"

Unaware we've met before, and not dumbfounded by her odd question, Knox answers on my behalf. "Laken. Laken Howell." Nicole and I recoil in sync when he adds, "Your new bodyguard."

"What?" Nicole gasps out in a shocked breath. "No!"

Her stern denial already has me on the back foot, so I won't mention the unpleasant taste that hits my mouth when I notice how Knox is holding her. His hand hasn't dropped from her waist even with them reaching his desired location, and they stand barely an inch apart when he twists her to face him.

I can't hear a thing he says to her through my pulse ringing in my ears, but they look cozy. *Extremely* cozy.

"Laken?"

"Huh?" I reply after shifting my eyes to Knox, my questioner.

He glares at me as if to say, *Get your head out of your ass*, before continuing. "I was just explaining to Nik how you've recently returned from a long placement with the correctional department and that you're wanting to go private, so I gave you a shot."

What the fuck is he on about?

Knox drops his hand from Nicole's waist before circling it around her balled fist and giving it a reassuring squeeze. "I know being the protective detail of a music starlet isn't what you envisioned when pondering a career in music, but we all have to start somewhere." His lips hover an inch from Nicole's temple when he nestles into her. The simplest gesture makes me want to smash his teeth in, but my feet remain rooted to the ground since I have no clue who the bad guy is in this situation.

It isn't looking good for me right now.

"And who knows?" Knox adds, his tone the loved-up one he uses while schmoozing. "After spending a couple of months in the presence of greatness, you might learn a thing or two about what it takes to be a chart-topping musician."

When Nicole stiffens at the end of his sentence, I stare at her like she isn't the woman I messed the sheets with last night while correcting, "I'm not looking for a career in music. I haven't considered it for a long time. But if it were ever on the table, I'd only want to produce it, not compose it."

I thought my reply would lower Nicole's angst, but it seems to have done the opposite. The vein in her neck works overtime as she shoots daggers at me.

I don't know what has her so worked up. I left her a note saying I'd be back as soon as I could.

It's more than Knox will ever give her.

He runs before they're even asleep.

"Composing and producing are practically the same thing," Knox chuckles out. "Either way, everyone starts at the bottom rung of Knox Records before being given the chance to climb the ranks."

"Knox Records?" I couldn't be more shocked if he had slapped me in the face with a fish.

Knox told me I was stupid when I mentioned wanting to go into music production during our final year of high school. That with modern technology, there was no money to be made in producing anymore. He tried to steer me away from it, but since music lives in my veins, I spent the first two years of my incarceration on the rec room computer, honing my craft.

I only stepped back when I realized inmates were paid for work that could be sold outside the prison's walls. I couldn't see River, but I could make sure he was well looked after, so I spent the last almost eight years making plates for electric vehicles.

The anger on Nicole's face softens when the disbelief in my tone can't be missed. "You own a record label? Mr. There's No Money to Be Made in Music founded his own label?"

Knox nods like it is no big deal he stole my dreams out from under me for the second time in my life.

"And Nicole…" I pause, swallow, then correct. "*Nikki* is one of your artists?"

"That"—I could have lived without his following four words—"and so much more."

Before either Nicole or I can object, Knox suggests for Nicole to get dressed before instigating her exit of the room with a gentle pat on her bottom.

I'd be lying if I said his somewhat innocent gesture didn't fill me with an equal amount of rage and remorse. I'm pissed he's treating Nicole like a lapdog who will do as told to ensure it gets fed, and she's allowing it to happen, but I'm also panicked that I stepped out on my best friend with his girl.

Did I fuck my best friend's girl?

Did I break the ultimate guy code?

Did Knox win again?

He owes me a lot, but if I've dogged him like this, if I did him wrong how I swore I never would, he won't owe me a damn thing.

There are lines I swore I'd never cross.

Lines that are looking mighty blurred right now.

Knox waits for Nicole to be out of earshot before drilling me. "What the fuck is wrong with you today? You're acting like an idiot with half a brain." He thrusts his hand in the direction Nicole went. "I've been talking you up all week, and then you look at her like a sleaze who's never gotten his dick sucked." He rakes his fingers through his hair, turning the tips on themselves. "And don't blame Candy for this. I know for a fact she sucks better than any vacuum you've ever owned." Before I can remind him real men don't pay for sex, he shocks me into silence. "Did your first PO meeting make you edgy? There was no need to shit your pants. Officer Barker is on payroll. That's why he didn't watch you pee."

He helps himself to a nip of whiskey from the bar in the corner of the room, firming my worry that this space is as much his as it is Nicole's. "The fucker is still adamant you need an ankle bracelet, though. It's got nothing to do with you and everything to do with him not wanting the big guys knowing he's dirty." He downs a double of whiskey before locking his eyes with me. "You can't come on tour with us if you refuse to wear a dog collar." He kicks at the hem of the pants I slipped into this morning a second after dressing Nicole in her nightie. "So I asked the tailor to give the hems extra flare. No one will know you're wired."

Since I need more than a minute to work through the first half of the conversation, I veer toward the latter. "I refuse to wear an ankle bracelet. I'm not a fucking criminal."

When he throws me an arrogant smirk, my jaw tightens.

Before I can remind him why I pled guilty, a commotion outside steals my focus. River has arrived at the presidential suite to the jubilant cheers of the posse of paid friends Knox has rarely been without since junior high.

"I'm trying to help you, man," Knox murmurs a short time later, demanding my focus back to him. "He's gotten used to this life…" After thrusting the whiskey bottle at River, he waves it around the room I'm still praying like fuck isn't his. "I honestly don't know how he'll do going back to…" His gesture this time cuts like a knife. He tosses his hand at my chest, degrading me and my parenting skills with one quick motion. "But I guess that choice isn't mine to make." He throws back the equivalent of half a glass of whiskey before slamming the bottle onto the crystal bar. "He's your brother, so he's your responsibility." He sighs. "I just wanted to help you. You're family, and without you, none of this would have been possible." He once again highlights the luxury of the room. "I want to share my fortunes with my brother and make this a real family business."

When he notices my defenses are weakening, he calls River into the room.

Just like every time River joins a conversation, he hands out a dozen hugs before he takes over it. "Did you hear, Laken?" He holds up a pricy-looking buttoned-up shirt with his name and a job description stitched on the front. His smile is one I've never seen before when he announces, "I got promoted to head of marketing."

"Hold on a minute," Knox interjects, halving his grin. "I said the position is yours *once* you get your brother's permission." He slaps his shoulder before pulling him in to noogie his head, hopeful a bit of banter will lower his disappointment. "But I'm sorry, man. It doesn't appear as if Laken wants to go on the road with us. He has plans." He locks his eyes with mine. Since it's been a long time since he's looked me in the eyes, I can't quite read the emotion they're displaying. "Plans that don't involve us."

"That isn't what I said," I deny when River's bottom lip drops into a pout.

You'd swear I expressed more than I did when River asks, "So we're doing this? Are the Three Amigos back in business?"

"No." I backtrack again when my snapped reply devastates River more than when the judge handed down a ruling of twelve years. "Maybe. I don't fucking know. I need a minute to think. My head is swirling." I won't mention the state of my gut. I feel seconds from barfing.

I hardly slept last night, and I've not eaten since dinner, but hunger isn't the cause of my nausea. It's from trying to work out what the hell is going on. Nicole acted like she didn't know me. River seems more eager to hang with Knox than with me, and I just sprinted across the city to attend a meeting with my PO, who is supposedly on Knox's payroll.

That's too much shit to wade through less than twenty-four hours after leaving a maximum security prison.

When I flop onto the sofa in the corner of the room to cradle my head in my hands, the expensive thread of Knox's trousers brushes my elbow not even a second later. "Stop reading this as more than it is. If you wanna come on the road with us, come. If you wanna hang here until we get back, hang here." He waits for my eyes to lift to his. "I just assumed you'd want to be a part of this." He waves his hand around the room during the "this" part of his statement. "But I'll understand if you want to forge your own way in this world. I won't stop you. I just hope it won't fuck this up."

"This?" I ask when he doesn't gesture to anything or anyone this time around.

"This." He darts two fingers between us. "You're my fucking brother, man. My blood. I wouldn't be shit without you, so I don't want to leave you behind while creating greatness. I want you to get a share of the pie you deserve."

River takes the last half of his reply as literal pie. He rubs his hands together while licking his lips.

"And the perks aren't bad, either." Knox pushes off the sofa and moves deeper into the room. "Private jets. Presidential suites." The red hue on River's cheeks deepens with each word he speaks. "Endless women." He chuckles at River's beet-colored face. "And the who's who of the music industry." He gathers a coat tossed across the made bed in the middle of the suite. "It's the 'in' you're looking for but trying to deny, just with an official title that will keep BOP off your back until your probation ends."

His reply makes sense, but I'm still hesitant, and not all of it stems from what lines I did or did not cross.

"Why make me a bodyguard? I'm not exactly qualified for the role."

Knox's answer is the worst one he could give. "Who better to protect my girl than the man who'll stand at my side when we make it official?" After folding his coat over his arm, he twists to face me. "The limo leaves in ten. I hope I find you in it." He locks eyes with River. "Both of you." He squeezes his shoulder, silently farewelling him, before exiting the suite without so much as a backward glance.

His failure to look back reveals he's disappointed in me.

He isn't the only one.

"Are you fucking crazy?" River shouts a second after we're alone, his anger delivered with an excessive amount of spit.

"Language—"

"Oh, fuck off." His chest deflates as he lets out a heavy sigh. "Your double standards are so outrageous anyone would swear you got lumped with the extra chromosome."

"Hey—"

He doesn't give me the chance to reprimand him for picking on his disability. "I want to do this, Laken. I've been a part of it from the start and want to see it through. Nicole is..." I don't mean to groan but can't hold it back, and it gives away my hesitation in an instant. "Is that who this is about?" His brows furrow as he takes a moment to deliberate. "I thought maybe it was because you didn't like how Knox stepped up to the plate to take care of me when you left."

"I didn't leave, River. I went to jail." *For you, I went to jail for you.* But since I promised never to share that, I wet my lips before saying, "And I'm not angry about Knox taking care of you." *How can I be when that was our agreement?*

"Then what's your problem? You skipped into our room this morning, and now you're walking around like a bear with a sore head." He suddenly stiffens. "Did you hang with the road crew? They're not a good representation of the industry." Even with his voice not altering, I know he is mimicking something he's heard previously. His eyes rolled partway through his statement, and his hands are balled at his side, telltale signs his beliefs aren't on par with what he's saying. "And hanging with them will only get you fired."

"I didn't hang with anyone." Liar. Liar. *Liar.* "I just need a minute to wrap my head around everything. A *lot* has changed." Hating that the tension between us is already stale, I try to lighten the mood. "Like whoever thought you'd be excited about having your name on a business shirt?"

"I have to wear a tie, too." When I arch a shocked brow, he chuckles. "I almost told him to shove it, but I really like working for Knox Records. It's so much better than my last job." For the first time in years, vulnerability echoes in his tone when he glances at the people who greeted him with happy cheers and fist bumps. "They don't treat me differently. I'm one of the team. These guys are like family to me."

Conscious I have no right to strip his family from him for the second time in his short life, and that the matter of his guardianship is still up in the air, I give in to peer pressure far too quickly. "Then I guess we better pack."

River's eyes are on me in a second, hot and heavy. "Really?"

I nod before grunting through the strength of his hug when he crash-tackles me on the sofa. I was already seated, but you wouldn't know that for how far back he knocks me when he dives for me. "Thank you, Laken. I promise I won't let you down."

"You never have," I reply, returning his hug. "You just need to go a little easy on me, okay? This is all new to me."

He assumes I mean my position. I was more referencing the fact I chased my best friend's girl.

Knox hinted at marriage. That isn't something he jokes about. He only ever mentions commitment when he's giving excuses for his latest relationship's downfall.

"I'll teach you everything you need to know." I grant my lungs permission to breathe again when River stands. "We can start now." He mimics the stance of a bodyguard with his head tilted back and his arms folded in front of his inflated chest. "No more questions." I attempt to speak, but he beats me to it. "I said *no more questions!*"

"I—"

River's death stare would have any man freezing in their place.

Any man except me. "Knox said we had ten minutes."

His eyes bulge before they drop to my watch. "That was almost five minutes ago. We need to move fast." He grabs a pre-packed duffle bag from outside the room and tosses it into my chest. "Everything in the bathroom is mine."

"This is your room?" I ask, my tone more hopeful than surprised.

"No." He stops raiding the minibar before finalizing his reply. "But Knox organizes for new hair products to be delivered at each hotel he stays at, so he won't care if I take them."

I wonder if he feels the same way about his woman?

When I remain frozen, shocked by my snarky inner monologue, River forces me into a space that smells like a mix of my best friend's cologne and the body wash I licked off his girl last night.

10
NICOLE

A mix of emotions hits me when Knox sighs before gesturing for the limousine driver to begin our short trip to a private airstrip on the outskirts of Ravenshoe.

We're the sole occupants of a stretched black town car, which means the tension I've been avoiding like the plague the past hour can no longer be dodged.

Knox is angry. That isn't unusual. To survive the knocks of showbiz, he has to give off a prickly demeanor, but his mood this morning seems more reflected at me than the hype we're trying to create.

At one stage, I was convinced he'd heard my cries of ecstasy on the rooftop, particularly when he suggested we delay our departure time so I could stand in a steam-filled room to soak my vocal cords with moisture. But as the morning went on and my frustration about how quickly I fell for Laken's "I'm happy to wait" ruse settled, Knox's usually cocky demeanor shifted to edgy.

Desperate to ease the tension, I curl my hand over Knox's balled one and say, "It's for the best." When he looks at me, lost, I highlight one of our similarities. "I understand he's a family friend, so you want to help him, but there's only so much you can do to help someone before you eventually must step back and let them help themselves."

"I—" His reply cuts me off before the limousine staggers to a stop and the back passenger door pops open.

"That was a close call."

Butterflies form in my stomach as my head shifts through hours of footage to unearth the last time I heard that statement. It was last night in the elevator. Laken said it while entering—a mere second before his scent turned me into a lust-crazed idiot.

I'm expecting Laken to slot into the seat across from Knox and me, so you can picture my surprise when it is River's kind eyes that lock with mine a second before he wraps me up in a friendly hug.

The warmth of his embrace stops my disappointment from making itself known. His hugs are as heated as a furnace, and they melt my heart every single time he gifts me one.

"I'm so glad you could make it," I murmur when he sinks into the leather seat across from me. "I was getting worried you were going to turn down the position."

River is a brilliant artist, but he is an even better hype person. He can turn a dull situation into a raging party with nothing but his grinning face. That's why I suggested to Knox that he should give him a position on the marketing team launching my album. He has an eye for detail while also understanding color isn't the only thing you need to bring to the party to make it memorable. Love is by far the most important ingredient.

"And leave you in the hands of someone without an extra chromosome?" Spit sprinkles the air when he *pffts*. "I'd never do that to you, Nicole. You're my favorite person on the planet."

My heart launches into my throat when a voice oddly similar to River's projects from outside the limousine. "That wasn't what you said when you had me raiding *every* minibar in the presidential suite."

After filling the empty spot next to River, Laken adjusts the tilt of his head to shadow his eyes from the late-morning sun before saying, "He was worried you'd leave without him." He doesn't look at me while speaking. He doesn't even acknowledge my presence. "I told him you'd never do that. That family looks out for family. They have your back no matter what."

Even with his eyes not on me, I can tell the anger of his words is projected at me.

Why in the world is he angry?

He isn't the one who woke in a cold bed to discover their life's work had been stolen.

Knox appears blind to the tension ridding the air of oxygen. "I'll do anything for you, man. You know that." After shuffling to the edge of his chair, Knox slaps his hand into Laken's. "Welcome to the team. I appreciate you stepping up to bat for me again. I know it isn't the position you want, but your willingness to do this for me shows what a true friend you are."

When Knox pulls Laken in for a man hug, Laken's narrowed gaze shoots to me. He looks like he wants to hang me out to dry, like he wants to tell the world last night's escapades weren't consensual on both sides of the team, but instead, he mutters, "Thanks for having me."

I roll my eyes at their bros-for-life mantra before drifting to the scenery whizzing by the window. River is Knox's brother and hasn't been granted *any* special privileges—he was cleaning the toilets only last month—so why does Laken get to trample over everyone for one of the most sought-after positions at Knox Records?

Don't read that the wrong way. I'm not saying protecting me is every man's dream job. I am merely stating that most protective details see their position as a steppingstone in the industry.

The only person who hasn't chased fame is Hawke, and although he'd never admit it, that has more to do with whom he's protecting. He loves Jasper, Jenni and Nick's firstborn son, as if he is his own, and Harper, their adorable daughter, has him wrapped around her little finger.

So even Laken being a family friend of Knox's doesn't alter the facts.

There are more deserving people entitled to a promotion, so Knox should have given it more thought before handing the position to a blast from his past.

Wow. I had no idea how horrific Laken's rejection had burned until now. I sound like a bitter old cow instead of a woman who understands the terms of a one-night stand.

It would be easy to play it cool if he hadn't stolen from me.

That's where my anger stems. I wouldn't have cared about waking up in an empty bed if he had left my belongings alone.

Yeah, right.

If you believe that, you'll believe anything.

I zone back into their conversation when Knox says, "Anything you need to make this transition easier, let me know. *Nothing* is off limits." Unease grips me when Knox places his hand high on my thigh and squeezes it. "Except her. She's untouchable."

Before I can work out what he's playing at, the reason for his show of masculinity is unearthed when he removes his hand from my body to pull a contract out of his soft leather briefcase.

Knox makes all his employees sign a contract with a non-fraternization policy, and although he said it wasn't a requirement for artists—it's more to protect them than hinder their creativity—I happily signed it.

Knox's looks give any woman's eyes the workout of their life, but there are some lines I won't cross.

Messing around with the man in charge of my career is the first item on that list.

I almost warn Laken not to sign anything without having a lawyer look at it, but I can't get any words past the shock clogged in my throat when I notice he's once again shooting daggers at me.

If he wants to make out I'm the villain, I may as well portray one.

"Don't forget to mention that company perks are only to be utilized during *working* hours." I wait for Laken's eyes to align with mine before I lower my eyes to the complimentary condoms supplied by the stretch limousine company. The brand and use-by date match the condoms we diminished last night.

I can tell the moment their familiarity smacks into him. His jaw stiffens before his throat works through a hard swallow. "It won't be an issue," he murmurs after swallowing enough times to wet his throat with spit. "I won't have any need for company perks…" I would have preferred if he ended his statement there. Regretfully, I've never been overly lucky. "Not during *working* hours, anyway."

"Attaboy!" Knox says with a laugh. "I have no issues with you sowing your oats while we're on tour. I'd just rather you do it with the girls seeking free tickets instead of the ones I'm paying out the eye to bring the tour together." My back molars are already gnawed to stubs over him demoralizing the people we need to make my album a success, but I feel sick to the stomach when I can't take his final comment any other way. "If you want to pay for it, you may as well hire a *professional*."

I shoot my eyes up from my balled hands when Laken asks a short time later, "Have all employees signed this?" I assume Knox nods when a rustle flicks up the loose bangs framing my face, and am proven right when Laken continues his interrogation. "Including you two?"

When Knox's humored laugh doubles the heat of the glare Laken is hitting me with, my anger surges too fast for me to continue playing nice. "Why does it bother you if we've signed or not? It isn't like either of us are going to sleep with you." I thrust my hand between Knox and myself as I say the word "us" before locking eyes with Laken to ensure he can't miss my unvoiced words.

I won't make that mistake twice.

I thank my lucky stars for the driver's impressive skills when our arrival at the private airstrip allows me to exit the vehicle with a dramatic flair. I clamber out of my seat as if my ass is on fire before hotfooting it in the direction of a private jet idling on the runway.

It is on loan from Rise Up, a somewhat "good luck" omen from the men who didn't have two dimes to rub together before music gave them more than fame.

Since I am leaving Ravenshoe—a star-spotting haunt now as famous as LA—I'm screamed a range of questions during my brisk walk to the stairs leading to the jet. They aren't from fans wanting a piece of their favorite band. They're from members of the paparazzi desperate for an exclusive scoop on the group of friends who put Ravenshoe on the map.

"Is it true Noah and Emily's marriage is on the rocks?"

"Will you be back in time for Nick and Jenni's wedding? If sources close to the family are correct, it will be sometime within the next three months."

Wrong. Nick and Jenni are already married. As are Kylie and Slater, Rise Up's drummer. They just kept it a secret from everyone of no importance to them.

"Can you confirm or deny if Emily is expecting again?"

"Do you want to apologize to Kylie about the mishap that occurred last night?"

That question stops me in my tracks.

After cranking my neck to the middle-aged man livestreaming his "interview," I ask, "What am I meant to be apologizing about?"

His reply stabs me in the chest. "When you went home with her fiancé."

"I didn't go home with anyone last night." *Dirty, filthy sex with a stranger on a rooftop? Different story.*

"That isn't what *TMZ* is reporting," says a second pap with half a head of pink hair. "A reliable source informed them that you were seen leaving..."—she checks her notepad—"Mavericks at eleven p.m. on the back of Slater's bike." After scrolling on her phone for ten seconds, she spins the screen to face me. "See?"

"That isn't me."

I wore a Jenni Holt dress last night. The auburn-haired beauty on the back of Slater's bike is wearing cutoff jeans and a white singlet top oddly similar to the shirt Kylie, Slater's wife, had on last night.

"Kylie is mainly brunette, but her hair would understandably look more auburn if it was illuminated by dozens of cameras flashing."

I barely get two steps away when a snarky comment stops me for the second time. "Did you pre-plan your reply by yourself or while discussing with Slater how to keep your affair a secret from his heavily *pregnant* partner?"

"Listen, your source is *way* off the mark. I—"

Before I can complete my statement, a beefy arm wraps around my waist, and I'm carried up the stairs of the private jet.

"No more questions," the stern voice barks out when the paparazzi follow us.

They only back away when Laken plops me into a seat at the front of the plane before using his body to block their ability to snap my picture.

"I said no more questions!" He shoves the camera of the lead aggressor into his face before forcibly returning them all to the tarmac one push at a time.

With the jet no longer surrounded by the vultures of the media, Knox and River soon join me inside. Knox is too busy barking orders into his cell phone to check if I'm okay, but River hugs me to death like we didn't greet each other in the same manner only minutes ago, before he takes the seat across from me.

The pride on his face can't be missed when he slings his eyes to Laken, who is single-handedly manhandling over a dozen paparazzi into submission. "I taught him everything he knows." His chuckle returns my focus to him. "He's a fast learner." He takes his time drifting his almond-shaped eyes over my face before asking sincerely, "Are you okay, Nicole? Those guys can be pretty mean."

I nod. "Yeah. I've grown accustomed to it the past few years. I was just a little surprised they shifted their focus to Slater this time."

As a flight attendant places a glass of champagne down in front of me, River balances his elbows on the same glossed table. "Not just that." He nudges his head to the stretched town car, which is seeking an opening in traffic to return to the hotel. "With what happened in there? My brother can be a bit of a hothead, but I figured you'd be well versed on them since you've been dealing with Knox for the past year."

I'm left a little stumped. Not about his assumption that Knox is arrogant. I'm surprised by his admission that Laken is his brother. "I thought you said you only have one brother?"

The surprise in my tone slants River's adorable head. "I do."

"Knox?" I query, still lost.

The axis of my world is tilted for the third time today when strands of dark hair fall into River's eye when he shakes his head. "Laken."

"Laken is your brother?" I choke on my spit when his headshake shifts into a bob. "But Knox introduced you to me as his brother. He said he raised you since you were three."

My answers come from a voice above me instead of the man seated across from me. "Knox tells everyone that. Especially when he wants to get in her panties." Laken works his jaw side to side before gesturing his head to the seats at the back of the plane. "We should sit back there, River. We don't want people confusing us with the *talent*." He spits out my profession as if I'm a dog who performs for treats.

River stomps his foot down. "But I like it here."

"Now, River," Laken barks out, proving their relationship isn't a ruse. His tone is bossy and determined, almost on par with my father's stern tone when I act like a brat.

"Fine." After dropping his eyes to mine to issue a silent apology and hugging me for the third time in the past ten minutes, River stomps to the far end of the jet.

It takes Laken a little longer to shadow his stalk. I assume it is because he needs time to work his apology through his head before delivering, but am proven wrong when he places a gold-hooped earring onto the tabletop housing two untouched glasses of champagne.

My hand shoots up to my left ear when I recognize its design. My left earlobe is still missing the accessory only my right ear wore throughout our exchange last night.

I hadn't noticed I'd lost an earring until Laken pointed it out while gathering my hair in a fist. Since the earring's value was a pittance compared to the confidence bombarding me because I was on my knees in front of a man I'd only just met, I mourned its loss for three seconds before shifting my focus to making Laken as deliriously spent as I was when he had his head between my thighs.

"Where did you find it?" I ask, my voice high with shock.

"In your bathroom." I discover a reason for the angst in his tone when he adds, "Right next to a half-used bottle of aftershave."

"Laken—"

"I'm no expert, but you should probably mix things up this time around." When he nudges his head to my songbook, I snatch it up before he can threaten it more than he already has. "Not even country bumpkins want to listen to love ballads about homewrecking cheaters."

He leaves before I can offer him an explanation I'm not sure he deserves.

11
LAKEN

For the first four hours of the flight to Los Angeles, I pretend I'm sleeping.

Over the next hour, I flick through glossy magazines while acting like I don't recognize the name of the person featured on almost every page.

The shit the media makes out as factual is crazy. The articles are outrageous and expose why I would have much rather forged a name for myself in music from behind a sound desk instead of a microphone.

"It doesn't even look like her," I spit out while tossing the magazine with Nicole's supposed ass on the cover onto the table separating River and me. Its skid across the table mimics the jet's tires as it comes in for the landing. "The minute hint of red in that woman's hair is as lackluster as my beard. Nicole's hair is orange. As orange as..."

"An orange?" River fills in when an analogy evades me, his tone as firm as his grip on the armrests.

He's never been on a plane, but he handles the landing like a pro.

I was hopeful I'd slot into my position just as easily, but I should have given it more thought. I've been known to jump the gun when it comes to decision-making—especially when it effects River—but this is a whole new low for me.

How can I protect someone when I'm the man she needs protecting from the most?

While nodding in agreement to River's comparison, I slump low in my chair before once again slinging my eyes to Nicole and Knox at the front of the plane. "Does it not bother him that they're writing this shit about her? She's his…"

I can't say it.

I can't admit that Nicole is anyone's girlfriend but mine.

Which is fucked considering Knox is my best friend.

Unease curdles through my stomach when River unlatches his belt while saying, "To Knox, any publicity is good publicity."

Not one to sugarcoat things, I say, "That's shit."

"I know, and I plan to change it. I just need him to take me seriously." After pulling his backpack out from under his chair, River spins around the laptop he's been tinkering on for almost five hours. It shows a design for an album cover. It is simple but announces everything you need to know. Who the artist is and their field of expertise.

This one is straight-up country.

The pride in my voice can't be missed. "That's good, River. Real good."

"But too bland." River's sigh is silent, but I don't need to hear it to know his confidence is torn to shreds when Knox continues dissing his design while walking down the empty aisle. "It's no different from what every other Tom, Dick, and Harry is putting out. It'll get lost in a sea of millions."

"Conformity is a well-known trait of the music industry." I haven't studied music for years, but some truths never change.

River hums, agreeing with me, but Knox isn't as easy to get over the fence. "Not at Knox Records. We want to be different. Unique. We're not going to follow the masses. We'll carve our own road." The admiration in his eyes pisses me off when he flicks them to Nicole, who is making her way down the aisle even though the exit is directly across from her. "And the glory we'll achieve will all be thanks to her."

It dawns on me that Nicole isn't joining our discussion when she sidesteps Knox to enter the bathroom. This private jet only has one washroom. It is next to my seat.

I feel like shit so I may as well smell like it too.

Just when I think my mood can't sour any more, it nosedives off a cliff as Knox tells Nicole he'll join her in a minute. He doesn't keep his voice down or try to hide his intentions from the flight attendant collecting River's empty glass of coke. He proudly announces his intent to join the mile-high club, even with the jet no longer in the air, to anyone willing to listen.

I've never wished to be deaf until now.

Knox raps his knuckles on my chest, stealing my focus from the "in use" sign on the bathroom door. "I didn't come here to bust River's balls about his shitty cover design." I shift my eyes to River to silently assure him his cover is the perfect fit for a country-pop artist while Knox continues tossing out insults as if they're compliments. "I wanted to give you a heads-up so we don't face any incidents on the way out like we did on the way in." He props his ass on the armrest of my seat. I assume he's going to give me a rundown on the best way to protect Nicole from the vultures of the media, so you can imagine my shock when he says, "I'm not paying you to come between Nicole and the paps." Before I can remind him that I didn't sign any of the forms he tried to hand me earlier, payment details included, he adds, "Any publicity is good publicity."

"They're making her out to be a homewrecker. Every article I've skimmed the past hour is running the same set of false claims."

Well, I assume they're false. But what do I know? I thought Nicole was single when we hooked up, and I was soon proven wrong.

"And?" Knox asks, his voice humored. "You said she's in *every* magazine. Do you have any idea how much that type of exposure is worth? You can't buy coverage like this."

"But Nicole doesn't want fame this way."

Knox tries to act as if River never spoke. I don't let it slide, however. I peer past Knox, who's blocking my little brother from my view, before gesturing for River to continue.

Against Knox's grumbled warning for him to keep his mouth shut, River discloses, "She could have had a record deal years ago, but she didn't want it off her friends' backs. She wanted to make it on her own." He spins his laptop to face me. The screen is filled with a hideous album cover that makes Nicole look like she's starring in an infomercial for retro aerobics videos. Her clothes are fluro, her hair is teased out, and she's wearing puffy socks. "That's why she goes by Nikki J."

"The media knows who she is," Knox defends, his back up.

River's defenses are just as high. "Because you include it in every press release you send out."

"You what?"

That question didn't come from River or me. It came from Nicole, who is exiting the bathroom with a platinum-blonde wig hiding her identifiable locks. "We agreed that we would do this from the ground up. That it would be our victory."

Her "we" and "our" cut through me like a knife, but the glare she hits Knox with during her statement makes them more papercuts than fatal wounds.

"I tried. I swear to you, I did," Knox defends, his voice almost babyish as he tries to subdue her with charm instead of facts. "But no one was interested until your connection to Rise Up was exposed."

How the fuck can that be? Nicole had only seconds to prepare before her performance last night, and she hit it out of the park. I was in complete fucking awe and desperate for more, so how aren't disc jockeys rushing for the chance to play her songs?

I can't help the smirk that forms on my face when a groveling Knox follows a furious Nicole to the front of the plane. I'm not happy they're arguing loud enough to overtake the clicking of paparazzi cameras on the tarmac. I am pleased Nicole is standing up for herself and giving Knox some of the sass I sampled last night.

I wipe my smile off my face when I realize how disturbing I am being.

I fucked my best friend's girl, and now I'm sitting back and watching with eagerness as their relationship crumbles.

Neither are points I should peacock about.

"What do you think he's saying to her?" River asks, giving me an excuse for my inability to take my eyes off Nicole. "She's calming down pretty quick."

"She is," I agree, disappointed. "Do you know much about their…"—*nope, I can't say relationship, either, when Nicole is part of the equation*—"dynamic? Knox seems different with her."

He was more a do-as-I-ask-or-I'll-raise-my-hand-at-you man before I went away. He would have never chased a woman and pleaded for her to listen to him. He said there's too many fish in the sea to worry about the feelings of one.

"He is," River agrees this time around. "But I don't know if it's a good thing."

After taking his backpack to lighten his load, I bounce my eyes between his soul-baring pair. "What do you mean?"

He waits a beat before murmuring, "He's kinda obsessed with her."

"I get it," I stammer out before I can stop myself.

When that gains me River's upmost devotion, I try to crawl out of the trench I just threw myself in. "I mean, come on, look at her. She's gorgeous."

"She is," he agrees again with nothing but honesty highlighting his face. "So why doesn't he just sleep with her instead of women who look like her?"

"What?" My shock delivers my question so ear-piercingly loud, River's eyes aren't the only ones boring into mine. Knox's and Nicole's are as well.

Incapable of tattling while being gawked at, River walks to the exit. "We should finish this later."

"River..." I plead, desperate.

I hate cliffhanger endings.

I absolutely loathe them.

And although his expression is apologetic when he flashes me the quickest smirk, not a syllable escapes his lips as he exits the private jet to the frantic flashes of paparazzi cameras.

The crash of the paparazzi as we leave Van Nuys Airstrip is intense. Even wearing a disguise doesn't stop Nicole from being asked a hundred questions about her connection to a band I've never heard of during the short walk from the jet's stairs to a blacked-out SUV.

The West Coast paps' interview points don't veer far from the ones asked in Florida, but since Knox helms Nicole's walk to the awaiting car, they don't obtain the snapback response they forever seek when hounding celebrities.

Knox's gallantry makes it seem as if their shark-attack tenacity isn't the publicity he's seeking, and it has Nicole's anger slipping from the boiling point back to a gentle simmer by the time we reach a studio theater on the outskirts of Burbank.

Sitting across from them for sixteen miles hasn't awarded me any more knowledge than my five-hour stalk in the plane. They're as opposite as night and day.

Cocky and sweet.

Showy and humble.

Taken and fucking taken, so stop looking and do your damn job!

With Knox's raised brow matching the sentiments of my conscience, I jerk up my chin in farewell like I'm planning to place more than two feet of distance between the SUV and me before sliding out the back passenger door.

There are no flashing bulbs to contend with, nor a rush of heated bodies priming for the best shot. If you exclude the beggar seeking a dollar, there isn't a single soul on the footpath separating the SUV from the old theater about to host a dress rehearsal for Nicole's upcoming shows.

"Now do you understand why I said what I did on the plane?" Knox asks, startling me when he sneaks up on me unawares. "This studio is booked under Nikki J. The private jet was on loan from Rise Up. The two are not the same."

Stealing my chance to reply that they could be if he loosened the reins a little, he bobs back into the SUV to assist Nicole out before once again guiding her steps by placing his hand on the small of her back.

12
NICOLE

When a frustrated sigh whizzes from my nose, the makeup artist preparing me for my first full dress rehearsal says, "It could be worse. You could be doing the makeup for the artist instead of preparing her for gigs with the who's who of late-night broadcasts." As I flash her an apologetic stare, Bonnie adds, "It's fine. I'm not at all envious." Thankfully she smiles during her reply, or I'd have no clue she is being playful. That's how mellow her tone is. "We all pave our own road to success. Some just get lucky a little sooner than others."

She stops there, but I know the words she can't express for fear of reprimand.

She believes I am only here because of my connection to Rise Up.

The sucky part is she's right.

Nikki J isn't scribbled on the whiteboard outside my dressing room.

Nicole Reed is.

Knox said it was an accidental slip-up on the tour organizer's behalf.

I don't believe him.

When we entered the performance hall without the fanfare of the private airstrip, his ego slipped off a steep cliff. He wants the hype more than I do, and he gets it when two backup dancers spot my name on the door before it's fixed.

"Oh em gee!" the tinier of the duo screams, almost shattering my eardrums. "It's you, isn't it? You're Nicole Reed..." The part I always loathe arrives quicker since she only needs to read the malicious gossip made up about me instead of manufacturing it. "You're the woman who almost ended Nick and Jenni's relationship."

"That isn't true," I bite back before cursing my stupidity to hell.

I'm meant to deny any connections to Nicole Reed by reminding fans that everyone has a twin, even someone as famous as Jenni Holt, who is often mistaken for Slater's deceased sister, Serena.

"I can't believe this," squeals the pack leader. "I can't believe I'm dancing for someone who intimately knows the band members of Rise Up."

After snapping my picture like permission is no longer needed, she hooks her arm around her friend's elbow, then skips down the hall, telling everyone and anyone who will listen that they're about to meet Rise Up.

With my frustration extending further than my shirt collar, I yank off my wig before scrubbing a hand over my dry eyes.

My eyes aren't burning because I flew across the country in the equivalent of a sardine tin. They're dry from how often I dragged them to Laken's half of the plane during the five-hour trip.

I wanted to ask him why he took my songbook and what his plans are for the song he stole, but since I also wanted to kiss away the crease his forehead hasn't been without for a second today, I kept my stalk to a distance.

The fact I care about his crinkle frustrates me more than having my stage name thwarted so early into our West Coast tour.

The dubbed "Hannah Montana Ruse" was doomed from the start, but I thought I'd at least get a handful of lesser-known gigs under my belt before being forced out of the cloak of anonymity a stage name offers. Then people might have attributed my presence at social events to my talent instead of my association with Rise Up.

There's no chance now.

I still want to forge my own way in this industry. It'll just be a ton harder since my name is rarely mentioned when it isn't attached to megastars of the music world.

Could this day get any worse?

My commentary becomes factual when a familiar voice asks, "Ready?"

Since I'm still giving Knox the silent treatment, Bonnie answers his question on my behalf. "In two seconds." She coats my lashes for the third time before mopping up the mess I created when I buried my head into my hands as I wish I could have the sand. "Beyond gorgeous."

"Thank you," I praise, my mood not as chipper as hers.

I'm grateful for the honesty in her tone, but I'm still feeling wretched. It's been one argument after another to keep my real name out of any lineups we secured, so to discover Knox was slipping it in with the feelers he sent out was like a direct punch to my stomach.

I feel winded, and I haven't belted out a single lyric yet.

Knox said the music we produced was creating the buzz for my upcoming release. Now I'm skeptical if anyone has even listened to our sample.

Do you have any idea how panicked that makes me? People can't tell you your baby is ugly even when it is. It isn't acceptable, but they have no issues telling you precisely what they think about the babies developed outside your womb. Songwriters, authors, and poets are forever scrutinized, and only the super-determined make it through the carnage unscathed.

I'm not exactly sure where I stand. Some days, I feel like I'm in the middle of the ferocious flames, being charred on all sides, and others, I only experience the slightest burn of imposter syndrome.

Today's scalds are more personal than professional, though.

Desperate to get dress rehearsal over with so I can hide my still-blurry head under a mountain of pillows, I swivel my chair to face the door before slipping out of it.

My butt scarcely lifts from the leather padding when Bonnie forces me back on it.

When my surprised eyes dart to hers, she asks, "Aren't you forgetting something?"

Upon spotting my confusion, she nudges her head to the wig that cost more than my first car. If I was going to wear a disguise, I wanted it to look authentic. That hairpiece is as genuine as you can get. It is just several shades lighter than the brunette look I was aiming for.

Knox will swear until he is blue in the face that blonde artists outsell dark-haired artists three to one. I don't know where he gets his statistics from, but since his claim was at the end of a long day, I nodded like I believed him and bookmarked our argument for another day.

I've not yet had the strength to bring it up again, and I'm glad I didn't waste my breath.

A disguise is pointless when everyone knows your name.

"What's the point?" I say to Bonnie, my voice as low as my shoulders.

My question is rhetorical, but Bonnie doesn't know that. "The point is, you've *always* wanted to do this on your own." I almost *pfft* until she shocks me into silence. "And let's not forget that every person here today signed a contract with an ironclad NDA bulking up half the dossier." I want to squeeze her to death when she clicks her fingers while saying, "So they can hype themselves up all they like, but the instant they leave this studio, their mouths will need to be as glued shut as their legs if they don't want to be slapped with a lawsuit." Her legs reference is lost on me until she mumbles under her breath while packing away her supplies. "Although I wouldn't blame them if they wanted to break the contract for him." Her eyes sling to the left. "He is as delicious as a root beer float with extra whipped cream during a scorching-hot Fourth of July alcohol-free barbecue."

When I follow the direction of her lusty gaze, my throat dries. Laken is loitering outside my dressing room with his thick arms crossed and his brows pulled together, looking bored.

He isn't there by choice. Knox stationed him there in case the media mixed up the rehearsal date schedule. Excluding the two dancers from earlier, no one has stalked these halls seeking anyone of interest. Even Bonnie was in my dressing room when I arrived.

I snap my eyes away from Laken before I can work out why I still want to kiss away the crease in his forehead when Bonnie whispers, "I bet his lips taste like sin and a hint of whiskey."

"They're more sweet than tangy."

If Bonnie's mouth gapes any more, she'll ruin her perfectly symmetrical lined lips. "Say what now?"

Eyes wide that I spoke my statement out loud, I snatch up my wig like it doesn't need a hundred bobby pins to keep it in place before joining Knox in the hallway.

Bonnie's playful tone jingles down the hall faster than Laken's sigh when Knox's hand lands in the middle of my back. "You can run, sweetheart, but I know the perfect shade of lipstick for your alabaster skin, so you won't stay away for long."

13
LAKEN

"You killed it tonight. They couldn't get enough," Knox lies while guiding Nicole into the elevator of an opulent hotel smack bang in the middle of Hollywood, his hand still hovering and driving me insane.

"Are you sure?" Nicole asks, her tone not as confident as the steps she uses to force a gap between them. "Because they looked a little... shocked."

"It is the first time anyone has heard these songs. Everyone acts differently when they can't sing along with you. You watch. They'll be singing over you during tomorrow's rehearsal."

When Knox slings his eyes to me, seeking backup, I leave the lying to him by waving a room keycard over the panel and selecting the penthouse suite. I can't tuck Nicole in like I did last night, but can I call myself a bodyguard if I don't get my mark to her hotel room safely?

As Knox continues telling Nicole how she "rocked the socks off her performance," I think back to the number of times I cringed while watching her bump and grind across the polished dance floor with two dozen fluro-boosting backup dancers.

It was bad.

Bad bad.

I'd feel like an ass saying that if it weren't true, but there isn't a better word in the dictionary to describe her performance.

Nicole's voice could captivate anyone, but the lyrics were off, and whoever composed the music should be shot.

They took what should have been a love ballad and tried to jazz it up—jazz hands included.

While removing the fishnet gloves that match the stockings covering her scrumptious legs, Nicole says, "Maybe we should invite some spectators to the next couple of rehearsals? That way, we can get proper feedback before real-time shows."

Knox tries to shut down her suggestion, but when Nicole reminds him of his forever bias, the truth can no longer be denied.

I fucked my best friend's girl one floor above the room they shared.

I'm a fucking dog.

"You must be conscious of your bias to make ethical commentaries." I don't need to look at them to know they're flirting. Knox's laugh gives it away when Nicole says, "And you, my friend, will never be alert to that." He only ever uses that laugh on the girls he wants to bed.

My teeth grit when Knox replies, "It's what you love about me the most."

Love? When has he ever used that in a sentence when referencing a woman?

"But if it will ease your conscience enough that you won't keep me awake half the night tossing and turning, I can organize that for you." With his hand once again possessively hovering above the curve of her ass, he guides her out of the elevator when it opens on their floor. "Though we'll have to be mindful of fines. We promised exclusivity."

"I'd rather face fines than public humiliation." Nicole's voice drops to a whisper before she asks, "What if they boo me?"

"They won't boo you. You're a fucking star."

When Knox once again looks at me for backup, I give him the honesty I should have given before accepting his job offer. "You are. A real ten out of ten." I hate lying, but my morals aren't exactly upstanding right now, so I blurted out the first thing that popped into my head while recalling the acoustic performance she awarded me only twenty-four hours ago.

Fuck, is that all it's been?
A measly twenty-four hours.
It seems more like a lifetime ago.

"Really?" When Nicole's eyes land on me again, hot and heavy like she's dying for an ounce of integrity, I lower my eyes to my feet.

If I have to be honest with her, I'll have to be honest with everyone—Knox included.

That isn't something I can do right now. Not when River's guardianship is in his family's name.

I feel Nicole's hope fade to oblivion before she stomps away.

"Fuck me," Knox breathes out once she is out of sight. Resting his hands on his head, he peers at the ceiling. "Way to have my back, man. How will she prep her throat before performing if she's still not talking to me?" My silence returns his head to its original position. "You really think I'll let anyone else in on that action?" He rocks his hips forward while pretending to grab a fistful of hair. "Jizz is better than any throat lozenge on the market."

You'd swear I'd spent the last decade at a nunnery for how long it takes me to decipher his reply. Then, in under a second, I go from wanting to fall to his knees and beg for forgiveness for trying to ruin the best thing that's ever happened to him, to wanting to rearrange his face with my fists.

Even if I hadn't bedded his girl, I'd still feel the same.

Implying *any* of Nicole's talents are compliments of him is as disrespectful as it gets. His... *jizz* didn't give her the voice that stops you in your tracks and makes your hairs stand on end.

It didn't make her vocal range unreachable for even the greats in the industry.

If anything, he'll fuck it up with stupid choreography and compositions that should have been left in the eighties.

"A throat spasm will be the least of your worries if you let the public get hold of a single snippet of footage from her performance tonight. That shit was bad. *Beyond* bad. It looks like it came straight out of an eighties aerobic instruction video."

"It wasn't that bad."

Knox grins like I'm playing when I warn, "Don't make me dig through your old pornos to make a liar out of you. You masturbated to Susan Powter's fitness video more than any other DVD in your stash." I point to the door Nicole walked through only minutes ago. "She was wearing the same fucking outfit."

"For a reason," he says with a laugh, unable to deny my claim but for some stupid reason finding it humorous. "The eighties are making a comeback."

"Since when?"

"I don't know!" He throws his hands in the air, suddenly over our conversation. "Probably sometime between you bouncing on your obligations and waltzing back in like nothing's changed."

That's a below-the-belt hit, and I refuse to let it slide.

Fuck him and his belief I owe him something.

It is the opposite. He owes me years—ten long fucking years—so he doesn't get to speak to me like I'm a piece of shit his boot picked up while strolling through a dog park.

"You've always been a prick when things don't go your way. Glad to see some things haven't changed." His expression alters when I say, "You can shove your job where the sun doesn't shine. I'm out."

He follows me in the direction of what I assume are the rooms since Nicole went that way. "Laken, man, I'm sorry." He stops me from leaving by placing himself in front of me. I could push him out of the way, but his following words leave room for nothing but breathing. "She might be fucking pregnant, and I'm not handling it right, so I'm taking my shit out on the wrong person."

"Nicole's pregnant?"

"What?" His shock lasts for barely a second. "No." His confession doesn't let Nicole off the hook for straying while in a relationship, but it gives understanding as to why she did it. "It was someone I was fooling around with when we met." He scrubs a hand down his tired face. "It was nothing serious, but it continued a couple of months into… you know…" He makes a rude gesture with his hand. "I can't tell Nicole that, though. She'll leave me." For the first time tonight, the fret on his face is genuine. "I can't live without her, Laken. She is *it* for me." He locks his eyes with mine. They're wet with moisture. "I bought a ring. I just can't give it to her until I clear this matter up first." He sneers "matter" like he's talking about a business proposal and not a child. "What do you think?"

The diamond ring he shows me is enormous, over the top, and gives off an aura of wealth, but I hate it on sight.

Even more so when Knox announces, "Your mom helped me pick it."

"My mom?" I ask, shocked I can speak through the fury burning my throat.

First, he made me jealous. Then he brought my mother into our conversation like she spent our childhood baking us cookies and going to boy scout meetings.

This conversation couldn't get worse.

Knox grimaces before he nods. "She's been spending some time with River over the past six weeks." Before I can warn him about his stupidity, he adds, "Not alone. I'm not that stupid." He laughs at himself. "Says the guy panicked he got a hooker pregnant." He stores away the hideous ring, places his hand on my shoulder, then squeezes it. "That's why I need you here, watching my girl when I can't. It is the only way I can ensure your mother doesn't get her hooks into River again. If she goes for custody, and the judge is forced to pick between us, I'm reasonably sure he'll go for the guardian with no criminal convictions."

"She served time for driving under the influence." I can't believe I'm defending my mother. I just loathe that he's making out her charges were as immoral as mine, so I spoke before thinking. "And what do you mean 'us'? You said your father would sign over guardianship the instant I was paroled."

"That was the—"

A singsong voice interrupts us. "Knox…"

It's Nicole, and although she sounds as ball-breaking now as she did in the jet when she ripped him a new asshole, Knox acts oblivious. "I'll be right with you, baby cakes." He shifts his eyes back to me, waggles his brows like our conversation is nowhere near as serious as it is, and then asks, "We good?"

"I—"

"Are you really asking me to keep *her* waiting?" When he nudges his head to Nicole, who is leaning against the doorjamb of her room, wearing a nightie identical to the one she wore last night, my jaw tightens. "You'd never be so cruel."

I get cut off again. "Knox."

"She's impatient." While raking his teeth over his lower lip, he waggles his brows again. "Can you blame her?" He drags his hand down his body, his smile picking up. "I'm like a fine wine. Only getting—"

"More obnoxious with age." River grins about Knox's apparent heartbreak before aligning his eyes with me. "I thought I recognized your voice. It just took me a bit since you sound a little envious." After almost knocking me over with a welcoming hug, he takes a second swipe at Knox's massive attitude. "That never happens when it comes to him." After gesturing his head to Knox, he nods it in the direction he came from. "I set the DVD player up. Do you want popcorn?"

"What kind of question is that? Of course he wants popcorn. It is a movie marathon. Only a psychopath wouldn't want popcorn during a movie marathon." Knox messes up River's recently combed hair before heading toward Nicole's room, to which the door is now closed. "And make sure you keep the volume up. Things are about to get rowdy." He cups the doorhandle before spinning to face us. "Although you should probably have an early night. Rehearsals start at five."

"In the morning?" River and I stammer out in sync.

Knox nods before cracking open Nicole's bedroom door. "The alarm in your room has been pre-set." He preempts my question before I can ask it. "It is the third door back from the room River will be snoring in before the second section of credits roll."

"I'm staying here? With you?" I try to keep my tone neutral during my last question. I fail.

A groan rumbles in my chest when Knox fans his arms out wide before saying in a showy tone, "Welcome to life in the fast lane, baby. I sure fucking hope you can keep up."

If it isn't bad enough I have to sleep in the same hotel as the couple I'd rather destroy than help guide toward marital bliss, I have to share a suite with them as well.

This is as fucked as it gets.

14
NICOLE

"I knew you wouldn't stay away for long." Bonnie places down her brush kit before digging through her makeup cart for my favorite lipstick. "All smart career women buy the testers of discontinued stock." She laughs at my ick expression. "Let's see who's grossed out when you win best dressed at the Grammys next year."

I love her optimism, but it is a little too soon to be hedging bets like that. "Are we doing a full dress rehearsal again today? I thought yesterday was a one-off."

"It was," Bonnie agrees. "But since the gallery is about to be brimming with music buffs dying to sample all you have to offer, Knox figured we should give them the full shebang." She peers down at her makeup chair. "So get your cute little ass over here and tell me all the goss while we make you as glamorous as that hunk of man meat you're hogging to yourself."

"I'm not hogging him—" My phone ringing saves me from explaining how I knew she was referencing Laken instead of Knox.

Everyone assumes Knox and I are banging boots. They would never suspect Laken since he hasn't looked me in the eyes since our night on the roof.

"I'll be back in a minute. I need to take this."

Bonnie waves to announce she heard me before she goes back to sorting through her makeup cart.

Jenni's voice roars out of my phone's speaker before I can attach it to my ear. "Why the hell are we only hearing about this now? You slept with a stranger but waited forty-eight hours to update your friends."

"I can't help that you were traveling halfway across the world with no cell service."

I veer past Laken standing guard in the dressing room hallway and enter the alley at the back of the dance studio.

"It's okay. I don't need a shadow out here," I assure Laken when he attempts to follow me out.

"Is that him? Is he the Adonis you screwed senseless before you knew he was your new bodyguard?"

I cup the phone at the speaker end to ensure Laken can't hear Jenni, before shifting my pleading eyes to Knox. "The alleyway is locked, and there isn't another person in sight. Does he need to follow me out here?"

I'm being a grump because I barely got an ounce of sleep last night.

That's two sleepless nights in a row.

Get your mind out of the gutter. My lack of sleep last night had nothing to do with multiple orgasms and everything to do with the fact the man who stole from me was sleeping only doors down from my unlocked room.

I was up half the night checking my songbook was where I hid it.

Yeah, right.

My hurt is intense, but the memories of my night with Laken are stronger.

Knox finally caves after taking in my fluttering eyelashes for almost thirty seconds. "Five minutes—"

"And not a second more," I quote, finishing one of his favorite sayings.

Knox looks pleased I know him so well.

Laken appears disgusted.

"I'll meet you on stage." Knox presses his lips to the edge of my mouth before guiding a disgruntled Laken inside.

They're barely out of earshot when Emily says, "Your messages painted him as an ass, but he's smoking hot. There's no doubting that."

"So fucking hot," Jenni backs up.

Shocked, my eyes dart down to my phone. I gasp when I realize my endeavor to stop Laken from hearing them accidently switched our phone call to a Facetime chat.

"That ass..."

Jenni stops, swallows, then gleams excitedly when a voice in the background says, "No one else, Jen."

Past Emily's sweater-covered baby bump, I watch Jenni crash-tackle Nick onto a day bed in a massive dining room and kiss him senseless.

Once he's breathless, she murmurs over his lips, "No one else."

I grin like a loon when Noah joins our chat. "I think you were right. We should have packed bleach." As Hawke's grumbly laugh trickles through my phone speaker, Noah rubs Emily's stomach before drifting his dark, moody eyes to me. "How are you doing, Nik? Ready for us to come on a world tour with you yet?"

Nerves echo in my reply. "Hopefully one day."

Noah bobs down to pick up his adorable five-year-old, Maddie, while saying, "Tell me when you're ready, and we'll get everything settled here before joining you back in the States."

"And leave the biggest European tour known to man for my little tour dates? Don't be outrageous."

"We'd do it for you, Nicole," Emily says, her voice as sweet as her daughter's dimpled grin when she spots Aunt Nicole on her mother's phone screen. "In a heartbeat."

I "tickle" Maddie through the screen while saying, "That's because England is cold, and you grew up in Florida. Give it time. You'll soon acclimate to the bipolar weather."

Emily huffs but doesn't deny my claim. She hates the cold as much as she does the groupies who forever throw themselves at her husband.

When Maddie's mouth fills the screen with a big yawn, Emily steals her from Noah. "I better put her down for a nap. She didn't sleep much on the plane."

"I'll take her," Noah offers, stealing Maddie back. "Then you can talk to Nicole about the song she sent through last night." His eyes are back on me, teasing and playful. "It was stuffed somewhere between checking if we'd arrived okay and news about a *smoking hot date*." He mimics Emily's voice during the last half of his reply.

Giggling, Emily barges him out of frame. "Go put our daughter to bed." If her next words are meant to be whispers, she needs to take a lesson on being quiet. "Then I'll help lick your wounds after Nicole updates me on *everything* that happened *two... whole... nights... ago*."

With Emily's reply hinting at a gossip session, Jenni rejoins our conversation. "Spill, Nicole. I can see the debauchery all over your face."

"You cannot—" Raised voices cut off my reply. They sound excited. Almost giddy. "Oh my god," I murmur when I peer in the direction from which the voices project. A line stretches from the entrance of the dance studio and down an alleyway on the opposite side, spanning several blocks. "They can't be here for me. Surely."

"Who? Show us," Jenni and Emily demand.

I spin my phone to face the crowd, gasping along with my best friends as the line grows by the second.

"This is it," Jenni murmurs. "This is the moment you've been waiting for."

Butterflies tap dance in my stomach when I remember my face is without makeup. Emily and Jenni have natural beauty, but I look like a sheet of paper on stage when the bright lights reflect nothing but my pasty-white skin. "I need to go. I have to get ready."

"You—"

"Not so—"

I cut them both off with a promise. "I swear on Colette's grave that I'll call the instant this is over and tell you everything."

"*Every*thing?" Jenni double-checks like a deprived housewife who doesn't get her kinks untwisted daily.

"*Every*thing," I pledge before air-blowing them kisses and hotfooting it inside.

I've only just stored my phone away when a conversation in my dressing room slows my steps. "Have you known Nicole long?"

"No." Laken's chuckle would sound authentic if he didn't grind his teeth together at the end of it. "We only recently met." He waits a beat before adding, "I'm her bodyguard."

"Her bodyguard?" I picture Bonnie's dark brows raised into her hairline when she breathes out, "Wow."

"Don't make it sound like that. It's nothing important."

I stand tall with my shoulders back when Bonnie *tsks* him. "How can you say that? That girl has a gift."

"She does." I won't mention how wildly my heart beats during Laken's confession because I need to store oxygen for the brutal blow he hits my lungs with two seconds later. "But not like this. The only thing I should be protecting her from is excessive jazz hands and a hideous eighties getup."

I almost cuss Knox's vision to hell until Bonnie says, "The eighties are making a comeback." I wish she would end their conversation, but regretfully, she continues. "But I've heard rumors from the girls that things aren't great. I was hoping it was jealousy."

Laken digs the knife in deeper. "Believe me, it isn't."

A brief stint of silence prevails before the last person I want to see busts my watch.

Laken startles when he spots me at his station, and although he looks me in the eyes for the first time in twenty-four hours, the remorse in them doesn't match the callousness of his words.

"Did you tell them it's only been a little over thirty hours since we…" He wets his lips with a slow, teasing lick to get across his point. "Or were they talking about another random stranger you hooked up with before me?"

15
LAKEN

You're a fucking ass.

A complete and utter prick.

You don't deserve a woman like Nicole, much less the ability to add her name to your stats.

When my inner monologue becomes too honest to ignore, I cuss my arrogance to a painful death before stomping backstage at a dance studio brimming with chatty teens and a handful of scruffy-looking adults who appear oddly out of place.

I didn't mean to make out Nicole is a slut. My anger got the better of me, and I took it out on who I believed was responsible for the black tar filling my heart.

Nicole isn't solely to blame. Knox's confession last night that my mother is back in River's life started my downward spiral. Then, the constant bend of mattress springs from Nicole and Knox's room pulled the tracks out from beneath me.

I tried to drown out their antics by shoving a pillow over my head before drowning my sorrows with a bottle of whiskey. Nothing worked. Even drunk, I couldn't escape the noises of someone getting down and dirty in a room only two up from mine.

It killed me hearing them, and it's had me acting like a bear with a sore head ever since, but not even alcohol poisoning gives me the right to disrespect Nicole the way I did. I was out of line, and if I'm honest, I'm hopeful my giant step out of bounds will get me fired.

I tried to talk to Knox again this morning, but he's refusing to acknowledge that I'm not the best person to protect Nicole.

With him not willing to listen, I took a dig at the person he refers to as the "love of his life."

Knox has changed a lot from the man I once knew, but not even someone as laid-back as him would let his girl be called a whore and not have something to say about it.

Partway down the hallway that saw my personality stoop to the level my conviction automatically lumps onto my name, I'm stopped by Knox. "Where are you going? I need you out there." He jerks his chin in the direction I just left.

"I need to speak with… *Bonnie*." You have no fucking clue how close I came to blurting out Nicole's name. "I won't take a minute."

He twists me away from the dressing room and shoves me back toward the stage area. "There's no time. I need you out there with the masses, protecting Nicole like you're paid to do."

"It's fine—"

"It's not fucking fine, Laken!" he shouts, his roar rattling through his hands on my back. "You have no fucking clue what half those people out there are willing to do for a hundred dollars. One guy offered to kidnap Nicole for a little extra on top of the chair-filling fee I paid him to be here. So go back to the stage and stand where I fucking put you so none of those greasy homeless fuckers get close enough to sniff my girl's shampoo."

I don't know what part to work through first. My shock he paid the audience to be here, or my worry that he let in the person who offered to kidnap Nicole for such a measly amount.

I settle on the latter.

"Is he here?" When his focus remains elsewhere, I ask again, louder this time. "Is he here?" I shake him to force his eyes on me. "The fucker who offered to kidnap Nicole. Is he here? Did he show up?"

"Of course he did. He wouldn't get paid if he didn't show up." He peers past me, up at the bleachers a tour crew constructed overnight. "He's in the back row, wearing a stained Lakers cap. Why?" I'm halfway to the bearded man he pointed out when he shouts, "I didn't accept his terms."

"It doesn't matter. Do you really think a sane man offers to do something like that for a hundred dollars?"

I realize I'm asking the wrong person when Knox shrugs before signaling for one of the road crew to back me up. "Make sure he only roughs him up a little. We don't want another murder conviction slotted under his name before midday."

The man with tattoos skating up his arm startles.

I can't say I blame him.

Knox just made out I'm a notorious killer.

He could be right with how thick my blood is clogged with anger.

"Laken Howell?"

My brows pull together when I spin away from the police van housing a degenerate offering illegal activities for any denomination, when I spot a man in his mid-thirties wearing a dark suit and polished black dress shoes.

He looks like my parole officer, just not as sleazy.

"Can I help you?"

Confident I'm not about to run, he removes his hand from his gun and moseys closer to me. "I'm here on behalf of the Board of

Parole. It's about your ankle tracker." He flashes his credentials too quickly for me to see. "You were meant to be fitted with one before leaving Florida."

"My PO didn't mention anything about it." That isn't technically a lie. Knox mentioned it *after* my first meetup. Officer Barker only drug tested me.

The dark-haired officer nudges his head to the alleyway, requesting we take our talk somewhere private. I agree with his suggestion since I get eyeballed as often as the backup dancers eyeball Nicole.

Once I've joined him near an industrial bin, the unnamed officer states, "Officer Barker was unaware of your intention to travel so soon after release."

"He wasn't the only one." I take a moment to breathe out my frustration before asking, "Will this affect my probation?"

"It could..."—his pause isn't extensive enough for me to do anything but wait—"if you don't agree to be fitted with a GPS tracker now."

"Now?"

He grins at the shock in my tone before heading for a dark sedan parked a couple of spots up.

After throwing open the back passenger door, he gestures for me to enter his vehicle as if I'm a criminal.

I guess to him, I am.

I startle when my slip into the car has me butting shoulders with a beautiful brunette. She is ten times hotter and a couple of years younger than the man standing guard outside.

She must be accustomed to being ogled, as she gets straight down to business despite my creepy gawk. "Have you worn a tracker before?"

Spikes of dark hair flop side to side when I shake my head.

"These guys are foolproof." She gestures for me to place my foot onto the middle console between the driver and passenger seat and lift the cuff of my pants as she pulls a state-of-the-art tracker from a bulky briefcase. "You can do anything in them. Shower. Eat—"

"Fuck," the man outside tacks on, his tone playful. His spirited nature makes sense when the brunette's cheeks turn the color of beets as he adds, "You'll learn that one day. I'm still in with a shot of arresting him. I just need Regan to stop hiding his assets so well."

I realize their relationship is more friendship based than romantic when she rolls her eyes at his insinuation her other half is dirty.

After banding the strap of an anklet tracker around my ankle, she advises, "The only thing you can't do is remove it." She locks her chocolate-brown eyes with mine. "If you do, you'll be swarmed by law enforcement officers in minutes."

Her tug on the strap digs the clasp of the anklet so firmly into my skin it maims.

"Sorry." The brunette accepts a plain white handkerchief from the guy outside to dab up the droplets of blood careening down my foot before she fixes the tracker in place with less gore. "Sometimes I'm stronger than I realize."

She hands the bloody handkerchief to her partner before checking that the tracker is working on a handheld tablet.

Several heart-thrashing seconds pass before I'm given the all-clear to leave. "Everything appears to be in order." She farewells me with a smile and dampens my eagerness to leave by reminding me to be mindful of my surroundings. "And be sure to let Knox know we've caught up with you." She waits for me to look at her before she finalizes her statement. "He wasn't overly obliging when we visited your hotel last night. Anyone would swear he didn't want you speaking to us, or he wanted you to finalize the remainder of your sentence behind bars."

16
NICOLE

By the time Laken graces us with his presence, dress rehearsal is over, the crowd has diminished, and he missed my first standing ovation.

The crowd went wild at the end of my set. They stomped their feet and hollered as if it weren't little ol' me up on the stage, belting out lyrics like their approval was the only thing capable of keeping me alive.

They loved every second of my performance, but you wouldn't know that from how Laken shoots daggers midway through Knox's praise. "I told you you had nothing to worry about. They couldn't get enough."

As I wipe my sweaty head with a towel from the wings of the makeshift stage, I reply, "Thank you. This performance really put my mind at ease. I feel so much more confident about your vision now."

It is the fight of my life not to roll my eyes when Knox says, "You should have never doubted me." But I defy the inevitable since Laken supplies enough eye rolls for the entire crew. "I've only ever wanted what's best for you."

"I know. I'm sorry." When Laken's hooded eyes burn into me a second after I loop my arms around Knox's shoulders to issue him my thanks with a hug, the anger that steamrolled into me when he made out I go home with a different man each night returns full force.

He belittled me as if I were a whore, so I may as well act like one.

"Although there's still room for improvement."

"Such as?" Knox asks, pulling back, his expression telling. He wants to shut down my suggestion before it's heard, so I start with a point I know he will entertain for at least a minute.

"I think we need to ramp up the sexiness of the choreography. Give them a taste of what could be offered if they play their cards right."

Knox isn't the only one shocked by my suggestion. Bonnie's mouth gapes open, and several dancers' eyes bug out of their heads.

Laken's expression remains impassive. It exposes he's happy to call me a whore, but he doesn't believe I have what it takes to be one.

I'll show him.

"Imagine plucking a random man out of the audience each night and giving him the performance of his life." I walk the length of the stage, pretending to seek a participant in the sea of one before spinning back around to face Knox. "You, handsome gentleman, would you be so kind as to join me on stage?"

He grins at the showiness of my voice before gesturing that he's already on the stage.

"Not there," I murmur before taking my impromptu performance to a never-before-reached level by pointing to one of the chairs the backup dancers use during the chorus of "Glitter," a debut single on my album releasing next week. "There."

"There?" Knox double-checks.

While grazing my teeth over my lower lip in a way I hope is sexy, I nod.

"All right, I'll play along." He shoots his eyes to Laken, shrugs like he's clueless I am using him to make his friend jealous, then plops his backside onto the dining chair I'm planning to strut around like a stripper does a pole.

"If you're going to do this…" Bonnie says when I join her in the stage's wings to switch on the music, "you better do it good." She removes the cloak I placed on at the end of my performance, leaving nothing but a skin-tight leotard and fishnet stockings. "Don't leave *anything* on the table. If you want a man of *that* caliber to get jealous…"—once again, her eyes don't sling to Knox during her reply. They lock on Laken, who is now glaring at Knox more than he glared at me earlier—"you need to ensure he knows *exactly* what he's missing out on." She twists me to face the stage just as the opening of "Glitter" booms from the speakers. "Now show him what he'll never get again if he doesn't pull his head out of his ass."

With a pat on my bottom, she forces me back under the spotlights.

It's hot under the lights showcasing my every move, but this has nothing to do with twenty-thousand-watt lightbulbs and everything to do with the heat of Laken's stare as he watches me bob and weave around Knox like he paid for the privilege.

I should be singing. That's the main part of my performance, but I can't get any words out. I'm too busy trying to remember the routines I memorized when watching *Moulin Rouge* with Jenni and Emily at the Sydney Theatre Company during the first half of their world tour last year.

I can't kick my legs as high as the stars of that show, and I don't have a skirt to flare, but if the bulge that rubs against my leotard when I end my performance by straddling Knox's lap is anything to go by, my moves are just as provocative.

"We might have to put an under-fifty clause on ticket sales," Knox breathes out slowly after waiting for the dancers' applause and catcalls to slacken. "We don't want an old geezer having a heart attack when you send all the blood in his body rushing to one area."

His response is what I'm aiming for.

It is merely coming from the wrong person.

After dismounting Knox's lap and acting oblivious to his whine, I spin to face the imaginary audience before bowing to their illusory applause.

I'm on cloud nine and the most confident I've ever felt... until I sneak a peek at the seat Laken's hip was butted against at the start of my performance.

The entire row is empty, and Laken is nowhere to be seen.

17
LAKEN

*A*s I squash my phone to my ear, my blood still hot from how close I was to returning to prison, I spin away from Knox's gleaming face.

He's only experiencing a minute portion of the performance I was awarded from Nicole two nights ago, but it pisses me off to no end.

It is right up there with him fucking with my freedom for the second time in my life.

It is lucky River called when he did because I don't know how much longer I could have held back from vocalizing my anger for the world to hear. I'm a ticking fucking bomb seconds from detonation.

Halfway to the exit, I say, "You need to speak up. I can't hear you."

"It's Mom…"

That's the only part of River's reply I catch, but the panic in his tone is potent enough that I only glance back at Nicole for half a second before I complete my exit of the dance studio in a sprint.

As much as this kills me to admit, Nicole's safety falls more on Knox's shoulders than mine.

I won't make the same foolish claim with River, though.

"Don't go anywhere. I'm on my way."

"Laken?" River asks when the stomps of my shoes are softened by the carpet pile in Nicole's SUV I assign as if it is my private mode of transport.

"Yeah." I place on my belt before gesturing for the driver to return to the hotel.

The crack of his reply breaks my heart. "I'm not at the hotel." He only sobs when he's hurting. He doesn't feel pain like the rest of us. The only way you can hurt him is by breaking his heart.

"Where are you?"

Another sob before, "*We're at the—*"

His voice is replaced by one I haven't heard in a long time. "The transfer of guardianship you issued your friend's family won't hold up in court."

"River is over eighteen. He doesn't need a guardianship order anymore."

My mother *tsks* me. "I bet the judge we're about to see will disagree with you. River's disability requires management—"

"Management you haven't supplied him for over twenty years."

I smack the headrest in front of me with my fist. I thought I was angry watching Nicole dance for Knox only minutes after finding out he almost screwed me over, but that has nothing on this.

I can fix the mistakes I've made with Knox and Nicole with words.

I'll need a lot more than that to put my mother back in the box she should have never crawled out of.

"What do you want, Ma? And don't act like you want to get to know your sons. You've *never* wanted that."

As her mind ticks over with the endless possibilities she wrongly believes I can supply her, River uses the silence to his advantage. "I told her about my new job. I thought she'd be proud of me. I'm sorry, Laken. I should have never said anything."

"This has *nothing* to do with that. I just want to ensure you're being properly taken care of."

She's a fucking liar. The number of lies she's told me means I've been skilled at sniffing out liars since I was eight. That's why I was so blindsided to discover Nicole isn't single.

After requesting the driver take me to the closest courthouse, I ask, "How much do you want?" When another stretch of silence passes between us, I plead, "Be reasonable, Ma. I don't have a bottomless pit of money."

"But he does." She doesn't need to say Knox's name for me to know who she's referencing. The first time she returned to Johnston Bay after a prolonged stint of absence was a month after Knox and I were photographed in a local newspaper. We'd won the state championship, and she was eager to see if the win came with a large, glossy check.

"Not anymore," I lie. "His father cut him off when I went to..." I stop talking when I recall I usually keep that portion of my life quiet. My shame is too high to share my incarceration as if it's worth celebrating.

"Jail?" my mother fills in, reminding me her ears are always to the ground when it comes to who she can siphon money from. "The apple didn't fall far from the tree, did it?" I assume she's referencing her short stint behind bars before she says, "He went back there more than he came to visit his boys." I look down at my watch when she brings it up. "That's where he got that stupid piece you show off like it's valuable and where he'll end up again when he gets out of his latest court-appointed rehab stay." She gets back on track before it truly sinks in that this is the most she's ever shared about my father. "Fifty thousand."

"Ma—"

"Fifty thousand or River comes with me to Milwaukee. I've already purchased his bus ticket."

"A bus? I don't want to go on a bus." River's voice loudens as he tries to snatch back his phone. "Don't let her do this, Laken. Please. I like the family I have now. I don't want to go to Milwaukee."

"You won't go to Milwaukee, River. I promise."

It takes half a dozen more pledges before he settles down enough for my mother to hear a pledge she doesn't deserve. "I'll get you the money, but I need a couple of days."

"You have until midnight."

"Ma…"

A phone cracking splinters down the line before River's upset breaths. "She's gone," he murmurs just as I arrive at the front stairs of a courthouse to pull his wet face into my chest.

"Can this wait?" Knox asks after joining me in the office that separates my room from the one he shares with Nicole.

I'm meant to be confronting him about the probation breach he almost instigated, but my mother has left me no choice but to leave that hanging in the wind for a couple more days.

I can't exactly ask a favor after ripping him a new asshole.

"Nicole is *extra* playful tonight." Even with him trying to get out of the meeting I requested, he sits on the bulky leather chair behind a wooden desk, then makes a tipi with his index fingers. "I've always wondered how she'd dispel the rush of endorphins that'll hit every time she performs live."

134

I don't know if he's obsessed with the scent of his fingers or if he's sniffing up the leftover white powder he's convinced no celebration can be without when he breathes in deeply through his nose.

Whatever it is, it bolsters his cockiness.

"Could have never imagined anything like this." He connects his loved-up eyes with mine. The lust in them makes me sick to the stomach, but I'm not sitting across from him for any benefit of my own. This is solely about River, the person I pledged to protect long before I knew what love meant. "You should have stuck around for the show. It ended on a *high* note." He makes a gesture no man over the age of fourteen should make. "Actually, I'm glad you left. Your absence meant she didn't need to keep quiet. She screamed so loud my ears are still ringing."

The love I have for my brother can never be discredited after tonight. If not for him, I would have ended this meeting five sentences ago with my fists.

Instead, I get to the point. "I was wondering if I could get an advance on my salary?"

Knox's nonchalant reply shocks me. "Of course. Whatever you need."

I wait, expecting more.

I'm not often proven wrong.

"But…"

He builds the suspense by leaning forward like he's going to ask for another ten years of my life.

I breathe a little easier when his terms aren't as stark as predicted. "You can only pay me back with funds from *this* position." He circles his finger around his desk as if Nicole's stage is in the middle. "You have to see it out to the end. No more 'I'm not qualified for this position' or comments about needing to protect Nicole from excessive jazz hands."

He heard that?

"I saw the way you handled that grifter today. He was cuffed and in the back of a police van before Nicole even went on stage." He commends me like he wasn't the cause for additional muscle in the alleyway earlier today. "Nice work covering our bases with a police presence. It kept the crowd at bay and had them acting like true fans meeting their idol. Nicole has no fucking clue they were paid to be there." He steers the conversation back on course like it never strayed from his objective. "How you handled things today proves you're the right man to protect Nicole. I want your word that you'll stay at her side twenty-four-seven. If she's awake, you're awake. If she's asleep, you're asleep. If she's fucking—"

"I get it. You can stop spelling it out."

"Then lets fucking shake on it so I can get back to the party." By party, he means Nicole, who is tipsy after one too many wines. "We're meant to be celebrating!" I assume he's referencing Nicole's first taste of fame, but I am proven wrong. "The kid may not be mine, so I'll soon be free to move ahead with my plans." He waggles his brows before holding out his hand in offering. "So, do we have a deal?"

Even while reminding myself that this isn't about me, it is the fight of my life to accept his handshake.

I'm given an out when I recall he's clueless about what he's signing up for. "Don't you want to know how much I need and what it's for?"

He couldn't look more cocky while shaking his head. "Your mother is in town, and the cash cow she milks anytime he looks close to getting cashed up was recently paroled. I know what the money is for, and since she is as predictable as your willingness to do *anything* to protect River, my guess is fifty K." He doesn't give me a chance to get over my shock. "You'll pay that back in a month, easy. Perhaps two."

"That's a salary in excess of three hundred thousand dollars a year. That's too much."

"Not when you're guarding the next superstar of pop, and you have a point one percent share in all her future earnings," he showboats, his tone confident. "The fact she's your future sister-in-law is merely a bonus."

Once again, I could have lived without his last comment, but I don't get riled about it this time. I needed his help. He pledged allegiance without breaking a sweat, so I'll protect his girl even with the only threat to his happiness standing directly in front of him.

18
NICOLE

"It's going to be so much fun. I can't wait."

I gush along with the backup dancers while showing them to the door. It's late, and I'm exhausted. With today's rehearsal running over by four hours and Knox inviting everyone back to the suite for pre-celebratory drinks about my first radio interview Monday morning, my limbs feel like Jell-O.

A long soak in the tub is the only item on my itinerary tonight, but first, I need a bottle of water to soothe the spasms in my throat.

"We'll see you Monday after your first live performance!"

Bella and Ellen wiggle their fingers at me in farewell before walking to the elevator arm in arm. Ellen's shyness explained her stunned expression the first time we met, but Bella's demeanor remains a mystery. She is a little standoffish—*except when it comes to Laken*.

Their flirty banter over the past three days would convince you that they've met before, and with tonight giving Bella unlimited access to Laken outside of office hours, she ramped up her efforts to get to know him better.

She clung to him like a leech and was the sole cause of my dry throat.

Ignoring how she followed him around the set was easy when you're trying to perfect the sexed-up choreography a stern bout of jealousy encouraged, but it is virtually impossible when it's occurring directly across from you.

When Laken didn't shut down her flirting like he does at rehearsals, I spent half the night forcing vicious words into my stomach instead of spewing them out of my mouth for the world to hear.

My jealousy is frustrating. I honestly don't know how to handle it. I don't have much experience with it, and although I could ask Emily and Jenni for advice, the last time I did that, I had to fend off walking STD billboards.

I also shouldn't be asking advice about a man who presents one way before doing a complete one-eighty only hours later. I could have sworn Laken looked remorseful when Knox stopped him in the corridor outside of my dressing room three days ago, but nothing but haughty arrogance has hardened his features since I tried to claim back some of the confidence he bashed to smithereens by saying I needed protecting from my hideous dance moves.

I've never felt as self-conscious as I have the past five days. I want to blame the change up on my upcoming late-night show gigs, and learning that the man paid to protect me requires an ankle monitor, but it feels like more than that.

I didn't even balk when Knox told me about Laken's shady past. I'm not one to judge, but hoping Laken's new accessory would scare Bella away should have been the last thought on my mind.

As I break through the kitchen door, I yank down the wig making my scalp itchy. The lush fibers brush against my shoulder as I recall that the hotel replenishes the water bottles in my room every morning.

"You'd lose your head if it weren't attached," I murmur to myself while pivoting on my heels halfway into the kitchen.

"Ouch," I sob with a groan when my quick spin has me crashing into a firm chest.

While rubbing my stinging nose, I lift my eyes to the person shadowing me so soundlessly that I didn't hear their steps. "You should watch…" My words trap in my throat when my eyes lock on to a pair of familiar angst-riddled eyes.

For the umpteenth time this week, Laken has followed me into the kitchen. Since Knox is running an errand, it is the first time another presence hasn't dampened the hold he placed on me the instant he entered the elevator last week.

The tension is as immediate now as it was back then, and I want to forget how much it hurt waking up alone the morning following our fun night.

It was the same three nights ago when I got a little excited with the champagne in the limousine. I was almost tipsy enough to act recklessly, but before I could, Laken ordered Knox to deliver a package on his behalf like he was running the show before he ordered me to bed like a child.

I told him to shove it, but he was quick to remind me that not a single decision made while intoxicated is a good one.

I was on the verge of tipsy when I met him, so I couldn't exactly argue.

It's been three days, but I can still hear my bedroom door's bang when I slammed it shut after my dramatic stomp to my room. I acted like a child, but the tingles I'm experiencing now are nothing close to childish.

How can you be mad at someone and want to kiss them to death at the same time?

It is preposterous to have such starkly different responses for one man.

"What are you doing, Laken?" I ask when I can't avoid the energy crackling in the air for a second longer.

I hate the hope in my tone that he's followed me to issue an apology for his erratic behavior the past five days, but not as much as I loathe his reply. "I promised Knox I wouldn't sleep until you slept, eat until you ate." He works his jaw side to side. "Fuck until you fucked."

Although it should be easy to harness my callous tongue since he doesn't have a gorgeous blonde draped over him, I seem to have lost the ability to act cordially around him. "Oh… should I have checked that you'd finished with Bella before showing her out? I hope I didn't spoil your fun."

Incapable of acting nonchalant about the thought of him with another woman, I sidestep him before making a beeline to my room.

My hurried steps slow when Laken whispers, "If you want me to apologize for ruining your fun for the second time this week, you're shit out of luck."

"You didn't ruin anything," I fire back, detesting that he thinks he's affected me in any way. "But would it kill you to admit you were wrong?" I thrust my hand at the living room like the audience from three days ago are messing up the Persian rugs with the dirt from their shoes. "They *loved* my performance. They couldn't get enough."

My mouth gapes when he uses my words against me. "You must be conscious of your bias to make ethical commentaries."

"So you still listen to me even while acting like I'm not in the same room as you?!" I angrily shake my head when he doesn't flinch at the anguish in my tone. "You're an ass."

"Me?" He follows my storm across the pristine marble floors, his stomps as pounding as my heart. "What I said to you that day was wrong, but come on, you didn't give me much to work with."

I stand in front of him, chest to chest, lips to lips, groin to groin. "People have one-night stands all the time. That doesn't make them whores."

"No, it doesn't," he agrees, shocking me. "But you should have been honest. You should have told me about him! I shouldn't have been blindsided the way I was."

"Him? Who the hell are you talking about?"

I take a startled step back when he shouts, "Knox! You should have told me about Knox." He looks like he hates the world when he spits out, "I went from hearing you moan my name to hearing you moan for him."

He couldn't have shocked me more if he had slapped me, but we're interrupted before I can get a word out. "What's with all the shouting?" River exits his room, scrubbing his tired eyes. "I can hear you over Allie and Noah's fight." He darts his eyes between Laken and me. "And the tension feels about the same too." His shocked eyes settle on his brother. "Lake—"

"Go back to your room, River. I'll be with you in a minute." His tone drops several decibels. "Nicole is about to go to bed. Alone. Again." I might have missed his next set of words if my heart hadn't been at my feet. *"For the first time in days."*

I want to wipe the arrogance from his face and slap his callous words from his mouth, but since only half the scenarios in my head involve my hand, I squeal out my frustration before stomping into my room and slamming the door with as much force as I used days ago.

That man! That egotistical, self-righteous, arrogant, *beautiful* man has me wanting to pull my hair out, but instead, I race for the safety blanket I'll never be without even with them currently halfway across the world.

"You can't tell him things aren't as they seem."

I glare at Jenni's half-shadowed face, shocked by her comment. It is early morning in London, and with two children under six and a rock-star husband forcing her to burn the candle at both ends, she appeared to be having a sleep-in before I called.

"He thinks I'm an adulterer." I had an inkling Laken had mistaken Knox's position in my life when he mentioned finding my earring next to a bottle of aftershave, but it became blatantly evident during our argument. "I can't let him believe that."

"Why?" Jenni asks through a prolonged yawn. "Noah showed me the songs you've sent through the past few days. He said they are your best to date. But they're not Rise Up material." My heart sinks until she adds, "They're Nikki J lyrics. You've been endeavoring to unearth these songs since signing with Knox Records. They're your pot of gold under the rainbow."

I flop onto my bed before tossing an arm over my glossy eyes. "I doubt Apollo would agree with you."

"Then Apollo is a dick." I grimace when Nick's head pops onto the screen of my phone. I woke him too. His bad bedhead can't hide this fact.

Nick is as cocky as Apollo, and before Jenni joined his life, he was just as much of a player, but he's never once looked a gift horse in the mouth and turned his nose up at it. "I told Noah he was crazy if he didn't consider at least one of your songs for our next album." My heart warms when he confesses groggily, "He said he couldn't do you wrong like that. That family doesn't stab family in the back. He wants you to succeed and knows your new songs will ensure that."

"Knox—"

I want to squeal in frustration when I'm interrupted again. How can I work through my confusion if I'm not given the chance to voice my worries?

"I woke up to hundreds of alerts for Nicole." Jenni swivels her phone to the door of her room. "Oh, hey. I was just about to call you." Emily enters the room with her laptop balanced on her hand. "I know you can't afford a publicist right now, and you don't want me working for free, but I set up some Google alerts for your debut radio interview Monday morning." My groan gets gobbled up by her confession. "I set them up as your friend, *not* your publicist. You can't turn away help from a friend." Excitement highlights her face. "Anyhow, there were *hundreds* of alerts overnight." She clicks her keyboard a handful of times. "Someone in the audience leaked a video of your last rehearsal. It is all over the net..." Her words trail off as her brows inch together. "Oh..."

"What is it?" Jenni asks before I can.

Her eyes scan Emily's laptop screen for several terrifying seconds before her expression backs up Emily's unvoiced worries.

I sit a little straighter. "What?"

"It's nothing," Emily gabbers out before snapping her laptop screen shut and peering at me through Jenni's phone. "You know how bad some critics treat new talent. They'd rather cut you down while you're still in the minors than wait for you to hit the majors."

"The reviews are negative?"

"No." She brushes off my worry with a wave of her hand. "Not all of them." When the FaceTime screen advises her my camera is in pause mode, Emily warns, "Don't google reviews, Nicole. It is the first advice I give all new artists. Let me correlate the feedback and give you the true response before you believe the keyboard warriors hiding behind computer monitors."

Her warning comes too late. I've already hit the mother lode, and it is as painful as it gets.

"Ouch..."

My one hurt-filled word tells them everything they need to know.

I found hundreds of comments under the leaked video.
Not   a   single   one   of   them   is   positive.

19
LAKEN

*M*y pillow smashes into the wall separating my room from Knox and Nicole's when a breathy feminine moan churns my stomach more than my argument with Nicole.

I've managed one restless night in the past five. *One.* It was the night I convinced Knox to drop off my mother's "ransom" so she couldn't milk me of more of his funds.

My mother would have left me for dust the instant I handed her the bundles of cash in a gym bag, but with Nicole too tipsy to make decisions for herself, and Knox notorious for overlooking consent, I made out I'm not schooled on my mother's inner workings.

I thought I had won the battle when Nicole stormed to her room.

Turns out my asshole radar isn't my only feature on the brink.

Knox made up for his one night of absence multiple times over the past three days. He and Nicole are acting like newlyweds, and their actions had me giving Bella more attention than she deserved.

She could be a decent girl if she didn't have dust for brains and if she stopped belittling her friends on the belief it would big-note herself.

There's no "bros before hoes" logic as far as Bella is concerned. She's as bad as Knox when steamrolling anyone to get what she wants.

When the grunt of a man seeking a quick release bellows through the air vent, I give up on my quest to sleep. After stuffing my legs into the jeans hooked over my bed, I tie on my running shoes sans socks, then hotfoot it out of my room.

I only last thirty seconds in the living room before the moans of a couple in the midst of ecstasy find me again. They're too loud to be drowned out by the minute slithers of liquid in the bottom of the bottles Knox's road crew polished off during the celebration of their upcoming tour.

Thank fuck no amount of jealousy had me missing the "Open 24 Hours" advertisement for the hotel bar in the building's lobby.

I'm leaving the penthouse suite in less than a minute and entering a noticeably empty establishment.

With the earlier hour, I'm not surprised. It's a little after three in the morning.

The bartender in the corner of the cozy space, watching a rerun of a Red Sox game, greets me with a head bob, but a slender blonde at the end of the bar, nursing a bottle of whiskey, doesn't acknowledge my presence.

While smirking about her lack of glassware, I sit three spots up before ordering a double of Buffalo Trace.

"I doubt there's a double left," the bartender replies while nudging his head to the only other occupant of the bar. "And she isn't willing to part with the bottle for me to check."

"He can have it," the blonde offers after overhearing his gripe. "But I'll need a fresh bottle if I'm"—*hiccup*—"gonna keep drowning my sorrows."

When she slides the almost-empty bottle of Buffalo Trace across the counter, she flashes the quickest portion of her side profile.

"Nicole?" I sound in disbelief. Rightfully so. Her words were so poorly slurred that the hairs on my arms failed to stir when she spoke. And let's not forget the part about how she's currently being screwed to oblivion upstairs.

Nicole's sob is low and brimming with shame. "Nicole Reed is no longer with us. She was buried in a shallow ditch by Nikki J sometime within the past three hours."

When the bartender approaches her with a freshly opened bottle of top-shelf whiskey, I signal to him that she's had enough, before transferring my ass to the barstool beside hers.

I try to think of something to say to lessen the heaviness on her slumped shoulders, but forever diplomatic and still pissed she didn't apologize for blindsiding me the way she did, I get straight to the point like any decent bodyguard would. "Does Knox know you're down here drinking?"

Stupid question.

If he did, he would be down here with her, sniffing out any dips in her morality he could use to his advantage.

I give Nicole a few minutes to reply. When nothing but a commentator bragging about the best player in the league sounds between us, I ask, "Are you all right?"

"No."

For how long it took her to configure a response, I expected more.

"Do you want to talk about it?"

This reply is quicker than the last but just as short. "No."

"Are you sure? I'm a shit fucking listener, but I can pretend to be almost anything."

"Like a good guy?" After almost slipping off her chair, she locks her eyes with mine. They're bloodshot, but the red rims around them have nothing to do with alcohol. She's been crying. "What do you want, Laken?"

Confident she won't remember our conversation in the morning, and still desperate for answers, I say, "I want to know why you're pissed at me." With one truth comes another. "And why you dogged me like that."

She spins to face me so fast that the shot of whiskey the bartender served me from the recently opened bottle clatters to the floor. "I dogged you?" Her *pfft* sprinkles my face with spit. "You're not the one who woke up in an empty bed."

"I went to run an errand." When she rolls her eyes, I defend myself like she isn't my best friend's girl. "I left you a note."

"Let me guess, you wrote it in my songbook?" She doesn't take in my head bob before knocking me on my ass. Figurately. I'm already seated, remember? "Before you *stole it*."

"I didn't steal anything. I'm not a thief."

"Then what did you do to get that?" She kicks my ankle tracker with the toe of her pump. "Knox told me you defrauded the government, but I'm not sure I believe him." She looks at me as if she trusts me more than him. "Is it true? Did you defraud the government?"

"Pretty much so," I bite back, over both our conversation and the constant repercussions of a hasty decision I made years ago while under the influence. "I lied to keep a promise I'd made to River. I guess some people would see that as defrauding the government." When my reply has her looking at me in a way she hasn't previously—with pity—I say, "Grab your purse. You're at your limit, so you won't be served more alcohol tonight."

She yanks out of my hold when I curl my hand around her elbow. It isn't hard. I'm barely touching her, but she makes it seem as if I'm squeezing her heart of blood. "I'm not going anywhere with you."

"Why the fuck not? You had no problems spending time with me when I buried my head between your legs."

She swings for me. Her hit isn't an open-handed slap or a fairy tap to my stomach. She swings for my face with her fist and almost takes me down with one punch.

After righting my head to its original position and working my jaw side to side to ensure nothing is broken, I once again curl my hand around her elbow before tugging her off her seat. "I'm not asking, Nicole. We're leaving. Now."

When her heels digging into the carpet get me nowhere fast, I wrap my arm around her ass, then toss her onto my shoulder. The wig she's using to hide the shame on her face falls to the ground as her fists whack into my back.

"Put me down! Just because you're the first man to give me head doesn't make you the boss of me." Her reply blasts excitement through my veins. It only lasts as long as it takes to remember Knox is a selfish man. "No one is the boss of me!"

She beats into me until we enter the elevator, and its lurch as it springs into action swirls her stomach more than the whiskey she's struggling to keep down.

"I'm going to put you down now, but don't take that as me backing down. I'll carry you all the way to Ravenshoe if it's the only way I can guarantee you'll make it to your bed in one piece. Do you hear me, Nicole? I'm not playing with your safety like this, and you mean too fucking much to me to sit back and watch you fall."

I take her silence as acceptance of my warning.

She sways when I place her onto her feet, but she doesn't bolt for the elevator panel to select the next floor as I'm anticipating. Instead, she hits me with a mood-sobering fact. "They hate me. They said I should quit singing and join the circus because that's where clowns belong." Her eyes are on me, wet and full of pain. "I should have listened to you. You tried to warn me. I just..."

"Handed your voice to someone else." I'm not asking a question or trying to make her feel bad. I'm endeavoring to show her it's okay to put your faith in someone who doesn't deserve it. We all make mistakes. I'm a walking billboard for them. "There's no shame in that. You've just got to remember that no one knows you better than you. Not Knox. Not your friends. Not even me. *You* know *you*."

When the elevator arrives at our floor, she blinks several times before helming our silent walk to her room. I stray my eyes to the floor when she commences stripping out of her coat and slinky dress at the foot of her untouched bed.

The reason for her hundred nightcaps makes sense when my eyes land on her iPhone dumped on the rug under her bed. It is playing a live broadcast of her rehearsal earlier. I know it is from today because she executes a kick that took her three days to perfect.

The belittling snickers booming from her phone speaker and the thousands of comments underneath the video can't be missed. They mock Nicole without concern for the consequences because they can hide behind a screen.

Nicole can't do the same.

No one in the public eye can.

"Don't pay attention to anything they say." I switch off her cell and place it on the bedside table before pulling down the stiff bedding. "The paparazzi aren't critics. They're not even your fans, and since they're clueless about what it takes to produce an album, they can't rate its salability."

"But the commenters are the people we need to buy my album."

Nicole quickly removes the tear that falls from her eye, but not fast enough.

I still see it.

"If the pressure is too much—"

"I can handle the pressure." One truth always encourages another. "I'm just not sure I am the right person for this job. I'm shy—"

"Bullshit." My word is spat out of my mouth like a bullet. "You're just hoping your shy act will be more appealing to the masses than a woman who knows what she wants and won't quit fighting until she gets it."

"It isn't an act." *Hiccup.* "I'm not acting."

"Bullshit," I repeat. "You weren't shy when you fell to your knees to suck my dick." Her inhalation exposes she's more turned on by my lewd comment than disgusted. "You weren't shy when riling me about a supposed prostitute addiction." That awards me a genuine smile for the first time in five days. "And you weren't shy when you sang with nothing but the tap of a pen against a sheet of paper as backup." I pluck up a pen from her bedside table and tap out the composition we arranged the night we met. "You're not shy, Nicole. You're scared of falling because you think no one will be there to catch you." Her glassy eyes bounce between mine when I admit, "That might have been true a week ago, but it isn't anymore."

"You..." She either takes a moment to think or swallow back vomit. I'm not exactly sure. "You stole my songbook. You took the first words I'd penned in a *long* time and made out they were yours." The instant the words leave her mouth, she knows they're a lie. She's merely struggling to understand how that is possible. "What did I miss?"

"I don't know." That's the most honest I've been in almost a week... perhaps even a decade. "But I will find out. I promise you that."

Nicole accepts my pledge with more faith than I deserve. She dips her chin in thanks before climbing into the middle of the bed on her hands and knees.

When I tug up the blanket at the foot of the bed to cover her bare legs, her veins too primed with whiskey to understand the AC is chilly, I discover where she hides her most valued possession.

Her songbook topples out during the blanket's rolls and flops open at newly penned lyrics.

I want to kiss the ~~sadness~~

arrogance from your face,

> make you my biggest mistake,..
> but I'm not sure how much
> more I can take,
> since you always look at me
> as if ~~we might break~~
> you're attending my wake…

The wetness of the crossed-out words announces this verse was recently written, much less its positioning in the songbook. It is toward the back, the last of the used pages.

Stunned by how plump the book has become over the past five days, I flick through the new creations.

Nicole's songbook was flat as a tack only days ago. Now it is brimming with lyrics, musical compositions, and cover design ideas stuffed into the spiral edge.

Each song is constructed with a similar premise—forbidden love. It is a risqué subject that will sell like hotcakes when composed with the right music.

"This is what you should be working on, Nicole." I raise my eyes to her, the pride on my face unmissable. "This is what your audience wants to hear. It's what they *deserve*." I find the first song I spotted before spinning her songbook to face her. "There's nothing needed to produce this. The hard work is already done. You just need to lay the tracks in a studio. And this…"

I flick back and forth between the pages, seeking the song she wrote the night we met. It is a long and tedious search that comes up empty-handed at the same time I notice slithered remains of torn pages in the spirals of the binder. It's gone, and so is the note I wrote.

"You ripped them out?"

Why would she do that? The note is understandable. I kept things rather basic. But the song was about fresh and exciting love and the butterflies you experience when you know you've stumbled onto something great. It was a love ballad through and through, but her best work to date. She's potentially thrown away millions of dollars and even more fans.

Her words are more upset now than slurred. "It was like that when I found it." She sinks her head onto her pillow, the weight on her shoulders too much to bear. "Well, I didn't find it. The maid who cleaned your room did."

"My room?" I check, certain I heard her wrong.

Through quivering lips, she replies, "I didn't realize anything was amiss until a loose page slipped out when I was preparing to leave the jet." She yawns before the alcohol drooping her eyelids shifts her words to whispers. "I was so mad at you that I let Knox off the hook too easily. I want to do this on my own. I deserve for *my* voice to be heard."

"Then do that. Fight for this"—I wiggle her songbook in the air—"with that." I tap it against her slow-rising chest, right where her heart is. "Don't give them any choice but to listen."

While clutching her songbook close to her heart, Nicole nods before asking, "Will you help me?"

"Knox—"

For how intoxicated she is, her words come out strong. "Doesn't get a say on who is a part of my team." Her blinks slow as her head sinks more deeply on her pillow. "I want you to be a part of this. I want you to be a part of me." As her words filter into her drunk head, her eyes pop open, glassy and shocked. "A part of us..." When she's still not convinced she has her statement right, she twists her lips and then tries again. "A part of—"

"How about we discuss it more when your veins aren't primed with whiskey?"

Needing to leave before I want to pretend the tension burning between us has nothing to do with her intoxication, I brush back the stray strands on her forehead, press my lips to where they lay, then head for the door.

Partway there, Nicole whispers, "Thank you, Laken."

It is the simplest of praises but the most impactful for me.

I can't recall the last time someone thanked me, and I've done far more for certain people than get them into bed safely after a night of drinking.

When I struggle to find a fitting reply, I spin to face Nicole to issue a response without words. I realize my internal fight was pointless when I spot her in the middle of her bed. She's out cold, and her pillow isn't the only thing about to be soaked with drool.

After saving her songbook from near disaster—and spending far too many minutes staring at the perfect details of her unblemished face—I head for the door for the second time in the past ten minutes.

Partway out, I hear whispered voices coming from the living room of the suite. Assuming it's River seeking where I disappeared to for the umpteenth time the past week, I head in that direction instead of walking deeper down the hallway where the rooms sprout off.

My heart beats at an unusual rhythm when I spot Knox in the entryway.

He isn't returning to the suite after running an errand.

He's showing a busty redhead out.

His hand hovering on the small of her back announces this, not to mention the sloppy farewell kiss he plants on her lips a second after opening the door.

What the?

After telling her he'll be in touch soon, he watches her stalk to the elevator, before removing her lipstick from his face in the entryway mirror. It isn't solely smeared on his lips, and it has my anger reaching a point where I can't hold back the groan rumbling up my chest.

"Laken... ah... hey," he pushes out when he hears my grumble. His eyes dart to the door the redhead just walked through before they return to me. "How long have you been there?"

"Long enough," I reply, certain if I don't start matching his lies with some of my own, I'll never get a truth out of him.

"Fuck." He rakes his fingers over his scalp before giving me the most pathetic excuse in the book. "It isn't as it seems." When I *pfft* him, he backtracks quicker than I can snap my fingers. "Well, it is. Clearly, you recognize Candy from Ravenshoe. How *could any man forget that face*? So there's no use denying what she does for a profession." He always rambles when nervous, but I don't call him out on it since it also makes him the most honest. "After a frantic few days, I needed to blow off some steam. I figured since I was too worked up for my usual outlets, I should take it out on someone paid to handle it." He speaks as if hiring a prostitute is as normal as ordering takeout. "Is everything okay? Is Nicole—"

"She's sleeping," I interrupt, hating that he brings her up so soon after walking a sex worker to the door, but also hopeful. Maybe Nicole said what she said because she's had enough of Knox's crap. "And most likely going to be hungover in the morning. Have you seen the stuff they're writing about her online?" When he nods, I breathe out a long, tedious breath. "The comments are brutal. They're tearing her to shreds."

"I know," Knox replies, shocking me further. "It is a fucking shit show."

"Then why weren't you there for her? Why hire a hooker when your girl needed you more?"

He throws his hands up like we're in a boxing ring and not the living room of one of the flashy suites he stays in like he has to prove something. "Are you really trying to give me relationship advice? You once thought a Valentine's Day gift was flavored condoms."

"In high school. I've matured the fuck up since then."

He laughs at me like I'm a sucker before sidestepping me to enter his office. As he cleans up evidence of his cheating ways, I stare at him like I don't know who the hell he is. Nicole is the best thing that's ever happened to him. She's intelligent, funny, and outstandingly beautiful.

Even with their wealth not on par, she is *way* above Knox's league. Yet, he's going to throw it away for a woman who charges by the hour.

When I say that to Knox, he dumps an open box of condoms into the top drawer of his desk, rights a wayward keyboard and mouse, then enters the attached bathroom to spray some aftershave around.

It is the same aftershave I found next to Nicole's earring.

He squirts the pricy bottle in the air until the scent of sex is replaced with spices and wood, then spins to face me. "There. Crisis averted."

I'm too shocked to speak.

Does he really think so little of Nicole that he believes a bit of aftershave will hide the hickeys on his neck?

"She's gonna find out," I eventually murmur, my tone hinting that I'm more hopeful than fretful.

Nicole deserves better, and she asked me only minutes ago to help ensure that occurs, so I refuse to stand down this time.

"No, she won't," Knox denies, walking me to the door. "Because you're not going to say anything." My back is already up, but it reaches a new level when he mutters, "Bros before hoes and all that shit."

"Knox—"

"I'll stop, all right? I promise. I just…" He scrubs at his face before reminding me that things could be worse. "Wouldn't you rather me choke out a prostitute than harm the voice of the woman who will make us rich?"

I don't give a fuck about the money, but the thought of him with Nicole like that makes me want to rip off his nuts. I hate that she's being disrespected, but if I had to pick between Nicole or a prostitute soothing Knox's edginess, I'd always choose the latter.

Knox mistakes my expression. "That's what I fucking thought." He slaps my back like nothing will ever come between us, before barging me toward my room. "Now get the fuck out of my room so I can get some shuteye. It might be a rest day for the crew tomorrow, but there's no rest for the wicked."

He winks at me and then commences closing the door just as my eyes land on a cot in the corner of the large space.

20
NICOLE

"Nicole, are you awake?" The drilling of my temples feels nowhere near as bad when River's sweet tone jingles through my ears. "I've brought breakfast."

"You didn't need to do that." My words taste like garbage and sound husky since my throat is so dry. As I scrub the chunk from my eyes, I scoot up my bed until my back rests on the headboard. "Oh my god, that smells like heaven," I murmur when the scent of coffee, bacon, and fresh juice bombards my senses as River rolls a serving tray into my room. "Did you do a coffee run?"

Mindful of where my eagerness stems, River shakes his head before pouring me a generous serving. "Cream and two, please," he says, quoting the order I give the barista anytime we go out for coffee.

After stirring the beverage he only fills halfway, he hands it to me before wrapping me up in a big hug.

I'm grateful he planned for spillage. His hug is so affectionate he would have knocked me over if I wasn't sitting.

Once he assures me I'm not seconds from dying, he inches back before raising a brow. "We have muffins too, but Laken said you wouldn't want muffins. That your tummy would want greasy bacon." He spins to face the serving tray to show me the mountain of bacon under a silver dome.

"That's a lot of bacon."

"It is," he agrees. "But you don't have to share. Laken cooked enough breakfast for everyone."

My heart skips a beat. "Laken made me breakfast?" I assumed he ordered room service.

River's head only bobs three times before he screws up his adorable face. "He kinda made it for everyone. But the bacon is mainly for you. He wouldn't even let Knox have any, and they're best friends."

His reply shocks me as much as his admission that Laken cooked breakfast. Laken and Knox appear close, but I had no clue it was near best friend status. Their personalities seem too opposite for that. They're almost like night and day.

River shifts my focus back to him with a pleading tone. "If you're okay, can I go back to the kitchen now?" The excitement on his face is understandable when he rubs his hands together while saying, "I want to eat the muffins while they're still warm."

"Yeah. I'm fine. Thank you for bringing this to me."

"You're welcome." He skips to the door before suddenly turning back around to face me. "Before I forget, Laken wanted me to tell you he didn't steal your phone." He takes a moment to make sure he has his words right. "He *borrowed* it with the intention of returning it once the scum-sucking warts on the toes of the trolls trolling you have been taken care of." He stops, twists his lips, then asks, "Does that mean he's going to kill them?"

"No," I say with a laugh. "I don't think that's what he meant." I freeze like a statue when River pulls a face that announces he thinks differently. "Do you think that's what he meant?"

His silence has my heart beating faster than the jackhammer pounding my temples.

"No," River eventually murmurs. "Laken's a nice guy. He would never hurt anyone."

"Then why did it take you so long to reply?"

I'm riling him, but he gives me an honest answer I'm not sure I deserve. "Because he's different when it comes to the people he loves. He'll sacrifice anything for them." I don't know whether to swoon or laugh when he adds, "So if the paps start dropping like flies, you didn't see or hear anything."

I twist the imaginary lock on my lips before throwing away the key. "My lips are sealed."

He smiles like he did when I refused to let him clean the female toilet in the recording studio. Back then, I was the only female on staff, so there was no way I would make him clean up my mess. "If you're feeling up to it, movie marathon at two. I reserved the entire living room. I didn't have to pay. Knox said I could use it. Some friends are coming from rehearsal. It will be fun."

"Sounds good," I reply, confident now isn't the time to be alone.

I don't recall much of last night. No number of nips, however, could have me forgetting the slaughtering my career undertook when someone leaked footage of my rehearsal.

I'm one lousy publicity stunt away from giving up a career in music entirely.

"Okay, great. I'll save you a seat."

When he races out the door, I smile at his enthusiasm before sipping the caffeine he prepared for me.

What should be a heavenly awakening isn't. The coffee tastes ghastly, and I understand why when I peer at the serving tray. Only a saltshaker sits next to a pitcher of cream. There's no sugar to be seen.

I feel like death, so I can only imagine how bad I look, but since the comments last night assure me my crew has already seen me at my worst, I sling on a silky slip, then trudge to the kitchen for a clean mug and some sachets of sugar.

My throat dries for an entirely different reason than a hangover when I break through the kitchen's swinging door. Laken is at the cooktop, pouring pancake batter onto a skillet. He's barefoot and wearing nothing but a pair of low-riding sleep pants. Since he's facing away from me, I get to drink in the two dimples in his lower back I missed out on the last time I checked out his ass, as he was fully clothed.

When my throat works through a hard swallow, desperate for lubricant, its rough bob announces my presence. He spins around to face me while saying, "Just a few more minutes, River, then you..." His words trail off when he spots me standing in the entryway of the kitchen. "Hey..." His smile makes my hangover nonexistent. "Out of bacon already?"

I laugh. It is a foreign thing to hear with how wretched I felt last night. "Not yet." I shake the coffee mug before pointing to the sugar canister on the bench. "I think that was meant to be on the serving tray instead of a massive saltshaker."

"Shit." He tries to hold back his smile this time around. His efforts are woeful. As his grin gleams as evidently as his impressive V muscle, he says, "Let me grab you a fresh one." Before I can announce his job is to protect me, not serve me, he fetches a mug from an overhead cupboard, pours a generous serving of caffeinated brew, then passes it to me to finish its preparation. "Figure you'd rather guarantee you're not about to get a mouthful of salty dishwater than relish me waiting on you hand and foot."

I could leave once I've added cream and sugar to the mug, but only an idiot would give up this view. The daily rate at this hotel is astronomical because of the uninterrupted views.

It has nothing on the wonderment in front of me.

When I slot my backside onto a breakfast stool under the counter, Laken shyly grins before shifting his focus back to the pancakes. He works in silence over the next several minutes, his creations plucked from the plate at his side before they've had the chance to cool.

"This is the last batch, Nicole, so if you want some, you better beat back the masses and let your voice be heard."

Something about his statement doubles the output of my heart.

I can't pinpoint exactly what, though.

I drop my eyes to my mug when Laken cranks his head back. "Coffee is about all my stomach can handle right now."

He nods like he understands the cause of the swirls of my stomach before setting down a plate of bacon in front of me. "And bacon. Bacon and coffee are the *only* things needed to cure a hangover."

Before I can ask him how he knows I'm hungover, a voice at the side asks, "Did someone say bacon?"

Knox enters the kitchen a second before the excessive amount of aftershave he placed on and plucks up a strip of bacon from the plate, crunching through it with his teeth. The crispiness of the salty strip being eradicated should drown out the growl Laken hits Knox with. It is as apparent as the tension that deprives the air of oxygen when Knox presses his lips to my temple.

"I need to head out for a few hours. Will you be all right here, or do you want to come with me?"

Laken appears prepared to answer on my behalf, so I speak quickly. "I'm good here." Before I can configure a reason for the relief on Laken's face, I accidentally wipe it off. "I promised River I'd join him for a movie marathon."

Knox's growl is as rumbling as the one Laken released only moments ago.

It annoys me as much as it does Laken.

"I tried to save you." After plucking a second strip of bacon off the plate under grumbled protest from Laken, Knox salutes me before exiting the kitchen as fast as he entered.

It takes several long seconds for the tension to drop low enough for me to speak. "Is everything okay? I didn't do something stupid last night, did I?"

God, please don't let me have done something as stupid as sleep with Knox.

I will never forgive myself if I did something so foolish.

Although Laken's reply liberates me of worry, it also piques my suspicion. "You weren't the one doing stupid shit." His smile is only half the size of his earlier one. "Eat, Nicole. You'll need the energy."

"You need energy to watch a movie?"

Now his smile is more prominent than ever. "You do when it comes to River."

Hating that I'm pacing in my room, waiting for the clock to strike two like a loser without a date, I unravel the strand of hair I curled around my index finger and walk to my bed.

The lyrics I've been encountering nonstop over the past six days are still coming in strong and fast, but they're a little different today—more about second chances and forgiveness than the one who got away.

"Where are you?" I murmur to myself when my dig through the blanket folded at the foot of the mattress fails to find my songbook.

A hotel employee serviced my room while I was showering, so everything is where it is meant to be *except* my songbook.

Laken wouldn't have taken it again, would he?

He couldn't be so cruel. River said he cares about the people he loves, so why would he hurt me twice in one week?

I freeze when I realize how deranged my inner monologue is.

Laken doesn't love me.

He hardly knows me.

I'm the only fool carrying a torch for someone who hurt me.

My limbs harden further when a snippet of a memory smacks into me as fast as a bolt of lightning brightening the sky.

You mean too fucking much to me to sit back and watch you fall.

Another revelation quickly follows the first.

You're scared of falling because you think no one will be there to catch you. Lyrics flood me when the remainder of Laken's promise is unearthed. *That might have been true a week ago, but it isn't anymore.*

The memories slowly trickling into my mind are foggy but clear enough for me to slant my head to the pillow I lay on last night.

The surge of euphoria thickening my veins tells me I don't need to search my songbook when I find it safely tucked under my pillow, but I can't help but check.

Laken made the first song I'd penned in over a year better. He added the beat it needed without overwhelming the lyrics.

He made it a Nicole Reed original hit.

Regretfully the only musical compositions in my songbook are the ones I placed there, but mercifully they push another memory to the forefront of my mind.

This is what you should be working on, Nicole. This is what your audience wants to hear. It's what they deserve.

"This is what they deserve," I quote, my voice unhindered by the nerves it hasn't been without the past two weeks. "So it's what I *must* give them."

"Nicole, over here!" River waves me into the living room bustling with the road crew we're about to spend the next several weeks with on tour.

"Sorry I'm late. I was writing." The glee in my voice can't be missed.

The crew is too busy chatting amongst themselves to give my excuse any thought. The only one who pays attention is Laken. He's hogging one-third of the only sofa not overflowing with employees of Knox Records.

"I saved you a seat." River guides me to the three-seater couch I just mentioned. "If you'll sit, we'll start proceedings."

It could be my imagination or the dozens of loved-up lyrics I just wrote down, but I'm confident the gap between Laken's knees expands when River plops me into the seat next to him.

A surge of excitement runs through me.

Once my thigh is butted to Laken's, River drags Bella onto a makeshift stage before shifting his eyes to the person I should have known was his brother.

River looks at Laken in a way he's never looked at Knox.

He truly loves him with everything he has.

"Ready?"

River waits for Laken to give him the thumbs-up before he and Bella reenact a scene I'm certain I've seen before.

A remote will never be seen as anything but a microphone when a devastated River drops it to the ground as Bella says, "That is so wrong."

Before I can blurt out the title, Laken leans into my side and whispers, "Unless you want to watch *Never Been Kissed*, pretend you don't know which movie their skit is from."

When I twist to face him, the minty freshness of his breath exposes he brushed his teeth as recently as I did. "Isn't the point of charades to guess correctly?"

"This isn't charades." His breathy response prickles the hairs on the back of my neck. "You only want to guess correctly *if* you like the movie they want to watch."

"You don't like *Never Been Kissed*?" His screwed-up face makes me laugh, and that simple gesture doubles the tension teeming between us. "I love Drew Barrymore. She can do no wrong."

Laken shifts his eyes from my smile to River and Bella when someone from the sound crew shouts, "*Never Been Kissed*."

With a shrug, he stops the timer on River's phone before spinning the screen to face him.

"Yes!" River fist bumps the air before forcing his excitement onto Bella with an ecstatic hug.

Once her cheeks are as red as mine from how often Laken's thigh brushes mine during their celebratory dance-off, he aligns his eyes with his brother's. "Bet you can't beat that."

"Don't count your chickens before they're hatched, River." When River and Bella sit in their spots next to mine, Laken stands before holding out his hand in offering. "Ready?"

"We're playing?" I ask, shocked.

He plucks me from my seat before anyone answers my question and spins me to face the dozen faces eagerly watching us.

Their interest is even more daunting than when I'm standing in the wings of a stage, waiting to perform.

I'm also not convinced my ego can take another battering so soon after the last.

It could pummel my confidence beyond repair.

"I can't—"

"You can do this, Nicole," Laken interrupts, his breath hot on my ear.

He steals my chance to announce I'm not as confident as he makes out by telling River to start the timer.

"I'm not ready to go it alone just yet."

Since my line doesn't come from a movie script, confusion mars the guessers' faces.

It doesn't linger for long. Only as long as it takes for Laken to say, "Now hold on to the railing." My heart thuds louder than my temples ever have when he places his hands on my hips to hold me steady. "Keep your eyes closed. Don't peek."

His fingers flex when I close my eyes before following the gist of his skit. "I'm not."

His voice is different when he says, "Step up onto the railing."

Rose's gasped breaths sound authentic when my mind drifts back to the night on the rooftop with Laken.

I swear nothing but millions of lights and people the size of ants are in front of me.

"Come on, keep your eyes closed." I flatten my back to Laken's chest when he asks, "Do you trust me?"

I nod before saying, "I trust you."

My arms are only just fanning out when a voice breaks through my daydream. *"Titanic!"*

Disappointed our skit was interrupted before we got to the best bit, I slump back before opening my eyes.

Ellen looks pleased she guessed correctly, but I'm disappointed when River checks the timer on his phone.

"Three seconds too slow." He bounces his eyes between Laken and me. "*Titanic* is out of the running for premium screentime tonight."

His rejection doesn't hurt as much as the brutal slaying I faced last night. Laken's grateful sigh eases it as he leads us back to our shared seat.

"Not a fan of *Titanic* either?" I ask as another couple commences performing a skit from the top one hundred romance movies of all time.

"Eh." He shouts out the name of the movie the backup dancers are performing before returning his focus to me. "I'd rather my romance stories end with an HEA."

"Me too," I admit, loving the ease of our conversations today. "Or I'll one star that book all the way to its grave."

His breathy laugh fans my lips, making me hungry, but before I can act on impulses for the second time this week, I shout, "*Casablanca!*" within half a second of Ellen saying, "Of all the gin joints in all of the towns in all of the world, she walks into mine…"

21
LAKEN

"Nicole..."

"She's okay," I assure Bella before she can shake Nicole's shoulder again. "Let her sleep."

Bella's brows furrow. "Are you sure? She's drooling on your shirt."

It takes everything to make my smile look like a grimace. Nicole lasted longer than River usually does during the movie marathon. She got through two movies, *Casablanca* and *The Notebook*, before her cheek landed on my shoulder, and her faint pants of breath on my lips made me the hungriest I've ever been.

She's been out for almost two hours, but I'd rather she sleep off her hangover than spend the next several hours puking her guts up.

When Bella stares at me with her hip cocked and her stance frozen, I realize I failed to answer her. "I've got plenty of shirts."

"I'm sure you do." The next half of her snarky reply hits me below the belt. "But should you be wasting them on a taken woman?"

Support comes from an unlikely source. "Is knocking boots really classed as being taken?" Ellen hits Bella with a saucy wink. "Because if it is, you've been taken ten times this month alone."

My jaw tightens at the thought of Knox and Nicole "knocking boots," but Nicole is shunted awake from an unlikely source before my frustration is vocalized.

River has returned from his room, where he went to practice his routine for the next movie marathon night. He's adamant *Never Been*

Kissed needs to be on the list of top romance movies of all time. His stomps are so loud they'd wake all the hotel guests.

"It's raining!" He never looked more excited. "It's pouring down." He thrusts his hand at the foggy window, showing how well LA is being drenched. "You know what that means, Laken." Before I can tell him he shouldn't let our mother's crazy antics influence him, he shouts, "Rain Karaoke!"

He snatches up the remote Ellen used for the win and commences belting out Creedence Clearwater Revival's "Have You Ever Seen the Rain."

I realize Rain Karaoke is no longer just our thing when the road crew starts singing the chorus with River before shadowing him outside.

"You don't have to," I tell Nicole when River shouts for her to hurry.

"Don't have to...?" She leaves her question open for me to answer how I see fit.

I raise my eyes to the roof before doing precisely that. "Sing in the rain."

"They're going to the roof to sing in the rain?"

The excitement her eyes held when she exited her room hours ago shines bright when I bob my chin. She looks like a kid on Christmas who Santa didn't skip because his mother was too cheap to buy her son a single gift.

"We have to go." She leaps to her feet like they haven't been tucked under her bottom the past two hours and plucks me from my seat, racing us toward the elevator banks.

"This way is quicker," I promise while throwing open the emergency exit stairwell and guiding her up two flights.

This hotel doesn't have a rooftop as elaborate as the one in Ravenshoe, but there's plenty of space for an impromptu rain-themed concert.

I firm my grip on Nicole's hand when she takes a startled step back as we arrive on the rooftop. River and a handful of the road crew have reached the final chorus of the song. The acoustics on the roof are spellbinding, not to mention how the musical half of the road crew uses everyday items to back up the performance. One uses the metal shutters on the air vent to mimic a tambourine. Another, a moving box for drums.

The "music" complements the singers, but the show's true star can't be denied.

River's voice is so on par with John Fogarty's husky tone that I get goosebumps.

I'm not the only one in awe. Nicole cheers and claps like a groupie when River ends his performance by falling to his knees, fanning out his arms, then flopping his head back so the rain can hide the tears he'll never admit are wetting his cheeks.

Our mother always sang this song when she got so drunk she thought the roof with loose shingles on a two-story bungalow was a good place for a six- and three-year-old to dance.

Once he's confident the rain conceals his tears, River forces me to remember not all our childhood memories are bad. He pulls Nicole and me into the middle of the noisy group before handing the "microphone" to me.

My first few lines are as rickety as the roof we used to stomp on, but I push my nerves aside when Nicole leans in to sing the chorus into the pretend microphone with me. Her voice doesn't have John's husky, mannish twang, but it stops several of the crew in their tracks.

They stare at her in admiration like I did on the rooftop almost a week ago, aware they're amongst one of the greats and fucking stoked to be a part of it as much as I am.

22
NICOLE

My eyes sling to my bedroom door when a tap sounds through it. When it remains closed, my visitor waiting for permission to enter instead of storming in like he owns the place, excitement trickles through my veins.

Knox usually enters without waiting. So that can only mean one thing—my guest isn't my manager.

"Just a minute."

Like a fool who didn't spend the last two hours rocking out to rain-inspired songs on a cool fall afternoon, I fluff out my hair that's drying and check my face in the mirror before granting my visitor permission to enter.

"Come in."

The excited patter keeping my heart rate high jumps astronomically when Laken's head pops into my room a second before his body. I can't exactly pinpoint what changed between us the past twenty-four hours, but it has caused a drastic uptick in the tension our exchanges are never without. He's no longer looking at me like he loathes me, and my trust that he's a good guy is almost as high on the scale as the fun day we've had.

I can't remember the last time I had a day off. It was long before I met Knox.

"Hey..." I angle my head to hide my smile when his tone sounds as elevated as my pulse. "I thought I should bring this back." He wiggles the hairdryer he's clutching. "It was a close call, but we might have saved the remote."

"Phew." Dramatically, I drag my hand across my forehead. "They charge thirty dollars for a nip of scotch, so I'd hate to see the replacement cost of a remote control."

My teasing smile slips when Laken mutters, "Lucky you went for the cheap stuff."

With the tension too playful for panic, I say, "So that's why I could smell your aftershave." While I continue to scrunch the ends of my hair, I plop onto the end of my bed. "I couldn't work out how it had gotten on my pillow." A smidge of shyness dips my tone. "I thought it was from you hiding my songbook under it."

My hope returns more potent than ever. "It slipped out when I tugged up the blanket." Like he needs to blame my nakedness on something, he adds, "The AC was cool."

"And I went to bed only wearing a pair of panties and a bra." I grimace. "Did I strip, or did you have to…" I make a gesture with my hand that I hope spells everything out since embarrassment is clutching my throat.

"That was all you. I kept my hands to myself." The disappointment in his tone during his last sentence saves my ego from a beating. "Both last night and the night we met." I know he's telling the truth before he even speaks the words I'm dying to hear. "I didn't take your songbook, Nicole. I didn't touch it." As he scrubs at his neck, a cuss word leaves his mouth. "That's a lie. I touched it to write you a note." His next set of words that crack out of his mouth like a whip proves he knows the sentimental value of my songbook will forever outrank its salability. "A note I wrote in the pencil I searched the rooftop room for so my addition could be erased." He licks his lips to loosen them up for his confession. "But I swear on River's life that I didn't remove it from the bedside table I placed it on when you straddled my lap."

Catching pneumonia is no longer an issue with how hot his comment makes me. I'm burning up and struggling to sit still. And we won't mention the look he gifts me when I pledge, "I believe you." My shoulders sink as air whizzes from my nose. "It just sucks we don't know where it went because that song could have been a goldmine." I pull my songbook from its hidey-hole and plop it onto the bed. "Apollo said it was probably the only decent thing in there." I nudge my head at my songbook. "The rest are worthless."

Laken couldn't look more shocked if I had told him we were related. "Is he a fucking idiot?" He doesn't give me a chance to reply. "He must be because there are *several* hits in that one teeny-tiny little book."

"Will you show me which ones you think have potential?" My question leaves my mouth before I can comprehend that I'm taking the word of a man I only met a week ago over a producer who's been in the industry for decades.

After jerking up his chin, Laken places the hairdryer onto the bedside table before filling its void with my beloved songbook. Only days ago, I would have ripped it from his grasp. Now, it seems as if it couldn't be in safer hands.

"This one is good, but there's something off with the lyrics. They feel moodier and more morose than the newer ones."

When I peer down at the song he's referencing, I gulp. "I wrote that when I was angry."

It was the first lot of lyrics I penned after believing he had violated the last gift my sister had given me. "What about this one?"

> You can act interested, but your heart can't lie,
> She'll never capture your attention like
> the woman who first caught your eye,
> She's a prop, a gimmick, not your one true love.
> She won't be the one you pick

when ~~it comes~~ push comes to shove.

As Laken continues reading the lyrics I wrote while jealous about the attention Bella was bestowing him, I watch his face for any clues.

He gives nothing away. Not a single hint.

He keeps his thoughts locked up tighter than a vault until his eyes lock with mine.

The pride in them gives him away.

"This is good, Nicole. Real good."

I wait for a "but."

It regretfully shows up only seconds later. "But..." I could kill him for the delay. "Aren't you writing this from the wrong perspective?" When I peer up at him, confused, he works to ease it. "If your creativity comes from your life..."—he flicks through my songbook—"which this screams is the case, why is she jealous? Why aren't you writing about how he feels watching her with him? And how it tears him to shreds knowing he can't have her like that. You make it seem as if the jealousy is one-sided and only coming from her." His eyes pop before he throws open my bedside table drawer and rummages through the limited items inside.

"What are you looking for?" I ask when his frustrated groan rumbles through both our chests.

"A pen and a piece of paper," Laken replies, still hunting.

Shockingly, I snatch my songbook and favorite pen before thrusting them into his chest.

You'd swear I'd given him the key to my heart when he asks, "Are you sure?"

The fact he seeks permission weakens my hesitation in an instant.

When I nod, his grin stops my heart before he plops his backside onto the bed beside me. "This could be a perfect duet."

After mouthing the lyrics I penned for the start of the song, he commences jotting down his own set.

> I act disinterested because it
> is the only way I can survive…
> Watching you with him kills me,
> I'm not gonna lie…
> The smiles you once gave me
> made me believe I was alive…
> Now I'm struggling to find a way to thrive…
> I don't want you to be a prop,
> a gimmick, or the one who got away…
> I want you to be the only woman
> I love each and every day.

"Don't touch it!" I shout when Laken almost scraps the entire thing at the end of the final line. "This is the beginning. We move *up* from here."

After flicking through his verse and mine, I make a handful of adjustments before seeking Laken's opinion.

My heart refuses to beat while I wait for his approval. And when I get it, it is like all my Christmases have come at once.

I squeal like I'm years younger than I am before I flick to the next song in my songbook.

"Now work your magic on this one."

By the time River announces he's not waiting a second longer to eat, my bed is covered with composed song sheets, and my heart is the fullest it's ever been.

Although I never imagined it occurring in a hotel room thousands of miles from my hometown, this is what I envisioned when I conjured up what producing an album would entail.

It should have never been "that isn't right" or "that's not the vision we're going for." It was meant to be an inspiring time that encouraged both creativity and originality.

Laken gave me that.

He gave me back my voice.

"In a minute, River," Laken murmurs, his focus fixed on a song we've been working on for the past hour. "Let me finish this one first."

"You said that three hours ago." River stomps his foot. "I'm hungry now."

"I won't be a—" I curl my hand over Laken's and squeeze it, stopping him mid-denial.

When he peers at me in shock that I want to place anything between me and a guaranteed multi-platinum album, I shrug like it isn't a rarity. "I haven't eaten since breakfast…" I check the time on his retro watch. "That was almost seventeen hours ago."

"See," River bursts out, unaware the only thing I'm craving right now is more of Laken's musical genius but I'm setting it aside solely for him and his hungry tummy. "Even someone with a brain as big as Nicole's knows the importance of eating." He rubs his stomach like he didn't eat two buckets of popcorn and multiple boxes of Maltesers during *Casablanca*. "And there's no better brain food than overloaded tacos."

"Tacos?" Laken asks, his brow high. "You're upset that we delayed a food binge that will have you spending the rest of the day on the toilet, crapping it out?"

"Tacos don't make me poop," River denies, his lofty tone hinting at his fib.

Laken's brow inches higher and higher and higher until River has no choice but to rebut his lie. "Still worth it."

After hitting him with a sassy look I can't help but smile about, he spins on his heels and stalks away.

Laken and I shadow his exit shoulder to shoulder only two seconds later.

"I told you tacos—"

"Yeah, yeah, save your lecture for when I'm not about to shit my pants," River interrupts, glaring at his brother. He nudges his head to a café outside our hotel that's preparing for the early morning breakfast rush. That's how late our song session ran over. It is almost dawn. "You should probably buy dessert." His adorable almond eyes sling to me. "This *won't* be pretty, and my bathroom has no air freshener."

"Dessert sounds great." I spin to Laken to hide the humor on my face before asking, "Care to join me?"

"I'd love to."

I want to pretend his quick response isn't because of his brother's warning, but when River's backside squeaks louder than his shoes as he races through the rotating door of our hotel, my hope slithers.

Don't get me wrong. Even while purchasing tacos from a food vendor a couple of blocks up from our hotel, the pride in Laken's eyes didn't diminish. He just seems a little uneasy when we're alone.

Anyone would swear it is a conscious effort for him to keep his hands off me.

I realize that might be the case when his hand only warms the small of my back for half a second as he guides me toward the café.

"Eat in or takea—"

Laken is interrupted by a familiar set of chants.

"Nicole, is it true Rise Up went on a European tour so they'd miss your public humiliation?"

"Nicole, would you like to comment on claims you're pregnant with Nick's child?"

"Nicole, have you seen the video blowing up on social media about you?"

Although there are only half a dozen paparazzi for Laken to remove from the café, I'm swarmed by members of the public in less than a nanosecond. The paparazzi linked my name with Rise Up. That type of exposure only ends one way.

With me almost being trampled.

The crash is immediate. Within seconds, I'm overwhelmed by requests for autographs and selfies.

"Move back," Laken demands before he curls his arm around my shoulders and pulls me into his chest. "Keep your head down." He's not ashamed to be photographed with me as the Rise Up band members should be but aren't. He's trying to protect my head from the number of phones and cameras shoved in my face during our short walk from the café to our hotel. "Get the fuck back!"

As he seeks the assistance of the security team in the foyer of the hotel, I'm grabbed at the side by a man double my size and yanked out of Laken's grip.

"Nicole!" Laken's voice is as stern as the panic that grips my throat when the crowd realizes I'm in the open.

They race for me so fast they knock me over.

I'm certain it is over, that today was my last hurrah, but Laken arrives out of nowhere and pulls me into his arms before I'm trampled alive.

His heart thuds in my ear as he barges through the crowd with no concern about how many phones and cameras he breaks. He is a man on a mission, and after thirty heart-whacking seconds, he breaks us through the hotel entrance and the security team assigned to the foyer takeover and subduing the crowd.

"What the fuck was that?" Laken asks, his focus not on me.

When I wiggle, requesting to be placed down, he sets me on my feet before marching to stand chest to chest with a man he seems to know.

"You couldn't see them swarming her?" Anger seethes in his words as his eyes bore into the blond gent who is wearing the same outfit as the rest of the security personnel, just flashier. "She almost got fucking trampled."

"Mr. Samson instructed that we were not to intervene in any exchanges between Ms. Reed and members of the media," the man fires back, his tone not as tempered, his stare not as raging.

"I don't give a fuck what Knox told you! He's not in charge of Nicole's safety." I'm expecting him to say, "You are," so you can picture my shock when he bangs his chest while adding, "I am. And I'm telling you to do your fucking job or stand down so someone not willing to compromise on morals for a couple of measly dollars can do the position right."

The man tries to make out he's not accepting bribes from Knox. He stammers and splutters, but the only words he eventually gets out are, "It won't happen again." He peers at me over Laken's shoulder. "You have my word, Ms. Reed."

His word means nothing to me, but I accept it purely with the hope it will weaken Laken's anger enough for us to return to our suite without blood being spilled.

It takes Laken a few seconds to walk away, but once he does, the tension amplifies instead of lessens. That might have more to do with him curling his hand around mine to walk me to the elevator than anything.

I've always seen hand-holding as intimate. It is above a man's hand on the small of a woman's back, or him taking the lead to ensure she doesn't face any encumbrances during their walk.

It is a man standing at his woman's side, supporting her and showing she is his equal.

Only floors from the penthouse suite, Laken loosens his hold. It isn't what you're thinking. He's not snatching his hand away because the wetness between our palms has exposed my like of hand-holding. The hand I used to cushion my fall is cut up and bleeding.

"You're bleeding." He sounds as devastated now as he did when he shouted my name after I was ripped from his arms.

"It's just a scratch," I assure him, hoping it will lower the angst on his face.

You'd swear my arm was scheduled for amputation when he says, "On your playing hand."

Before I can speak another word, he scoops me into his arms like he did outside the hotel and exits the elevator on our desired floor.

I'm not exactly sure what the scent is when we enter the suite, but mercifully, it isn't horrible. It smells similar to the scented oils Knox's masseuse used anytime she did one-on-one visits at the studio.

"Laken, it's fine. It doesn't even hurt," I promise him when a second after he plops me onto the vanity in my bathroom, he hunts for the first-aid kit in the medicine cabinet. "It won't affect my jazz hands at all." I raise my hands to give him the jazz-hand-performance of my life. "See. Perfectly capable of disgusting any man over the age of twelve."

Laken doesn't see the humor in the situation. "This isn't funny, Nicole. You could have been seriously hurt."

"But I wasn't. You got there first—"

"After letting them rip you from my arms." His hands are in his hair, tugging and violent. "I fucked up. I let you down."

I twist to face him, our bodies awfully close. "You did no such thing."

He acts as if I never spoke. "God, what if they'd—"

"Don't force scenarios in your head. They never end well."

"They could have killed you, Nicole. And it's my fucking job to protect you. I'm meant to stop situations like that from happening, not encourage them."

When his eyes lock with mine and I see their vulnerability, a thousand lyrics fill my head, but only one line from them matters. "You saved me."

"No."

I stop the shake of his head by placing my hands on each side of his prickly jaw. I'm meant to be expressing my gratitude for his quick thinking and assuring him that he's the one who stood up to defend me while others sat by and watched my downfall, but the only matter that gets broadcasted is how uncontrollably crazy I am about this man.

    I tried to fight the pull.

    I tried to brush off my jealousy as anger.

    Nothing worked.

    I'm besotted, and I'm done pretending I am someone I'm not.

    So, after hooking my thumb into the belt loops of Laken's pants, I tug him forward and seal my lips over his mouth.

23
NICOLE

My boldness wouldn't have dipped even if Laken hadn't immediately returned my kiss. The tension is too thick for that. The lust is too firm. It's been boiling for hours, and nothing will stop it now that it is finally spilling over.

Our exchange moves at a lightning-fast pace. There's no time to be savored and appreciated. We need to fuck to quench days of tension. Then we can take it slow and relish every moment.

As my hands fumble with the opening of Laken's trousers, his mouth drops to my neck to drive me wild with desire. He kisses me hurriedly, his mouth suctioning as his hand cups my breast to toy with my nipple.

One brush of his thumb over my budded peak puckers them both even more, and goosebumps break across my skin. It feels divine but almost too slow.

I want to be taken hard.

Consumed.

I want to be fucked.

"Please," I beg, desperate to answer the pleading thuds of my clit that haven't been quiet for a single second today. Its pulse has been frantic since breakfast, its beat as noticeable as the ping of the button in Laken's pants when he yanks on the zipper so ruefully that it bounces across the tiled floor.

His eagerness sends a pleasing shiver through my body and doubles my boldness. A second after he yanks his pants past his delicious ass, I slot my hand between his mouthwatering V muscle and his cotton boxer shorts. I stroke him in rhythm to his pants hitting my neck as he rolls the stiff peaks of my nipples between each index finger and thumb. It is a fast, needy pace that announces I wish to make him as unhinged as the urge to come is making me.

I'm desperate to be beneath him, to be stretched by him.

Desperate enough to beg.

"Please, oh, god. Please. I need more."

I push on his head until it falls from my neck, past my breasts, and then to my stomach.

"Shy, my fucking ass."

When I glare at him before continuing with my quest for his mouth to add to the mess his smile caused my panties, Laken's lips rise against my blistering skin. But instead of teasing me for my eagerness, he encourages the unladylike gap between my legs by placing his head between them and blowing a hot breath across my panty-covered slit.

"Oh, god." I'm not sure if I murmur this comment or shout it out loud. I can't view the world in the same way. How could I? The only man who's ever given me head is sucking my clit into his mouth through my panties and swirling his tongue around it, his impatience too noticeable to ignore.

He hasn't removed an article of clothing. We're both fully dressed, yet we're making out like we're at a club where clothing is optional.

After dragging my panties to the side, Laken feasts on me like he didn't just consume four tacos for supper. He licks, sucks at me, and drives my clit wild with his tongue.

Once I'm drenched front to back, he stuffs a thick, blunt finger inside me, making me gasp.

Need flares through me as one husky moan after another leaves my mouth. I'm burning up everywhere and seconds from detonation. But Laken doesn't stop.

He continues to devour me.

Consume me.

Make me senseless with need.

And I love every damn minute of his attention now as much as I did when we worked on songs he promised will be worldwide hits.

When Laken adds a second finger to the first, the stars floating in front of me augment to fireworks. They're bright and blistering and announce the same thing.

I'm about to come.

"I can't hold back."

My warning has only just left my mouth when a brutal climax slams into me.

I ride the wave for as long as possible, my moans as loud as Laken's grunts as he tries to keep up with the deluge. He annihilates every drop of my cum with so much eagerness a second orgasm quickly follows the first.

It is the strongest, most prolonged, most blinding climax I've ever experienced.

It takes everything from me, so by the time I blink through the haze it caused, Laken's boxer shorts have joined his pants around his knees, and he's fisting his cock in his hand, attempting to strangle the beast.

My inner muscles flutter when I take in the droplet balled at the end. Pre-cum leaks from his cock, but before I can sample it, Laken fills his hands with my ass and shuffles us to the only solid wall in the room.

Since I refuse to shower with an audience, the frosted glass wall separating the washroom from the main part of my room has offered me a ton of privacy I haven't had since Knox became a part of my life.

I can't say the same this time around, though.

When Laken braces my back against the cool material before slipping my panties to the side, I'm confident my shadow can't be missed.

Although I can't recall if Laken closed the door on his way in, at the moment, I don't care. Nothing but the subsequent chase is on my mind, and the race is so fast every muscle in my body pulls taut when Laken lines up the head of his cock with the opening of my pussy and prepares to drive home.

"Nicole…" I can barely hear Laken over the pounding of my pulse in my ears, but there's no doubt whose name he speaks when he sinks into me for the first time this week.

The mutual growl we release when he takes me to the base of his cock tears through the last remaining shred of control I have left. I beg him to take me harder, to fuck me how I've never been fucked. I tell him I want to feel where he's been for the rest of our working week.

He does *precisely* as asked.

He pumps in and out of me until my moans turn ear-piercing, sweat dribbles down my back, and I'm overwhelmed for the third time tonight.

"Fuck, siren."

Laken tries to power through the tight spasms of my pussy, he tries to put them into the background of his mind, but the instant I clamp around him, hungry for him to lose control, his thrusts stop. Once he's buried deep inside me, he loses the battle.

He shoots his load inside me, the throbs of his cock as brutal as the hammering of my clit and as hot as the tension that will forever fire between us.

"Jesus Christ," Laken breathes out heavily, his words as shaky as my thighs.

He sets me down before taking a staggered step back. "Fuck." This expletive isn't voiced with the same lusty tone he used seconds ago. He looks disappointed with himself. Somewhat guilty.

I have a clue as to why when the snap of my panties settling back into place occurs only half a second before a blob of cum soaks into them.

We forgot to use protection.

"Fuck." He tucks his rapidly deflating penis away before shooting his hands into his hair. "Fuck!" he screams again while tugging on the spiky locks.

"It's okay," I assure him. "I'm on contraception, and I can back it up with the morning-after pill."

His eyes shoot to mine so fast, his swift movement makes my head as dizzy as back-to-back orgasms. When the disappointment on his face grows the longer he takes in my ruined panties, I yank down on the hem of my skirt until it hides the evidence of our blunder.

"It isn't that big of a deal, Laken. I'm clean—"

"So am I," he promises, his mood edgy. "But I shouldn't have been so reckless. I was meant to show you that you deserve better than him, not lower myself to his standards." My stomach gurgles when my foolhardiness returns to bite me in the ass. "I have a condom in my wallet, but I chose to pretend I didn't because I wanted to claim you in a way I'm confident Knox never has since he's paranoid about unwanted pregnancies." The guilt on his face doubles. "I should have *never* disrespected you like that."

"Laken—"

I'm interrupted by the person causing Laken's near meltdown entering the bathroom without bothering to knock.

When Knox realizes I'm not alone, his wide eyes dance between Laken and me for almost thirty seconds. I assume he will criticize me for overworking my vocal cords so close to a live performance, but I am proven wrong when he says, "I was talking to Dallas downstairs. He mentioned you had a run-in with the paparazzi." He steps closer like the tension in the air isn't as thick as it is. "They were so eager for an interview, they knocked you over."

"It wasn't the paps who knocked her over."

Knox acts as if Laken never spoke. As he steps even closer, the concern in his eyes silences me. I've never seen them hold so much worry, and he once threw me to the wolves with no backup.

Apollo's feedback that day was brutal.

It was the same day I had to strain to hear a single melody.

"Are you okay?" He drags his eyes over my body like more than lust and sweat marks it. "When he told me what had happened, I felt sick to my stomach."

"I'm fine. Laken—"

"Should have never taken you out alone." His words are spat from his mouth like daggers and directed one way. To Laken's half of the bathroom. "His stupidity could have gotten you seriously injured." He inches back before shredding Laken's confidence to pieces. "He could have gotten you killed."

"No. What happened wasn't Laken's fault. He..." When I direct my focus to the man who needs to hear my words the most, my reply clogs in my throat.

The other half of the bathroom is empty, and Laken still doesn't know the truth.

Jenni slouches back in an armchair with ski jackets tossed over its rolled top before connecting her eyes with mine. "The last part is kind of hot and disturbing at the same time. What are your thoughts?"

"About him not using protection?" I sound daft. Rightfully so. I spilled an entire day's worth of chemistry onto her without coming up for air.

When Jenni jerks up her chin, I shrug. "I thought it was okay."

She sees straight through my lie.

With only an arched brow, she has me caving like a virgin at a sex club. "It was hot."

"So *fucking* hot," she adds, emphasizing on my reply.

"And it isn't like it is solely Laken's fault. I could have told him to put on a condom. I didn't because..." I trail off when I realize I sound like the harlot in "Glitter."

Jenni would never let me off so easily. "Because...?"

I try to think of a respectful way to finalize my reply. When I fail to come up with a valid point, I murmur, "I wanted him to be my first."

"To take you bare or...?"

I roll my eyes at her insinuation I'm as innocent as my pasty-white skin and ginger locks make out. "Tony—"

"Doesn't deserve a mention." She shivers like I dated him when he was bald before saying, "But Laken..." She breathes heavily out her nose and then shivers for a completely different reason than horror. "I think he's ticking all the right boxes."

My eyes adopt a look of love when I murmur, "I think so too."

"Then you have to tell him."

My words blurt out of my mouth in quick succession. I always talk fast when nervous. "Tell him what? That I—"

She reminds me so much of the teenager I met when she interrupts me. "That you *loooove* him."

"Don't be ridiculous. I've only known him for a week."

My cheeks couldn't get any redder when a deep, mannish voice joins our conversation. "And?" As Jenni twists her camera to announce our discussion isn't private—I should have known; our conversations are never private—Noah sits straighter on the couch he's sharing with Nick and Emily. "A week. A month. A year. It shouldn't matter. Don't put value on time." I swoon along with Emily when he locks his dark eyes with Emily's translucent pair. "Pay attention to who you feel yourself with the most. The people you feel yourself around the most are your tribe. They're the support network you'll seek time and time again when things get rough, and the ones who will keep you going no matter how bad the day." I remember I'm not the only one who has suffered through the loss of a sibling when he returns his eyes to mine and says, "Issue doubt to the people who instill doubt, but don't base someone's value in your life on how long you've known them, or you could give up something great."

"I'm sorry," Emily butts in, her voice charged with emotions, "I'm gonna need to hump my husband for a couple of minutes. To save everyone being grossed out, meeting adjourned."

Noah pulls Emily onto his lap, causing her to giggle before the shuffling of feet announces the group has agreed to her offer to defer their meeting.

"If you had told me you were in the middle of a meeting, I would have waited." That's a lie. I was dying to decompress, so I would have shared regardless of who was listening. You don't need better proof of this than the knowledge our conversation started while Knox was still in the room with me.

"Noah told me to take the call," Jenni says after moving our conversation to the kitchen of the mega-mansion they're using as a home base for their Europe tour. "And I'm glad because his input was pretty compelling. I've known you for…"

"Eleven years," I fill in when math fails her. She's more a design and art kind of girl than a math and equations girl.

"And not once have I seen you like this. Your face is glowing. You can't stop smiling even when you're complaining. And—"

"I'm not complaining. I am just…"

I've got nothing.

It's for the best since Jenni keeps talking. "Sex is good. But it isn't *that* good." She breathes out heavily like she can't believe she's about to speak the words she does. "You have to tell him the truth. If it isn't how you feel, at least let him off the hook for thinking he's messing with his best friend's girl. It isn't like the tension will stop when he knows the truth. You'll just have some groupies throwing themselves at your bodyguard instead of you." When I pull a face, she laughs. "Don't worry. You'll still get your fair share of male fans' interest, but you should prepare yourself for the attention Laken will get when he's linked to you. Some women only want what other women have, and Laken is a hottie."

"Jen…"

"No one else." She dispels Nick's jealousy with three little words before shifting her focus back to my nonexistent relationship. "I'll stay by my phone in case you need backup."

"You want me to tell him now?"

"Ah, yeah. We're not going the suspense route. We've done that for a week already. I need to know the outcome like yesterday." Her claps boom down the line. "So hustle, lady, before this momma gets nagged for morning tea."

Morning tea? It's barely dawn.

"All right. I'm going," I announce when Jenni's brow gets lost in her hairline. "But you really should watch how many times you scowl. You're closer to thirty now than twenty. Laugh lines will soon be confused as wrinkles."

I smile when she gags. "Thanks for the reminder."

She nods when I say, "I'll call you when I'm done."

"I'll be waiting."

After breathing out my nerves and disconnecting our chat, I open my bedroom door and tiptoe down the hall.

Don't ask me why I'm tiptoeing. It just seems like the sensible thing to do since I have no clue how Laken feels. Maybe it is the thrill of the forbidden maintaining his interest more than I am.

"Nicole!" In his eagerness to wrap me up in one of his famous hugs, River slips off the couch and races my way.

His steps are thunderous. They could wake the dead.

And they do.

"I thought you were going to have a power nap after talking with the girls?"

I return River's hug before spinning to face Knox, my questioner. He's standing in the doorway of his office, his shoulder butted against the glossy wood.

"I was. I just—"

"You heard me," he interrupts, his smile picking up. "I should have known. These walls are paper-thin." He takes a moment to read my neutral expression before asking, "So, what did you think?"

"About?" I ask, confused.

"The gigs I've secured you. The Late Show. Peterson. Bobby Macguire."

My mouth falls open at his last name drop. "Are you serious? Bobby Macguire wants to interview me?"

He nods. "And that's only the beginning. The label's phone has been ringing off the hook."

"Oh my god." After the brutal beating my ego took only days ago, this is better than anything I could have anticipated—though not quite as good as how Laken ended our fun-filled day.

Nothing will ever top that.

A snippet of doubt creeps in when Knox's demeanor seems off. "They specifically asked for me, right? They're not expecting Rise Up to attend with me?"

"Rise Up wasn't mentioned once. They want *you*, Nicole. They're so desperate for an interview that they're offering incentives to ensure you sit across from them first. They are talking two to three live performances per interview."

With my excitement too high to wrangle back for a moment longer, I throw my arms around Knox's neck and hug him tight. "I can't believe this. I'm so excited." I inch back so he can see the sincerity in my eyes. "Thank you so much."

"You're welcome." I'm shocked for an entirely different reason when he ups the ante of our innocent exchange. After gripping my head with both hands, he leans in and plants a sloppy kiss on my mouth.

His hold is so firm it takes me almost ten seconds to break free from his lip-lock, and by then, it's too late.

Laken has already witnessed it.

His balled hands announce this, not to mention the tightness of his jaw.

I doubt he'll believe my "we're only friends" line now.

"Laken, I—"

He spins on his heels and walks out the door he only recently entered before one-tenth of my explanation leaves my mouth.

24
LAKEN

"If you've come to apologize about this morning, walk the fuck back out of my office and close the door on your way out. I don't need to hear it."

I swallow down the brick that hasn't been freed from my throat for days but maintain my ground. "I—"

Knox drops his pen onto a stack of papers before raising his eyes to my face. They're not filled with the anger I'm anticipating. They're more glitzy than pissed. "Did I stutter?"

"No, but—"

"No buts, man." He leans back in his office chair and makes a tipi with his index fingers. "I don't need to hear your apology because I don't deserve one."

I stare at him like I don't know who he is.

Clearly, that's the case, because if my best friend were about to confess to fooling around with my girl not once but twice, he'd be doing more than falling to his knees to apologize.

He'd also be bending over to rest his cheek on the guillotine block.

My thoughts shift from my public execution to Knox when he says, "I don't know what magic trick you used, but you achieved something last night I've been endeavoring to do for months."

Nicole's face in the midst of ecstasy automatically flashes up during his reply, and it firms my hands into fists.

Mercifully, his response proves I didn't wholly fuck up my campaign yesterday by purposely forgetting to use protection. "You brought her out of hiding." He laughs a breathy chuckle. "The alias is gone. She's agreed to use her real name."

"And that's a good thing?"

"Are you fucking insane?" He doesn't wait for me to reply. "Of course it is. Nikki J can't open doors. Nicole Reed, though…" A showy wolf whistle whizzes between his lips. "Every talk show host this side of the state wants a piece of her. I've been booking gigs all morning." He drags his teeth over his lower lip. "Gigs you'll make sure she enters and exits safely." I can't tell what emotional response is liable for the flare that darts through his eyes. "Dallas told me about your run-in with him this morning. You were so eager to rough him up that you sprinted out of the bathroom like I'd busted you doing something you shouldn't have done."

"I was—"

"It's my fault. I asked you to eat and sleep when she does." I'm glad he keeps his last analogy off the list, or guilt may eat me alive as badly as it did when he reminded me how easily I swept the hotel security's stupidity under the rug. "I didn't realize you'd take it so literally, though. I guess I shouldn't be shocked. We have an agreement, and even when things blow up in your face, you keep your word. That's how I know you'll do the same this time around as well. You'll never let anything or *anyone* interfere with River's best interests."

The dip in his tone piques my suspicion, but before I can analyze it enough to respond, he joins me on the other side of his desk. "He's your baby brother, your flesh and blood, so you will always have his back first." He slaps my shoulder like not an ounce of fucking guilt is hardening my features before using the same hand to pull me in for a man hug. "So how about we stop with the shenanigans that have you forgetting you owe me fifty K, and we get this show on the road?"

Pulling back, he drags his hand under his nose like more than adrenaline is keeping him awake before gesturing the same hand to the door. "I need you downstairs, clearing a path. Dallas said the crowd extends beyond the parameters you set this morning." He speaks as if he didn't instruct them not to leave the lobby when Nicole gets hammered by the paparazzi. "A YouTube video blew up overnight. Nicole is all over social media sites."

When his cell buzzes on his desk, he silences it before bringing up the footage he mentioned. It is a grainy video of Nicole singing in the rain. "Whoever's stupid idea that was better pray she doesn't get sick. I'm not lying when I say she won't have a moment of rest over the next three weeks." Apprehension settles low in my stomach when he sits in his office chair before he scrolls to his voicemail. "Lucky you made her one day off worthwhile because her ass is mine for the rest of the month." He winks and makes a clicking noise with his mouth before pressing his phone to his ear. "Then hopefully not long after that... *forever.*"

His call connects before a syllable can fire from my mouth, and I'm dismissed from his office with an arrogant hand gesture.

"You're not wearing that."

I peer down at the shirt I threw on after endeavoring to free the guilt from my veins with a five-mile run before returning my eyes to River. I had to do something to lessen the clog, because even with

Knox reminding me of what I'm risking messing with Nicole, it took everything I had to leave his office, minus a confession.

Only during my exhaustive sprint did I realize I'm not trying to free myself from the burden of guilt my exchanges with Nicole have placed on me. I want to release Nicole from hers.

Busting them kissing in the hallway killed me, but after a brief contemplation I should have conducted when Nicole stared at me, brimming with remorse, it dawned on me that their embrace was emotionless and without a single spark. There was no fire behind their kiss. No connection. You couldn't even say it was fueled by friendship.

That is how lackluster it was.

So, instead of my run clearing the deluge, it added more ambiguity to the waters.

Something isn't sitting right with me about Nicole and Knox's relationship, and I'm determined to ensure it isn't anything close to the horrid thoughts filling my head.

When River coughs, alerting me to my ignorance, I ask, "What's wrong with my shirt?"

He waits a beat to silently read me before replying, "Knox said the places we're visiting today are filled with famous people, so you need to look the part."

Not asking permission, he enters my room before rummaging through my limited selection of clothes.

Once he has a pair of leather pants and a shimmery shirt in his hand, he holds them out to soundlessly gauge my opinion.

His choices are too horrific for a nonverbal reply. "No fucking chance."

"Language," he snaps out, mimicking my stern tone as he gets sassy. "And what's wrong with what I picked?"

I scoff as if he is blind. "The shirt is horrendous. And leather? You want me to wear leather pants in the middle of the day?"

He nods like I'm considering his suggestion more than telling him no. "All the rock stars wear leather."

"I'm not a rock star, River."

"You're not," he agrees. "But you're in love with one."

His reply hits harder than a punch to the stomach, but I act like he's not as smart as he is. "You don't know what you're talking about."

"Don't treat me like I'm stupid, Laken. I've seen the way you look at her. You care for her."

I'm always on the defense when forced to lie. "That's a bodyguard's job. They have to care for their target to ensure their safety."

I realize the lack of an extra chromosome doesn't make me more intelligent than him when he asks, "Who said I was talking about Nicole?"

With my shock rendering me speechless, he dumps the shimmery shirt onto my bed before heading for the door with the leather pants still in his hand. "If it takes displaying my frank and beans to get a girl like Nicole, I'll need the stiffness of leather." A chuckle rumbles in my chest when he says in a sassy tone, "The serving is too generous to leave my modesty in the hands of cotton."

"Cheese and rice."

When I stray my eyes to the cause of River's near cuss word, a lump forms in my throat and my pants. "Jesus fucking Christ."

I grunt through the jab River hits my ribs with before dragging my eyes down Nicole's slender frame. She's wearing a fire-engine-red dress that makes every man in a ten-mile radius want to gallop in a circle while squealing "wee woo wee woo" on repeat.

Nicole is beautiful. She is downright gorgeous. But today, she's neither of those things.

She's sexy.

Her hair is mainly pinned back from her face, her makeup is a natural palette, and the split in her dress shows off enough thigh to be daring but not enough to make her look easy.

There's only one downfall to her outfit.

She's exiting our hotel on Knox's arm, who's more formally dressed than me. He's wearing trousers instead of jeans, and a pricy leather jacket hides his button-up shirt.

"I told you all rock stars' wannabe partners wear leather. Even if it will reach ninety, you should have risked ball chaff for her."

It takes a few seconds for the "wannabe" part of River's reply to sink in, but I lose the chance to grill him about it further when the swarm circling Nicole like vultures kicks my naturally engrained protective side into gear.

After pushing past the men Dallas and I forced to the other side of the street only minutes ago, I band my arm around Nicole's waist and guide her to the awaiting limousine. My clutch could be seen as cruel. I do not mean to hurt Nicole. That is the last thing I'd ever want. I just refuse to consider a rerun of last night.

Nicole's face when she was yanked away from me killed me. It physically maimed me more than the kiss she shared with Knox.

So I refuse to let anyone take Nicole from me—even Knox.

The crush almost becomes unbearable when the camera lights' heat is added to the mix.

"Nicole, do you care to comment on the video that was uploaded last night?"

"Nicole, will any of the songs you covered be performed during your West Coast tour?"

"Nicole, how does it feel to have the number-one trending video on both YouTube and Insta Reels?"

Although as shocked as I am by the pleasantness of their questions, Nicole focuses on one thing.

Me.

"When you get a minute, we need to talk abo—"

"Move." With more aggression than needed, I push away the cameraman responsible for cutting her off, before dropping my lips to the shell of Nicole's ear. "We'll have plenty of time to talk once I've ensured you're safe. Can't call myself your bodyguard if I don't put your safety first."

When I make a break through the crowd by shoving more than using my manners, Nicole says, "That's one of the things I want to talk to you about. I don't think you should be my bodyguard anymore. I want you to—" Her words shift to a wince when a member of the public tries to execute the same pluck and yank routine the brute mastered earlier today.

Their bid is unsuccessful this time around.

Nicole only leaves my side when I place her into the back of the limousine and I'm yanked back into the surge of the crowd.

"Get the fuck back!"

Before my fist can send the grabby perp flying onto his ass, Dallas drags him back by the collar of his shirt and punishes his ribs with a quick one-two jab.

When the crowd thins, uneager to be served Dallas's style of justice, Knox uses the opportunity to slip into the back of the limousine with Nicole.

I'm about to follow him inside, but he blocks my entrance. "Jump into the SUV with the crew." He nudges his head to the tinted Escalade behind the stretched town car he's hogging like it only has two seats. "It's going to the same place." Nicole's eyes lock with mine a second before Knox slams the door shut, only just drowning out his mumbled, "I want some alone time with my girl so we can make a ton of memories."

25
NICOLE

"Why did you do that? Why are you insinuating *this* is more than it is?" I thrust my hand between Knox and me as I say the word "this."

Knox scoffs at me. "What are you talking about? I'm not *insinuating* anything."

My chest's erratic rise and fall is highlighted when I fold my arms under my breasts. "You asked Laken to follow us in the road crew SUV so you can '*make a ton of memories with your girl.*'" I mock his impish tone during the quoted part of my reply.

A lack of sleep isn't solely to blame for my bitchy attitude. It is mainly because of the distance Knox forced between Laken and me today. Between makeup and a two-hour appointment with a stylist, I haven't seen hide nor hair of Laken all morning, so he's none the wiser that the kiss he witnessed wasn't close to romantic.

"Yeah? And?" Knox murmurs like he can't understand what has me so worked up. "Are we not doing that?" He waves his hand to the craziness Laken just walked me through unscathed. The paparazzi are so eager for the perfect shot that they squash their cameras against the tinted glass of the stretched limo while jogging alongside it. "You're my *main* girl, Nicole, the *only* artist I personally represent. That's how much I believe in your talent and what I meant about making memories. I want to cherish every moment of your success *with* you because I've been there since the start."

"Oh…" The one time I want an interruption, I'm not granted one. It's what I get for acting so pretentious I assume every man wants to be romantically linked with me. "I thought you meant something else, which is understandable since Laken thinks we're together." I watch Knox for any signs of shock. When I fail to get a single smidge of surprise, I say, "Which is even more peculiar considering you're his best friend, so he could have only gotten that assumption from you."

"Best friend?" He chuckles while scrubbing at the stubble on his chin. "That's a stretch on our association."

Although there are thousands of truths in my head to call out his lie, I use his instead. "Family looks out for family. They have your back no matter what."

"Laken said that, not me," he denies, forcing me to delve deeper into memories of that day.

"I'll do anything for you, man. You know that."

Now I have him over the barrel, and he knows it.

He's so stumped he takes almost a minute to reply. "River is like a brother to me, has been since his first foster placement with my family when he was ten. But I don't know Laken as well as I do his little brother." He licks his dry lips while continuing to try to pull the wool over my eyes like the walls in his office aren't paper-thin. "I was already annoyed at how many times River went in and out of care, and I've never gotten over the fact Laken dumped his brother for good for a couple of ounces of cocaine."

"What?" That's as much as my disbelief will allow me to speak. Laken kicked out two road crew members during rehearsals last week for snorting lines in the dancers' bathroom, unaware that the man who hired them founded their addiction.

Knox kept his cocaine addiction well hidden until our days at the recording studio stretched well into the night. His coping mechanisms aren't ones I've handled before, but Apollo made out it is a standard practice in the music industry.

"Do you not find it strange that Laken left town for almost a decade before showing back up the week River got a promotion?"

Knox leans forward until his elbows balance on his knees. "They've been estranged for some time. I swear River told you about it the first week you met."

"He said no such thing. *You* told me he was *your* brother."

"Cut me some slack, Nicole. I said he's *like* a brother to me. It isn't my fault you misheard what I said." I didn't mishear anything, but he continues talking before I can defend myself, foiling my chance. "I guarantee Laken is only sniffing around now because he heard River's salary includes a percentage of your royalties. He knows he's about to hit the big time and wants a share of the pie he doesn't deserve."

I hardly know Laken, but I'm confident many points of Knox's story are as fabricated as the songs he wants me to sing. There's no truth to them. No heart. They're manufactured to tell a story no one has ever lived.

"Even when he ordered more tacos than his stomach could handle, Laken wouldn't let River pay for his meal." Knox's glare turns evil when I say, "However, you were adamant River had to reimburse you for the items he took from the minibar at our last hotel." I return his watch to ensure he knows I'm not the wallflower he thinks I am. "They're complimentary in the presidential suite. The 'perks' he deserves didn't cost you a single cent." I return his earlier scoff. "And neither did the room since I picked up the tab."

"I said I'd pay you back. I had some issues with my card." He's back on the edge of his chair, his expression no longer stern. "Why are you making it out to be such a big deal? Payment processing errors occur all the time."

"Because you're making out that Laken is only here for money. Money you supposedly don't have."

"I have money. I just couldn't access it when we were checking in. The banks were closed." He glances around at the buildings we're bypassing before shifting his eyes to the driver. "We need to make a detour."

"Where?" the driver asks, put off by the inconvenience, particularly since we've not yet lost the media tail scratching the paintwork of his pricy ride.

He tosses a bunch of metal credit cards over the privacy partition while saying, "Anywhere with an automatic teller. I wasn't aware my *loan* had a maximum seven-day repayment term attached to the offer."

"You're being ridiculous."

Knox's eyes snap to mine. "I'm being ridiculous? You're the one who has her panties in a twist about a guy she hardly knows." He stuffs his empty wallet into his trousers before sinking low in his seat with a frustrated headshake. "I should have never hired him. I just figured a job might keep him around a little longer this time." He peers past my shoulder like the crew's SUV is only feet behind us. I realize it is when its frame reflects in his massively dilated eyes. "River seems to enjoy his company."

"He does," I agree. "He *loves* his brother."

"As I do my mother, but that doesn't mean she won't try to fuck up my life at any available opportunity." His sigh ruffles the strands of hair Bonnie left down to frame my face. "I was stupid to hire him. I should have never let him back into River's life until he proved he had earned it." My heart sinks to my feet when he says, "I'll fix my mistake during your first interview. I'll let him off gently and promote Dallas to his spot."

"No," I shout, my fury unmissable when I realize the last words I spoke with Laken make it seem as if I want exactly this. "That isn't what I want."

"Then what do you want, Nicole?" His tone is higher and angrier than I've ever experienced. "You wanted me to hire River, so I hired River. You wanted to do your first tour on the opposite side of the country, so I booked your tour on the other side of the country. What more can I fucking do to make this easier for you?" He puts air quotes around "easier."

His question is rhetorical, but I refuse to let him guilt-trip me the way he tried to guilt-trip Laken this morning in his office. "I asked you to stop making your *brother* clean toilets he didn't mess." I spit out "brother" in a way he can't ignore. That might have been the first time I caught him in a lie, but I doubt it will be the last. "And I want you to stop squashing my voice. This is *my* career, songs, and life, so although you can have input, you will never have all the control. No one but me controls my destiny, and it's time you learn that."

26
LAKEN

"*Is* he trying to get her trampled?"

My heart lodges in my throat when my eyes sling in the direction River is looking. Instead of waiting for the road crew's SUV, Knox has taken it upon himself to guide Nicole into the building hosting her first live radio interview.

Even if she doesn't want me to be a part of her protective detail anymore, I can't sit by and watch her get hurt.

"Enter via the back entrance with the crew," I tell River a second after tossing off my belt and slipping out the back of the SUV.

I don't want to be forced to pick between saving Nicole or him because I honestly don't know who I'd race for first.

That's fucked to admit since River is my blood, but there's something about Nicole that brings out my protective side. Even if I weren't her bodyguard, I'd still protect her.

I also want to save her from experiencing a hurt I'm reasonably sure she's already experienced. Her lyrics hint that she's been hurt in the past, not to mention the little glimmers of sadness her eyes get when she takes a moment to reflect.

"Get back. Move!"

Nicole exhales in relief when I pull Knox's hand from her back and tug her into my chest. I shelter her with my body, ensuring it takes all the bumps and grazes of our short walk, but my gallantry seems pointless when I spot wetness in Nicole's eyes as we enter the foyer of the 92.1 LA Daily building.

"Are you all right? Are you hurt? Did they get you?"

She stops me from searching her body for injuries before blocking my line of sight with her classically elegant face.

Once she has the focus of my wandering gaze, she assures me, "I'm fine."

"But—"

She flattens her finger to my lips, grinning when her briefest contact causes the hair on my arms to stand to attention. "Now is not the time to squash my voice, Laken. Not just as it's about to be heard." Her tone is neither stern nor playful. It is more confident than anything.

When I nod, conscious that she's right—we're minutes from her first press conference; now is not the time for *any* neuroses to be aired—Nicole looks set to say more, but a lady with a clipboard and blunt bangs who's been endeavoring to interrupt us since we got here can't hold back a second longer. "We have twenty minutes until we're due on air."

Nicole gulps back the nerves the lady's snarky comment lodged in her throat before straying her eyes to me. "What I said on the way to the limousine isn't as it seems." The production assistant taps her foot, hurrying her along. "I don't have time to explain all the details right now. They're still a mess in my head, but once I have everything sorted, I will update you at the first opportunity."

"Now nineteen minutes."

Nicole's expression reveals how badly she wants to snap back at the fire-breathing dragon, but she keeps her cool, for the most part. Instead of crumbling under the strain of the woman's bossy demeanor, she tosses out a handful of her own demands. "Then you better point me in the direction of the producer's office because I have a handful of changes I want to make before we record today's segment."

Her determination makes me hard. She didn't pussyfoot around her demands. She straight up announced she's making changes with no room for negotiations.

The production assistant acts blasé, though. "Changes?" When Nicole nods, her self-confidence building the more her importance is challenged, the lady sighs heavily before gesturing for Nicole and Knox to follow her. "You'll need to be quick. We don't prerecord our shows."

After squeezing my hand in silent assurance of where her focus remains even with her about to wow the world with her voice, Nicole jogs to keep up with the lady.

Knox hangs back like nothing happening is of his choice.

His response is understandable. Until the crew's day off, he had everyone jumping on demand—myself included.

A power shift is long overdue.

I love my brother and will forever protect him, but I can't continue being guilt-tripped and bribed to keep the promise I made to him when our mother left, or I'll never be the man Nicole deserves. I'll only ever be a puppet.

When the tension reaches a point that can't be ignored, I ask, "You good?"

I hate what this is doing to our friendship, but I've already given him so much, so I can't give him Nicole as well.

At least not without a fight.

Knox shoots me a snarled glare like he's aware he is no longer privy to my deepest, darkest secret, before disappearing down a dark corridor like I never spoke.

It takes me a beat to shadow his stalk. I don't fear him. I'm simply aware of how short his temper is when he doesn't get his way. He's a spoiled brat, and he wouldn't care less if his actions put a dampener on the success Nicole is on the cusp of achieving.

He's yet to learn that it's okay to come second by putting someone else first.

"And this is your chair." The executive assistant for 92.1 LA Daily gestures her hand to a director's chair in the wings of a television-style set.

"Are these radio segments recorded?"

Smiling, she nods. "Every interview is live streamed on our social media sites and recorded in front of an audience who won tickets to be here." Some of the nerves I'm confident Nicole is facing hit me when the assistant nudges her head to the bleacher-like pews behind plain sheets of windowpane. "It looks like a fishbowl, but the glass helps keep any sounds the producer doesn't want included in the segment out and the singer's voice in." She hands me a set of headphones. "You'll see."

As the noises of a busy set trickle out of the headphones I placed on my head, the executive assistant attempts to go through the same steps with Knox, who is seated a couple of spots closer to the "fishbowl" than I am.

I say "attempt" because Knox snatches the headphones out of her hand a second after aggressively plopping into his seat.

When the unnamed woman peers at me, seeking support, I smile at her to assure her that nothing she said pissed him off.

I'm reasonably sure all his anger stems from me.

After wiring Knox's headset into the same system as mine, the assistant returns my smile before giving the crew the all-clear to move forward with their plans.

Nicole enters the studio only seconds later from a thick curtain on its right.

The boisterous cheer of the crowd when they spot her tugs my lips high at one side. They cheer, clap, and stomp down their feet, their vocal welcome strongly reducing the rose coloring of Nicole's cheeks.

She was anticipating a far worse greeting.

"Wow," the host murmurs down my headphones when the crowd's applause reaches an ear-piercing level. "That's quite the ovation. I've never seen them so eager." My back molars smash together when he leans into Nicole's side and whispers, "Imagine if Rise Up were to ever accept my offer of a sit-down interview. They'd take the fucking roof off."

His intro implies how their chat will go, but I'm still taken aback by the first question fired off his tongue once a fluorescent sign behind him announces they're on the air.

"So... Nicole... is Noah as hung as reports claim?"

Nicole's answer is the blanket response every PR firm would recommend she use. "Only his wife can answer that question."

"Come on... you don't need to keep quiet on your affair anymore. Rumors are Emily has shackled him down with another kid. He's not going anywhere. Not even for a girl as pretty as you."

The crowd hurries to the edges of their seats like their most salacious suspicions are about to be confirmed, so Nicole tries to let them down gently. "I hate to disappoint everyone, but there's nothing to share. Noah and I are friends."

When the crowd boos, her eyes sling to the wings of the stage for moral support. I can only imagine how horrifying this is for her. Being mocked over the internet is bad enough, but it's soul-crushing when the slandering is done in person by someone she thought would help propel her career to the status it deserves.

Unsurprisingly, Knox doesn't appear upset about the negative light being shone on Nicole. He keeps his eyes locked on his shoes, and his facial expression is arrogant.

Mercifully, Nicole's attention doesn't linger on him long enough for her to absorb his moody attitude. Her eyes find mine only seconds later, and within moments, she sits straighter like my presence alone inserted a steel rod in her back before she focuses on the disc jockey's next question.

"Would it ease your guilt if I reminded you that we're the only two people in the room? It's just you and me, Nicole. All alone. Sharing saucy secrets."

"That doesn't ease my conscience in the slightest," she replies without pause for thought. "How could it when there's one point nine million Los Angeles men I could have been seated across from today, but somehow, I got lumped with the likes of you?"

Emanual, the host who intended to cut Nicole down as brutally as the critics of her first YouTube sensation, gapes his mouth before he gauges the audience's response to Nicole's reply.

With them as in awe of Nicole's wittiness as I am, he changes the pace of his interview from an interrogation to a proper sit-down chat. "All right. I deserve that. But what can I say? I'm a horny dog when it comes to celebrities and their mating challenges." Once the audience's chuckles simmer, Emanual returns his eyes to Nicole. The humor in them is pushed aside for lust when he takes her in as a person for the first time instead of a prop for him to toy with. "Talking about celebrities, what do you think your chances are of becoming one with this?"

When he holds up a mock album cover that looks nothing like the one Knox assured Nicole would meet the market, Knox breathes out a snapped cuss word as my chest puffs high.

That's River's album cover—the one he designed on the private jet.

She used my little brother's design on a cover that will be sold worldwide.

I couldn't be more proud.

Knox is on the opposite side of the spectrum. "He's got the wrong fucking album cover," he tells anyone who'll listen. "That's not the right cover."

"It's giving me Swiftie vibes." Emanual tilts the cover to the audience when they hum in agreement. "Yeah? You guys feel it, too?"

Their praise makes Nicole smile. "I can only hope to emulate her."

"Rate your chances?"

"Of Taylor fandom?" she asks. Her smile vanished.

When Emanual nods, Nicole's breathy laugh whistles through her mic. "Zero to negative ten." As quickly as her confidence is swiped, it returns more potent than ever. "But with some tweaking and the right guidance, who knows… maybe I could have a handful of Taylor-worthy hits."

Her reply piques Emanual's interest as much as mine. "Tweaking? I thought your album was slated for release in…"—he checks his watch, which is as old school as mine—"nine days?"

"It is." Her honesty is a refreshing change. "It's just not ready for public consumption yet."

"What the fuck is she saying?" Knox is seconds from blowing his top. His ears are red, and he's tugging on his hair so fiercely that he won't need to wait to inherit the balding gene from his father to consider hair implants. "It's been ready for months."

Clearly, Nicole disagrees with him. "After a handful of tweaks, I'll be confident the audience is purchasing a part of me, not a manufactured hit designed for the masses."

215

Emanual looks stunned. He isn't the only one. I thought it would take more than a night of songwriting to have Nicole believing in herself enough to go against everything her record label wrongly told her was the right direction for her career.

It shows how vastly I underestimated her confidence.

"That is *not* something I've heard before." Emanual laughs when Nicole's face whitens. "It isn't a bad thing. It's just been a while since we've had an artist who places the demands of their heart above their bank balance." After drinking in Nicole's blush with more admiration than I like, he tells the live audience and the ones listening in that they'll be back after a short commercial break to hear Nicole perform "Glitter."

"I was hoping I could perform something else." Nicole gets Emanual and the live audience over the fence by announcing it's a song that's never been heard. "I wrote it recently with a... *friend* of mine."

When the producer seeks Emanual's approval, he shrugs. "It can't be worse than the garbage they were pimping before her YouTube video put her interview request at the top of the pile." He hits Nicole with a truth I'd rather he keep to himself, but with the honesty she deserves. "I was planning to cancel your interview today. The stuff your label was sending through was bad. I thought the trolls got it right for a change, that you'd escaped the circus with Madam Fleur and Dani Trace. Then I saw this..." He taps a tablet on his desk. "This is what we *need*. This is what we *deserve*. So if you're guaranteeing this is what we'll get..."—he once again highlights the video playing on his tablet—"you can perform any song your heart desires."

"She's going to fucking ruin me," Knox murmurs when Nicole promises to give Emanual's audience the performance of the year. "And when she does"—he turns his narrowed eyes to me—"I'll make sure you go down with us."

27
NICOLE

"You're fucking insane. You asked for an inch, then took it a mile." Knox thrusts his hand at the radio station our shared limousine is pulling away from. "First, you go off script by performing a song not contracted to the label. Then you tell him your album needs tweaks."

"Nothing that can't be—"

"Nothing at all. It's been finished for months now. *Months!* You made the label look like incompetent fools."

His glare lodges a brick in my throat, but I refuse to back down on the decisions I made this morning after our discussion slash argument in the limousine. "How? By striving to give the people we need to make the album a success an album worth buying? You heard what Emanual—"

"Emanual is a disc jockey getting too fucking big for his boots."

Even though I agree with him, I continue speaking as if he never interrupted me. "He was ready to cancel my interview. The only thing that stopped him was the footage that went viral on YouTube last night." The footage he stabbed his finger at was of me singing the only solo performance of the rain concert. The rest of the performances were duets with either Laken or River. "This is what we need. This is what we deserve." Instead of mimicking Emanual's southern drawl, I return my voice to its standard setting. "Laken said the same. That my fans deserve to hear *my* songs."

"Laken doesn't know what he's talking about. He isn't a music producer."

My heart speaks on my behalf again for the umpteenth time over the past twenty-four hours. "I'm still willing to risk it."

Knox's eyes are on me, hot and heavy. "Risk what?"

"I want Laken to produce a handful of my songs." When this idea popped into my head this morning, I thought lust had made me looney, but after having Marcus look over the work Laken and I had done the day before and hearing the crowd's response to the song we co-wrote, there's no denying the obvious. Laken has talent by the bucketloads. He could be a star, but unlike Marcus, he only wants infamy behind the desk because it is the only way he can do a job he loves and protect River at the same time.

A fragile soul can only take so much before it cracks, and although River's outer shell seems unbreakable, those who truly know him know it is a front he uses to protect himself.

That's why he never argued for better when Knox made him clean the restrooms after the stinky road crew messed them up, and why he never batted an eyelid when his services went unpaid for months.

It is also why Laken continually lets Knox walk all over him.

He deserves better, and I will make sure he gets it.

"What... are you... I..." Knox breathes out a low sigh before settling on, "This is the *exact* reason I demand all employees sign a nonfraternization contract. Just because they knock it out of the park beneath the sheets doesn't mean they'll do the same out of them." When I don't flinch at his insinuation Laken and I have slept together, he breathes heavily out of his nose. "Apollo will never go for it. He signed off on this weeks ago."

"That's okay. I don't need his approval or his studio." I hand him the details of a contact Noah shared this morning. "The studio hasn't been used for a couple of years, but it has everything we need to lay down some tracks." My voice isn't as confident during my next few sentences. "My contract states that creative control remains with the artist. That means the artist determines the songs, music compositions, and dance routines." I flatten my palm against my chest to amplify my point.

This is my choice.

"Your album releases next week." He stares at me like he doesn't know me. "Next. *Fucking*. Week. We don't have time to record more songs."

"We will if we make sacrifices." I show him the itinerary he forwarded to the team this morning. "Most of my interviews are either first thing in the morning or late at night. There are several hours to record in the middle of the day." I seem to be getting him over the fence, so I give him one final tug. "Preorder sales for my album skyrocketed overnight. It could go platinum opening week *if* we give them an album they deserve."

He shakes his head before running his hand through his hair. "This is insane, Nicole. You're going to make me fucking bald. But..." His last word isn't expected, and it is as shocking as his next two. "You're right. The chances of your album flopping are less likely if we mix things up like you did on the rooftop." The scrub of his jaw has him missing my swallow. When he said "rooftop," my mind went straight to my heated night with Laken, not us singing in the rain. "But I wish you'd stop dropping shit on me like this. I don't handle change well." He laughs before dragging his hand under his nose, making me wonder if his backflip is because my proof can't be denied or because he's under the influence. Either way, he sounds playful while saying, "Even when it'll make me a ton of money, I have to be dragged to the plate by the scruff of my shirt."

I didn't anticipate our conversation taking this route, but I'm incredibly grateful it did.

"So you're willing to give it a shot?"

By "it," I mean Laken.

Knox takes a moment to deliberate before jerking up his chin.

To show my gratitude, I wrap him up in a hug that would make River proud. "Thank you so much for believing in me and my vision. I won't let you down. I promise."

"I hate that you say that like I haven't had your back all along. Neither of us would be here if I didn't believe in you, Nik." He holds on tight, extending our hug long enough for the paparazzi to timestamp its occurrence into the record books. "But can I ask a favor?" He waits for me to inch back and bounce my eyes between his before letting me know things aren't as bad as I imagine. "Can I run a background search on Laken before offering him the position?"

"Knox—"

"Not just for your safety but River's as well. I want to make sure he's not left heartbroken again."

I hate myself for even contemplating planting the seed of doubt he's trying to insert in my head, but since I'm confident his PI won't find anything that will change my mind on how I feel about Laken, I give him the go-ahead.

"But keep it basic," I plead, not wanting Laken's privacy violated more than it already is. "Except when ensuring he knows we're not in a relationship." I drift my eyes to Laken standing outside the limousine as he pushes back the men and women who could ruin us before we truly start if they share the photographs they recently snapped of Knox and me with the world. "I like him."

So much so I don't want him to ever experience the guilt he felt this morning when he thought he'd betrayed his friend.

When Laken opens the limousine door, Knox makes it seem as if our conversation during the commute was nowhere near as serious as it was. "Like *like*? Or *like* like?"

I roll my eyes at the immaturity in his voice before accepting Laken's hand to assist me out of the stretched town car. Then I match its childishness when the briefest connection of our hands sends shockwaves darting down my spine. "I *like like* him."

28
LAKEN

Nicole has endured back-to-back interviews today, yet she looks as alive and hopeful during her final one as she did the first five. The radio hosts love her, and although she's had to handle an unfair share of narrow-minded questions about Rise Up, she breezed over them as she did during Emanual's interview before securing her audience's utmost devotion with her impressive vocal range.

The perfection behind her performances today has left many breathless.

The woman I met on the rooftop is the same woman the public are falling in love with. A down-to-earth and extremely beautiful individual with a country twang to her voice even though she's never stepped foot in the South.

They want the real Nicole—the raw Nicole—and the footage I uploaded to YouTube to counterbid the false claims of the keyboard warriors offered the perfect introduction.

Now she's sealing the deal one interview at a time.

I am as proud of her as I was of River when one disc jockey commented that Nicole's album cover complemented her unique style and flair.

I just haven't had a chance to share my praise yet.

Between making sure River's tears were tears of happiness and shuffling Nicole from one location to the next, we've not had a single moment to ourselves.

That won't be an issue in ten minutes. Nicole's last interview is scheduled to end shortly. It is being held on the rooftop of a hotel that's become a global sensation since it's been viewed over three hundred million times on YouTube in the past twenty-four hours alone, so any words we exchange won't be done in front of an audience.

The executive producer of the number-one radio station in the country thought the rooftop of our hotel was the prime spot to host their interview with Nicole.

They couldn't have been wiser.

The home-like setting squashes the nerves that occasionally bubbled up as Nicole was whipped from one studio to the next, and the acoustics are so on point, the co-host's microphone picks up my swallow when she asks Nicole about her love life.

"Is there anyone special in your life right now?" asks a lady with glistening green eyes hidden behind thick frames. "We always hear rumors about you with the Rise Up men, but they're just rumors, right?"

"Very much so," Nicole agrees, relieved that someone finally believes her.

"Even Marcus?"

Nicole's laugh reveals her nerves are surfacing, but she locks them down remarkably fast. "Even Marcus. We've never been anything more than friends." She furrows her brows before correcting herself. "We will never be anything more than friends."

"Because there's someone else you're holding a flame for?"

The female co-host is good at her job. Her demeanor makes it seem as if Nicole is chatting to a friend instead of the millions of listeners tuning in to the segment, and Nicole is opening up to her more than any other interviewer she's sat across from today. "Maybe."

When Nicole drifts her eyes to the sheets of plastic pane the production crew placed up to lessen the traffic noise from the streets below, the road crew hover in close like they're about to hear her sauciest secret to date.

This time, she gives them a snippet of her personal life they're dying to see. "It's fairly new, so I'm a little apprehensive to talk about it. I don't want to jinx it." A second audible swallow booms through the speakers that projected her earlier performance when she locks eyes with me, shyly smiles, then says, "It's even more daunting since I don't know if he feels the same way."

"That's the juicy sauce right there, ladies and gentlemen. Nicole Reed is in love."

The whites of Nicole's eyes glow brighter than the moon when her eyes pop open. "That isn't what I said."

"No," the male disc jockey replies, "you more *insinuated* it. But two plus two always equals four."

"Unless you failed math," the female co-host jumps in, laughing. "And she didn't admit anything more than that her relationship is in the teething stage."

The male host's reply is gobbled up by laughter. "It sounds like you're throwing her a lifeline, Tahnia."

"That's because I am."

"Why?" the male host instantly fires back.

"Because no one likes to talk about a relationship while it is in the teething stage." Her voice is so loud several of the road crew grimace when it squeaks through the speaker near their heads. "You should know that better than anyone."

When Tahnia's eyes shoot daggers at the male disc jockey, he tugs on the collar of his shirt before making a face only his co-host can decipher. "We seem to have gotten off track. I thought we were talking about Nicole's new-forming relationship?"

The audience, which is subsequently smaller than the others she's faced today due to the minimal floor space on the rooftop, laughs when Nicole butts in. "I'm more than happy for the focus to remain on Trent."

"Are you sure?" Tahnia asks. "This could be a great opener for I-like-you subliminal messages. The stars are out, the moon is bright, and I still have goosebumps from your performance. If you give him a taste of the magic you awarded us tonight, but in a more intimate setting, you'll know exactly where he stands by the a.m."

Nicole's words are so low, if she weren't wearing a microphone, I might have missed them. "He's already experienced everything I have to offer."

"What was that?" Trent asks with a cocked brow, his shock as staggering as mine.

Mindful he heard her mumbled comment, Nicole's eyes bulge as her throat works through a hard swallow. "Nothing. I didn't say a word."

They know she's lying, but since they're still riding the high of the biggest ratings they've had to date during Nicole's live performance, they let her off the hook.

"All right, girl. Don't say another word. We've got your back."

As Trent announces they're going to the phones to take some calls from listeners, I'm tapped on the shoulder by Miranda, Knox's accountant slash office clerk.

It is the fight of my life to take my eyes off Nicole—it's been like this all day, sneaky, longing glances and an unlimited number of playful hand squeezes—but I'm given no choice when Miranda stuffs a thin document with perforated edges into my hand.

"What's this?"

"That's your first pay stub." She highlights the 000001 written in the top corner next to my name before handing out stubs to the crew waiting for Nicole's interview to end so they can dismantle the set. It's been a long day, and everyone is exhausted. "You'll get one every week." She scans the crowd before asking, "Where's Mason?"

"He had to take a shit," replies one of the crew loud enough for the radio show's producer to glare at him. After mouthing his apology, he tells Miranda, "I'll take it for him. We're bunked in the same room."

His confession reminds me why I'm manning the rooftop without the sidekick who rarely left my side the past twelve hours. Nicole wanted River to be a part of the proceedings as much I wanted him to be, so she had a third director's chair added to her list of necessities by her second interview.

She also ensured there was no chance of her connecting her eyes with the wrong supporter first. My chair butted Knox's during her second interview, and it was closest to the stage.

I tried not to look into her diva demands too much. I miserably failed.

I've been prancing around like a soft cock all day.

"River went to bed early too. Do you want me to take his pay stub?"

"Ah…" I can't tell whether guilt or distrust hardens Miranda's face. "He… umm…" She scratches at her brow and releases a husky cough before admitting, "He doesn't get a pay stub."

"He doesn't?" If my voice were any higher, I'd check my neck for testicles.

Dark locks swish on Miranda's shoulders when she shakes her head. "His pay barely covers his board, and the rest Knox requested I put against his expenses."

Now my voice is fueled with annoyance instead of shock. "What expenses could he rack up that cost more than fifty K a year?"

Miranda's brow is lost in her hairline. "Fifty thousand?"

"That's Knox's going rate for his team. I've heard it a hundred times in the past week. Fifty thousand flat rate and a share of the royalties…" My words trail off when surprise softens Miranda's cut features.

"River is paid two dollars an hour, Laken. Before his… *promotion*"—she says the word like it doesn't hold the importance of its dictionary definition—"he only cleaned enough toilets to pay him a maximum of twenty dollars a week. His board is ten times that, so he owes Knox almost one hundred thousand dollars."

I try to simmer my anger by reminding myself Miranda isn't responsible for Knox's decision, but my concerns fire from my mouth like bullets from a gun. "What the hell are you talking about? He doesn't owe Knox a damn cent. We agreed that Knox would take care of River while I was away. That *all* his needs were covered. But even if that term was misunderstood like every other fucking agreement I made with Knox's family, what happened to the money I sent River each month?"

"I don't know," Miranda murmurs, her tone honest. "I handle all of Knox's accounts, both private and professional. Until a month ago, there were payments from a federal prison once a month, but there are no records of that money being forwarded to River."

"Maybe he used another account for River?" I don't know why I'm making excuses. I've had an inkling things aren't as they seem for a few days now. I just figured all my concerns were based on the feelings I've grown for my best friend's supposed girl.

Needing answers, I twist to face Dallas before asking, "Can you watch Nicole until I get back?"

I swore only hours ago not to leave Nicole's care in anyone's hands but mine, but Dallas was extremely remorseful about his fuck-up this morning, and he proved he's willing to do anything to protect her when he decked the paparazzo who shoved his camera in her face with enough force to mark.

I trust him to keep his eye on Nicole. Don't ask me to guarantee the same if her interview wasn't being undertaken on the hotel's roof.

When Dallas's head bob isn't enough incentive for me to leave, he adds words into the mix. "I won't let her out of my sight. You have my word"—he marks a cross over his chest tattoo hidden by his security shirt—"and my brother's."

Knox fooled him the same way as he fooled me—by convincing him to place his baby brother's needs before his own.

I slap Dallas's back in thanks before galloping down the emergency exit stairs. My adrenaline is too high to use the elevator. I need to disperse some of it in a healthy way before approaching Knox, because I can't guarantee I won't wring his neck if any of the thoughts in my head are true.

He's been acting like a dick all week, but his efforts today have topped the cake.

I honestly didn't know who the fuck he was when he stood across from me earlier and threatened me.

After everything I've done for him, I'm the last person he should be threatening.

"Knox," I call out when I enter the penthouse suites. "Are you here?"

He tapped out of Nicole's interview only minutes after it started, giving the same excuse as River. Exhaustion.

"Knox." When I notice a light under his office door, I rack my knuckles against the wood before pushing it open. "What the fuck?"

I spin away from the image of a woman with red hair on her knees before a man I once thought held a snippet of morals.

I was so fucking wrong.

"Don't act like this is something you've never seen before," Knox gabbers out like it's funny he's going through more prostitutes than underwear.

This redhead is the same one he walked to the door the other night.

"We once shared—"

"We didn't share shit," I fight back, pissed he's trying to bring me down to his level so soon after threatening to do exactly that. "You *hoped* I'd go sniffing for your leftovers. That isn't sharing."

"Leftovers you would have never had the chance to sample if it weren't for me."

With Knox's agitation unmissable, Candy says, "That's my cue to leave." After patting Knox's chest and assuring him he'll receive a discount next time, she flashes me an apologetic smile as she bypasses me in the entryway of his office before racing for the door.

When the slam of her exit booms down the hallway, Knox grumbles, "Thanks a lot, fuckhead. There's two thousand I'll never get back."

"You're worried about a measly two grand when you've been siphoning money from my brother for years?" My reply emulates the man I once was. A straight-to-the-fucking-point sharpshooter.

"What the fuck are you on about, Laken?"

Unappreciative of his mocking tone, I step closer to him. "The money I sent River every month. Miranda said it never moved beyond your bank account."

"What the…?" He exhales harshly. "She doesn't know what the fuck she's talking about. She's not in charge of my trusts."

"Trusts?" I ask, my anger too firm for confusion to make itself comfortable.

"Yeah, trusts. You know, where you put money for someone to keep it safe. That's where I placed River's money. I didn't want him wasting it on Twizzlers and sarsaparilla pop." His reply makes it seem as if I wired him a pittance each month instead of several thousand. "I'll take you down to First National tomorrow morning and sign the trust into your name. Then you can do whatever you want with it."

"I don't want it back. That money was for River. It was meant to help support him."

"My family is fucking loaded, Laken. We didn't need your money, so I put it away for him." My expression must show my trust is low, so he conceals his shaky laugh with a headshake. "What happened to you, man? You used to be cool."

If I was still seventeen, his comment might have stung. It doesn't have the same effect after spending ten years in prison for something I didn't do. "I grew up. Something you need to do quick fucking smart if you don't want to face the same cruel lesson I did."

Knox's back is up in an instant. "Are you threatening me?"

"How was anything I said a threat?" I watch him like a hawk before reminding him what's good for the goose is good for the gander. "I'm trying to stop you from falling through the cracks again because I won't be there to pick up the pieces this time, Knox. I'm not giving you another ten years of my life."

"You're trying to help me?" When I nod, he laughs. "Then why did you fuck my girl? Why steal the only sliver of hope I had for a good life?"

The angst in his tone makes me feel like a dog, but it won't stop me from standing up for myself as I should have a decade ago. "I didn't know she was your girl then." It seems as if tonight is the night for purging when I add, "I'm not even sure she's your girl now."

Knox glares at me as if he hates me. "Because you're an expert on relationships?"

"Because I remember Cecile's tears when she begged you to stop telling everyone you had slept together. You almost ruined her, Knox. Her father sent her to boarding school."

"Because she was whoring herself out!" he shouts, his voice reverberating. "Just like Nicole did when you came waltzing back into town like you owned the place." He bangs his fist on the desk. "She was *my* girl. I saw her first, and then you went and fucking ruined everything good about her. I loved her... I still fucking do, but you *stole* her from me. You *stole* her from your best friend."

"That wasn't my intention. I would have never touched her if I had known how you felt." When he hears my lie as readily as I do, I continue to try to pull the wool over his eyes. "Why do you think I fought so hard to stay away from her?"

"You say that like there's a possibility she'd pick you over me." With his ego beaten, he comes out swinging. "She doesn't want you, Laken. Not now or back then. She merely wanted to get back at me for the pregnancy scare."

My words are strained through a stiff jaw. "How the fuck could that be when you said she didn't know about that the night we hooked up?"

I don't mention this morning. Although I want to rub something more potent than salt into Knox's wounds, I'm not a man who airs his dirty laundry for the world to see.

I also won't talk badly about Nicole like that. If she wants Knox to know we hooked up more than once, she can tell him.

"I lied when I told you she was clueless." He looks me dead set in the eyes. "But that shouldn't shock you, should it? That's all I am to you. One lie after another."

"I never said that. Don't put words in my mouth."

"I saw the disgust on your face when you walked in on Candy sucking my dick." He scrubs at his jaw before spitting out words like venom. "Or was it hope that you'll have the chance to fuck my girl again when she exacts her revenge on the first perv she finds?" He rubs his hands together like he found a pot of gold under the rainbow. "That's not a bad idea. Force you together and get another guaranteed top-ten hit. With how fast a rival snatched up the first song you co-wrote, you'll pay back the fifty K you owe me in no time." His eyes are mocking when he locks them with mine. "What do you say, Laken? Want to take my whore for another ride?"

I'm over his desk and pummeling my fist into his face before any words past whore slip from his mouth. "Shut your fucking mouth before I force it to be wired shut."

I hit him for the second time and am swinging for the third, when my brother's frantic plea fills my ear. "Stop, Laken. Stop! We're family. We're meant to hug each other. We're not meant to hurt each other." He wraps his arms around me and yanks me back just as Nicole, Dallas, and a handful of the crew return from the rooftop. "I don't want to lose my family. I don't want to go through that again."

The joy Nicole's face hasn't been without for a second today is wiped clean when River's sobs reach her ears at the same time her eyes find Knox sprawled on the floor, bleeding and bruised.

Her words are slow and confused. "What's going on?"

"This maniac attacked me." As Knox wipes at the smear of blood dribbling from his brow, he stands. "I came down to make sure everything was ready for you to call it a night, and I found him rummaging through my office drawers."

"You're a fucking liar."

He adjusts his position to block me from Nicole's view. "He's crazy, Nicole. Deranged. He attacked me without warning."

I portray the man he's making out I am when he gets within touching distance of Nicole. My trust is hellishly low, so I don't want him anywhere near her. "If you touch a single hair on her head, I will bury you where you stand."

Knox doesn't flinch at the callousness of my tone because he is the only person in the world who knows for certain I am not a murderer.

That title belongs to him.

I simply took the rap for him when his father convinced me there was no way I could take care of River without his family's help. He said River would be placed in an assisted living facility within a month of Knox handing himself in because without Knox whispering in his ear, the numerous reports he'd concealed about our mother's abandonment would have reached the desk of Child Services years earlier.

His story was as convincing as the one his family lawyer spun when he said I'd be out in less than six months and the recipient of a hefty college grant for both River and me.

I've not seen a single dime.

I don't want a dime of his money, anyway.

I just want my life back.

Knox slants his head my way, smiles a bloodstained grin, then shifts his focus to Dallas. "Did you not hear what he said? He just threatened me." When Dallas remains as frozen as Nicole, he shouts, "Do your fucking job! Get him out of my damn suite!"

Dallas doesn't take a complete step. He's stopped by Nicole fanning her hand across his chest. "This isn't your suite. It's mine. I paid for it just like *every* hotel we've stayed at."

"You're taking his side? An ex-con you knew for two seconds before you opened your legs for him like the whores he sleeps—"

Nicole ends his sentence the same way my fists are dying to do but can't since River is still using his weight to pin me to the ground.

He hates when people fight, primarily when he classifies them as family.

As much as this sucks to admit, he sees Knox as more of a brother than he sees me. Knox took care of him in his formative years and gave him access to a lifestyle he would have never had access to if I hadn't taken the rap for Knox's mistake.

River thinks the sun shines out of Knox's ass, and I'm the villain threatening to disband his family for the second time in his life.

After righting his head, Knox works his jaw side to side before whispering, "Let's see if you still feel the same way when you read what the PI discovered about him."

When he pulls out a document from his desk drawer, River frees me from his hold so he can rock in the corner and mutter to himself, "You said you wouldn't use it against him. That you would use it to help him."

The world falls out from beneath my feet when it dawns on me what the document is. It is the form I was handed by Officer Riley when I was released from prison. The papers I trusted River would keep safe.

I can tell the exact moment Nicole reads my conviction on a record I should have burned. The color drains from her cheeks, and at the same time, her eyes fill with tears.

"Nicole—"

Knox cuts me off before I can promise her I'm not the man my conviction makes me out to be. "You haven't read the worst of it yet."

"Get your fucking hands off her," I snarl out when her scan of the second document he hands her has her knees almost buckling beneath her.

Nicole pushes Knox off her before sidestepping him to confront me head-on. "Is this true? Did you do what this states?"

"It isn't as it seems."

"He pled guilty," Knox interjects again. "It says so right there."

Nicole acts as if he never spoke. "Did you do what this says?" She doesn't give me a chance to answer. "Did you get behind the wheel drunk and crash into a fucking tree?"

She whacks at me with so much aggression Dallas has no choice but to intervene.

She'll hurt herself if someone doesn't calm her down.

As Dallas pulls her away from me, she continues to shout, "Did you flee the scene without checking if she had a pulse?"

Her knowledge of the accident Knox was a part of ten years ago is shocking. No one knows the details she's sharing. I was underage when I was arrested, and part of my plea agreement was that my record was permanently sealed, so how the fuck does she know so many details about it?

I learn this goes way deeper than her believing I'm a murderer when she breaks free of Dallas's hold and screams in my face, "Did you kill my sister, Laken? Were you behind the wheel of the car that was meant to deliver her home safely but instead veered into a fucking tree?" Tears stream down her face when she stammers through a sob, "Did you leave her to bleed out all alone?"

"No…" When she slumps forward before all my denial leaves my mouth, I catch her in my arms and pull her to the floor with me. "Nicole…" I roll her over until her head rests in my lap and her hair falls from her face. Her eyes are closed, and her mouth is slightly ajar.

I snap my eyes up to Knox. "What the fuck did you do to her?"

Knox's mocking tone breaks through the silence tearing me in two when he orders two men standing next to one holding a syringe to take Nicole to her room.

I try to push back the men I'm quickly realizing aren't from the standard road crew, but within seconds, the same sedative the doctor used to subdue Nicole takes effect. Then, the only fight I endure is the silent promise I issue River when our eyes lock across the room two seconds before blackness takes over.

I will make things right for both him and Nicole.

29
LAKEN

I'm startled awake by something sharp being rammed into my ribs. Despite the darkness of the room I'm waking in, my eyes squint like I'm standing inches from the sun, and my temples drill my skull like I have the worst case of heat stroke.

My body is acting like it's endured the workout of its life, and my mouth is drier than the desert, but my confused state isn't the most obvious sign that something is amiss.

I have no clue where I am or how I got here, and the anxiety it hits me with sees me attempting to snatch up the pointing object when it pokes me for the second time.

I say attempt because my hands don't move half an inch from the rickety chair my wrists and ankles are bound to.

"What the—"

"Don't worry. Everything is still in working order," says a familiar voice. "Regretfully."

After switching on a light, blinding me further, Knox pulls over a chair next to an industrial-sized boiler before straddling it backward in front of me.

Even feeling on death's door, I can't help but smile when I notice his bruised face. I don't know what day it is or how long I've been knocked out, but there isn't a drug on the market that will strip the image of my fists pummeling his face from my mind.

"Bet you wouldn't be acting so tough if I weren't restrained." I wet my lips to loosen up my words. I don't want anything to take away the actuality in my tone when I warn, "I'm going to take you down, Knox. I am going to fuck your life like you ruined mine." The more memories trickle through the haze, the angrier I become. "Her sister, Knox? Out of all the artists in the world, you had to sign your deceased girlfriend's sister to your label."

"Colette was never my girlfriend." The rage in his eyes simmers when he spots the surprise in my eyes. I never knew the name of the victim I'd allegedly stolen from her family. Knox's father said the less I knew, the easier it would be for me to move on after my brief incarceration. "And it's kinda fitting when you think about it. Colette's... what did Nicole call it?"—he hits me below the belt—"murder... saw me lose everything. So it's only fair her family returns it."

"Lose everything? What the hell are you talking about? Your parents are loaded."

"My mother is loaded," he corrects, his tone dipping. "She just wouldn't stop pushing. Prying. For some fucking reason, she believed I was more capable of committing the crime you were charged with than you, and she wouldn't give up hounding me until I snapped." He laughs like the only hospital he should visit to check his injuries is one for the insane. "She didn't just cut me off. She wiped my father clean. She took every. Last. Cent."

My admiration for Mrs. Samson slips when he murmurs, "On the agreement she never mentioned you or your arrangement ever again." Air whizzes from his nose as he struggles to hold back his laughter. "If you've ever wondered how much your freedom is worth, I can give you a figure. One hundred and seventy-three *million* dollars."

He wolf whistles like even he's impressed at the massive wealth his family accumulated since the slave era before he balances his elbows on his knees. "I didn't think she had it in her, but I reckon we might get close to that figure now."

Knox dumps a newspaper at my feet. Nicole is on the front cover. The article doesn't mention how she wowed her fans with back-to-back performances yesterday, however. It's talking about her "deranged stalker" and how he spent the last decade stalking her from his windowless prison cell.

"You fucking piece of shit." I fight like hell to get out of my restraints. My anger is enough to fray the thick woven material backed up with handcuffs but not enough to add to the cuts and bruises on Knox's face. "I don't know what the fuck you're playing at, but you've forgotten a vital part." I wait for his full attention before spitting out, "The girl you're trying to fool isn't dead this time. She wasn't left alone to die in the fucking car when you ran away like a coward. Nicole won't believe your shit. She's smarter than you give her credit for. She won't fall for your nice-guy act."

My blood boils when he smiles mockingly. "Nicole thinks I'm the only man she can rely on. She told me that only last night when she slept in my bed, snuggled in my chest."

I fight, thrash, and growl. "Let me out of these fucking restraints, Knox! You think you're all that, then fucking prove it! Stand in front of me toe to toe, you weak prick. Stop being such a fucking coward!"

"Even if I were to let you go, what would you do? Drag me to the police station and tell them I made you lie?" He shakes his head like he can't believe I'm so stupid. I don't understand his shock. I clearly am an idiot. I took the rap for him, didn't I? "That will only see you facing more charges, and you have *nothing* to prove your claim…" He scrubs at his jaw, hopeful it will hide the snide furl of his lip. His attempts are woeful. "Except perhaps how you weaseled your way into your victim's security team."

"You hired me. You offered me the position."

I chew on my words when he asks, "Where's the proof, Laken? I don't even have a signed employment contract to log in your defense."

My fight weakens when I recall stuffing his employment contract into his chest when Nicole got hammered by the paparazzi, but only by a smidge. "I won't let you get away with this. You lost your shit when you thought I'd stolen *your girl...*" I spit out my last words in a way even someone as fucked in the head as him can understand. Nicole was never his girl. "So how will you handle it when I upend your entire fucking world? You won't just be penniless when I'm done with you, Knox. You'll be rotting in a jail cell."

He swallows to clear the nerves from his voice before saying with a big sigh, "I kind of figured you'd get attached to the first person who feigned interest in you, hence me doing everything I could to keep Nicole away from you, so I put extra steps in place to make sure you'd heel like the dog you are."

The cuffs bend under the strain of my yank when he places a legal-looking document on top of the newspaper article. It is the guardianship contract my mother was meant to sign to relinquish all rights to River to me when Knox handed her the fifty thousand she demanded. Her signature is at the bottom of the legally binding document, but my name is no longer on the top.

Knox's is.

"There he is." I yank away from him when he tries to pat my head like I'm an obedient dog. "Should have known I only needed to use your brother to puppeteer you again. I'm sure she sucks dick good, but so do the other three hundred million fish in the sea." After mimicking the moves of a puppeteer forcing his puppet's motions, he collects the newspaper and guardianship contract from the ground, then spins to face the dimly lit exit. "Once she's earned back my share of my family's wealth, I'll shred this. Until then..."—he cranks his head back to face me—"I suggest you stay the fuck away. The restraining order Nicole requested this morning should be enough of a deterrent, but in case it isn't, you should know that isn't the only nationwide newspaper with your face on the front page. It's *everywhere*, and her fans are a crazy bunch of fuckers."

He salutes me before pulling open a heavily weighted door that streams sunlight into the room and darting through the opening.

"Help!" I scream, hopeful the thick steel door is for show. "Help!"

By the time the crank of the steel door opening booms into my ears, my wrists are bleeding, and the feet of the chair I'm restrained on are closer to the maintenance room I'm hoping has a hacksaw capable of breaking through my restraints.

"What the…?" Dallas's eyes shoot to me before they follow the droplets of blood my endeavor to escape dotted the floor with. I almost laugh when his eyes lower to the cuffs and he asks, "Do you have the key?"

"If I had the key, would I still be sitting here?"

He doesn't reply. He enters the maintenance room and returns with a Stanley knife and a screwdriver. The knife shreds through the rope part of my restraints like a hot knife through butter, but it takes a while for the screwdriver to buckle the steel cuffs enough for me to slip my wrists through the once-tight opening.

While rotating my wrists to ensure nothing was broken during my endeavor to free myself, I notice several needle pricks in my arm. I look like a drug addict.

I have a million questions in my head, but I focus on what matters the most. "Have you seen Nicole or River since last night?"

The first expression to cross Dallas's face is worry. It is closely followed by unease. "Last night?"

Were we not the only ones knocked out?

"When Nicole was given a sedative."

"Umm..." He wets his lips before confessing, "Knox ordered everyone out of the room not long after they sedated her. I haven't seen River or Nicole since then." He takes a moment to register the panic on my face before he pulls his brows together. "The stuff written about you is daunting, Laken. They're saying you were recently released from prison and were incarcerated for the death of Nicole's sister. Is that true?"

I almost lie until I remember that's what got me in this position. "Yes. But it isn't what it seems. I just don't have time to explain right now. I need to get to Nicole and River."

Dallas slows my steps to the exit. "They checked out days ago."

"Days?" I couldn't sound more shocked if I tried. "Nicole performed on the roof of this hotel last night. She's not due to check out for a few more days." My voice tapers the more I speak. My blurry head isn't responsible for the unease of my words. Dallas's faint headshake is.

"Nicole performed *three* nights ago. Then checked out the morning after..." He drops his eyes to my chest like the words Nicole shouted in my face were as bruising as my fists to Knox's cheek. "She hasn't been seen by the public since, and they're unhappy about that."

"Fuck." As my fingers worsen the thump of my skull, I try to make sense of everything. I'm aching, and my stomach won't stop gurgling, but that's because of the situation I find myself in, isn't it?

After a few moments of silent deliberation, I say, "Knox won't keep her hidden forever. He needs her out in public, selling the records." I check my watch, my shock too much not to balk when I realize three days have flipped over on its date mechanism. "She has a TV interview booked this morning. He secured a huge promotional slot after I put her singing in the rain on YouTube. He won't let her miss it."

"That was you?" When I nod, Dallas says, "That's not what's being reported on TMZ."

"Nothing being reported right now is true, but as I said earlier, I don't have time to explain." I flash him a quick smile in gratitude for his assistance before racing for the exit.

The midmorning sun streaming into the foyer of the hotel is blinding. It hinders my vision so well that I have no clue I'm walking onto a minefield until a piece of rotten fruit splatters on my shirt. "What did you do with Nicole, dipshit? Did you tie her to the boiler of her hotel?"

The haggler sends another piece of fruit sailing through the air as the crowd gathered outside the hotel, which Nicole planned to use as her home away from home, shifts their focus to me.

"Hey, isn't that the guy from Lateline?"

"That's Nicole's stalker."

"He's the convicted killer I read about in the paper."

"Get him!"

The last chant surges the crowd into a desolate onslaught. They peg everything and anything at me before rocking against the police barrier so furiously that it soon collapses.

My eyes bulge when they sprint for me like they do Nicole, but instead of begging for autographs and photographs, they threaten to dismember parts of my body and lodge them into any available orifice I have.

Only a foolish man would stand his ground when it's a hundred to one, so instead of waiting to see if they'll make true on their threats, I bolt down the sidewalk and weave in and out of the pedestrians hogging the last of the space.

During my sprint, it dawns on me how effective Knox's smear campaign was. Even men dressed in pricy suits recognize me when I dart by them, and I won't mention how many women snarl at me.

I'm the most hated man in America but also the most determined.

30
NICOLE

The afternoon sun blasts into my room when the curtains are dramatically opened. It is so bright, even with my eyes clamped shut, I risk a new wrinkle when I squint past the glare to see who's waking me.

"It's been three days, Nicole." I don't need to drink in more than the shadowy figure at the end of my bed to know who's attempting to drag me to the land of the living for the hundredth time in the past seventy-two hours.

I pissed Knox off when I canceled the interview I was booked to be a part of only hours after having my world ripped out from beneath my feet, so I'm aware of the desperation in his voice when he says, "Three days of canceled obligations. If you keep this up, you won't have a single fan left to purchase your album."

"I don't care," I reply, my tone honest.

I feel like a complete and utter idiot, so the last thing I want to do is show my face in public.

"What happened to giving the fans what they deserve?" He doesn't wait for me to formulate a reply, much less voice it. "Do they deserve to be ignored by someone they once thought loved them?"

"I do love them. I just... I..."

I can't face anyone if it means I have to admit I fell in love with the man who killed my sister. I'm not even accepting Jenni and Emily's calls right now. That's how horrible I feel. How ashamed.

Colette didn't die on impact. She was still on the phone with our sister, Petra, who she had called at the commencement of her trip.

Although she got a handful of words out after the horrifying crunch of the vehicle hitting a tree forced Petra to wake our parents, she was in too much pain to advise them of her location.

No matter how hard I try to forget them, I can still recall the screams that left my mother's mouth when the other end of the line went quiet.

They haunt my dreams to this day.

"It's all a farce."

"You're talking nonsense." Knox yanks my hands down from my face before forcing our eyes to align by bobbing down in front of me. "It was only a farce when you listened to your cunt instead of your heart. All women make the same mistake. You're just lucky you can put the publicity to good use." He plucks me from my bed, his grip firm enough to announce he isn't taking no for an answer, before he marches me toward the bathroom. "You have thirty minutes to get ready." His next words are mumbled. "It'll take you at least that long to fix the bags under your eyes, so get your ass moving."

The callousness of his words is shocking. He spent the first hour of my semi-conscious state apologizing on repeat. He said he had no clue Laken had been to jail, much less what he was sentenced for, and then when he found out who his victim was, he was physically sick.

While on his knees, begging for forgiveness, he cried—snot bubbles and all.

I truly thought he was remorseful for bringing up my family's pain so close to a time when I needed to be my best.

Now I'm struggling with more than guilt.

"Knox—"

He cuts me off by hurting me more. "Colette would roll in her grave if she knew how much you were giving up for the man who killed her." He acts ignorant to my quivering chin and wet eyes while waving his hand around the bathroom I tainted only days ago. "Wasn't this meant to be her life? Aren't you doing this for her?"

Since I can't deny his claims, I remain quiet. My love of music was founded through Colette. She was the true star of our family. She sang at church every Sunday and had planned to study music after high school. She had a true gift—a gift she wanted to share with me.

After gifting me my beloved songbook, she helped me write my first song. It was one of the songs I performed during my radio blitz. The audience ate it up, and I almost burst into tears when the radio production assistant gave her songwriting credits on the radio's website.

This was her dream as much as it is mine, so although Knox's hit is below the belt, he's right when he says she'd be upset that I'm throwing away an opportunity not many people get.

But that doesn't change the facts. "I'm not ready to go out in public yet."

"Then I guess it's lucky they came to you."

When I follow the direction of his narrowed gaze, I'm reminded that I still have a heart in my chest. The living room of the suite is in the process of being converted into a talk show set. A dozen production crew are setting up cameras, microphones, and two director chairs that will remain noticeably absent today.

My eyes sling back to Knox when he announces, "You'll do a sit-down interview on the couch, followed by a live performance on the roof since it's still set up with the equipment from your last performance."

I groan. Out of all the places he could have picked for me to sing, he chose the rooftop I thought would be a good place to tell Laken the truth.

Rooftops are our "thing," so I thought he'd realize relatively fast who I was referencing when mentioning the new relationship I was endeavoring to get off the ground.

Were our thing, I correct myself.

Upon hearing my gripe, Knox rubs his hands together while saying with a sly grin, "If you want a say in your career, Nicole, you need to occasionally get out of bed."

It's lucky he leaves the bathroom fast, because he is a mere second from being knocked out by the toothbrush holder I hurl at the door when my anger becomes too great to ignore.

⸻

After a long shower and an extensive hygiene routine, I feel semi-human.

My heart still feels wretched, though.

I can't believe I was so foolish to take someone at face value. I should have dug deeper into Laken's past before listening to the petitions of my heart. I should have instilled some of the madness Isaac undertakes anytime he hires a new team member.

I should not have trusted neither my gut nor my heart.

It is easier to acknowledge that now because I'm not standing across from the man who made the mountains seem so large and scary.

The way I felt when I was with Laken made the impossible feel doable. He made me believe I deserved this opportunity, and knowing it was a sham hurts.

As I flatten my skirt to ensure my outer shell hides my hideous insides, my mind drifts back to the memories that are being unearthed one grainy image at a time.

You'd swear from the look of devastation that washed over Laken's face when I asked him if he was the driver of the car that claimed my sister's life that he was as blinded by my accusation as I was when Knox handed me his criminal record.

I couldn't believe the names in front of me or comprehend how our lives had crossed paths again so soon after his release.

Laken was underage when he was charged, and although that doesn't usually conceal records for eternity, his lawyer was adamant there'd be no signed confession without a promise his record would never be made public.

While waiting for the authorities to locate Colette's crash site, my father was adamant the man who'd left his daughter to die alone in a cold, abandoned field would rot in hell, but after a private one-on-one meeting with the DA and the accused's lawyer, his opinion changed.

After a long talk with my mother that included more expletives than I've ever heard her speak, my father accepted the terms offered.

He's struggled to make peace with his decision ever since.

Colette's death changed him. It negatively impacted our family in a way I'll never truly be able to explain, but we sought comfort in the fact the driver was handed a far harsher penalty than he would have gotten if we had taken the case to court.

The coroner ruled Colette's death as an accident. The defendant had been drinking, but since it wasn't in excess of the legal limit, they believed his claim that he'd swerved to miss a dog. Add that to his sworn testimony that he abandoned his car to search for help, and he could have had an extremely lenient DA willing to offer a substantially lower sentence.

I realize I'm no longer alone when Knox waves his hand in front of my face. "Earth to Nicole. I've been calling your name for the past minute."

"Sorry, I was…" When I can't find an excuse that won't have me bursting into tears, I sidestep him before exiting the bathroom to collect my cell phone from my purse.

My heart leaps when I see how many missed calls and messages there are. Then it tries to break out of my chest cavity when it bleats with my FaceTime messenger tone.

As Jenni's name flashes across the screen, I drift my eyes to Knox to stupidly seek permission to accept her call.

Submissiveness isn't usually my forte. I'm just out of sorts.

When Knox's expression shifts to miffed, I roll back my shoulders before adopting the stance I should have taken a long time ago. "I either accept her call or invite them here to keep an eye on me. *If* they're not already halfway here."

Since he can't deny the accuracy of my statement, he says, "Five minutes. You're due on set in an hour and far from ready."

When he exits my room with a mocking laugh, I lower my snarl before connecting my video chat with Jenni.

"She's still not answering," she announces, unaware our call is connected. "The label will have to take a hit. I'm sure it won't kill Cormack. He's uber-rich—"

"Hey," I interrupt, stopping her both mid-rant and mid-packing. She's stuffing sweatshirts into a carry-on bag like LA is as cold as London.

A smile tugs my lips to one side when her eyes rocket back to mine so fast that one tear filling them dislodges. I'm not happy I've made her upset. I simply love how much she loves me.

We're like family.

"Nicole…"

When Jenni can't get any more words out through the frog in her throat, Emily takes over the campaign. "You scared us half to death. If River hadn't kept us updated, we would have been on your doorstep days ago." The tired droop of my eyes has her missing my surprised response at who's kept them in the loop. "How are you?"

"I'm okay."

Jenni sees straight through my lie. "No, truly. How are you?"

I flop onto my bed before confessing, "I feel like shit. My head is thumping. My skin is clammy and covered with bumps, and I'm reasonably sure I'm about to get my period." I do everything humanly possible to stop my mouth from spilling my next confession, but it blurts out before I can stop it. "I'm also heartbroken."

"Oh, honey…" A smidge of gaffer tape fixes a crack in my heart when Jenni ends her sympathy-filled reply with a demand for the men behind her. "Back to packing. The jet leaves in ten minutes. If you're not on it, you're staying here."

Knox hits me with a stern glare when I join him in the living room thirty minutes past the scheduled time of my interview. It took ages to convince Jenni and Emily to stay with their partners and children in the United Kingdom. It was almost as long as it took them to assure me I was not as stupid as I felt.

Laken didn't solely pull the wool over my eyes.

He convinced them he was a good guy as well.

Even Noah had nothing but praise for him when he interrupted my conversation with Marcus earlier this week to get his opinion on hiring Laken as a producer on my album. He usually keeps everyone at arm's length, his panic about losing them higher than a fear of living a lonely life.

"You should consider yourself lucky this show is prerecorded."

When I follow his stalk across the living room to tell Bonnie I've arrived, my heart faces its third stutter of the day. River is standing at the entrance of the corridor that leads to the bedrooms. His face is as white as mine, and his clothing is on par with someone about to attend a funeral.

Looking at him hurts. His genes can't be denied, even with an extra chromosome adding a cute edge to his sharp features. He has more than a handful of similarities to his brother, and the longer I drink them in, the firmer the guilt strangling my heart becomes.

When Knox notices the direction of my gaze, he snarls, "I told you to stay in your room."

"It's fine," I assure him, stopping his stomp to River and forcing the production crew's focus back to me. "He's not doing any harm."

Knox lowers his voice to barely a whisper. "I don't want you feeling uncomfortable."

Although I'd give anything to hug River until his shakes subside, my hurt is too high to do that right now. So instead, I tell Knox I'd feel more comfortable if he pointed me in the direction of the makeup chair.

"I won't win over anyone if I look like a ghost."

My inability to get over my hurt for someone undeserving of my wrath doesn't maim me as badly as expected when River's shakes lessen as Knox pivots away from him so he can guide me to the other side of the living room.

After soundlessly apologizing to Bonnie for my tardiness, I return my eyes to the hallway.

It is empty.

River is gone.

His emotion-packed retorts are on par with his brother's.

Too emotional to take all the blame, I shift some of it onto Knox. "What happened wasn't River's fault." When he looks at me, lost, I add, "You yelled at him for no reason."

Bonnie hums in agreement with me as Knox *pffts*. "That wasn't yelling."

"It was, and it isn't the first time you've done it in the past three days." I might have been high on the sleeping tablets a doctor prescribed so I could sleep off my grief, but they weren't strong enough for me to miss a handful of heated conversations between Knox and River.

Well, I can't really call them conversations since they were one-sided.

Knox looks set to continue arguing, so you can imagine my shock when he caves instead. "But I'll be more mindful of my tone from here on out." He hits me with pleading puppy-dog eyes. "Am I forgiven?"

I try to make it seem as if my heart isn't tattered into pieces. "Depends." I wait until he's almost frothing at the mouth before finalizing my reply. "Did the terms of this interview stipulate a buffet? I'm starving."

Knox bumps my shoulder with his hip before signaling for a production crew member to bring me a sugar-coated donut.

31
NICOLE

As Bonnie adds a generous helping of blush to my cheeks, the executive producer of the show impatiently waiting for her to work her magic asks to speak with Knox.

Bonnie's brows stitch as firmly as mine when Knox checks if I'm okay being left unaccompanied with Bonnie. "Of course she'll be fine." She *tsks* him before waving him away like she's been dying for a minute alone with me.

I realize that is the case when she asks a second after he leaves, "Now that that's out of the way, spill. What I'm hearing can't be true. Not Laken. He's the good apple in the bunch."

"It's true," I reply, my voice as high with shock as hers. "He pled guilty."

"I… It just…" She's a little more aggressive with the mascara this time around. "It doesn't make any sense. I saw how he looked at you and the pride in his eyes when you sang. It has to be a mistake."

"I wish it were…" I snap my mouth shut when I realize what I said. I'm giving away that I had feelings for the man who tore my family apart. My parents are still together, but it's never been as good as it was when all their children were sleeping peacefully under their roof.

I love Bonnie, but I wish she'd stop talking when she says, "I think I could forgive him." When I peer up at her, she laughs before bopping my nose with the tip of my favorite lipstick. "What? That man is fine. I'd even consider his little brother just to sample those genes."

"Bonnie!"

She laughs, grateful her taunt pulled me from my morose state. "That boy needs love. We all know he ain't getting it here anymore." She pulls the cap off the lipstick before leaning in with a sigh. "I'm glad you said something to Knox. I don't think I could have held my tongue for a moment longer." She gestures for me to pucker my lips. While sheening them up, she mutters, "You'll survive his wrath better than the rest of us. He's gone through road crew like underwear the past few days."

I had wondered why the crew today seemed so unfamiliar.

I had assumed they were part of the talk show's staff.

After a clear gloss to bring out the brightness of my lipstick, Bonnie steps back to admire her handiwork. "A priceless work of art."

"If only my insides matched my outsides." I squeeze her hand to assure her I deserve a sledging before shifting my eyes to the corridor the rooms sprout off.

God, I feel terrible about how I handled things earlier. River is as innocent as I wish his brother was. He doesn't deserve the brunt of anger any more than he deserves to be yelled at by Knox.

Not willing to leave River upset for a moment longer, I ask Bonnie, "Do you think we can stall them for a few more minutes? I need to speak with River."

"Honey, they're so eager, they rocked up before the sun. I'm sure a couple more minutes won't hurt them." Her sassy attitude dips when her eyes lock on Knox on the other side of the living room. "You just might need a detour." She nudges her head to Knox. "He's extra clingy today, and you won't get a single truth from River with him gawking over your shoulder." A second after her eyes pop open, she knocks the glass canister she uses to clean her brushes off her makeup cart. It lands in my lap and sees me leaping to my feet. "I'm so sorry, Nik. I was rushing. I always make mistakes when I rush."

Catching on to her ruse, I say, "That's fine. I've got another skirt in my room." I shift my eyes to Knox, who is watching our exchange with an arched brow, before assuring him, "I'll be back in a minute."

He peers down at my ruined skirt before jerking up his chin.

I mouth my thanks to Bonnie and race for the corridor, but instead of darting into my room, I continue down the hall until I'm standing outside River's room.

"River, have you got a minute to speak?" When my question produces nothing but silence, I push open his door. "River…" I stray my eyes to the attached bathroom before dragging them over his empty bed. It looks like it hasn't been slept in. The corners are pulled tight, and the pillows are propped against the studded headboard.

When I notice a thick book in the middle of his bed, I pace closer. The sun peeking through the drawn curtains at the side of his room reflects a phone book that's been out of print for years. It's open on business listings, and multiple motels and hotels have been crossed out in red ink.

River's search was extremely thorough. He's gone through dozens of listings; some look like they were scratched out more than once.

I drag my fingertip over a listing for a two-star motel several miles from here before pacing toward the window responsible for the chill in the air.

"River…" I call out again, hopeful he's not upset enough to forgo the prime spot for my upcoming performance.

The acoustics on the roof are incredible, but they're even more wondrous from the fire exit stairs only one floor below since they're bounced off the buildings surrounding ours.

When I find the fire escape empty, I attempt to close the window. River has been a bit sniffly since our concert on the rooftop, though he'll never admit that.

No matter how hard I pull, the window doesn't budge. I learn why when a gust wafts up the curtains. River propped the window open with his tablet, which is odd considering it's one of his most valued possessions. I can still recall how misty his eyes went when I gifted it to him on his birthday. I'd pre-downloaded all his favorite shows so he could watch them anytime he wanted. He didn't need to wait for Knox to be finished with the television.

My brows stitch when I notice a Post-it note stuck to the screen of his tablet.

Nicole's eyes only.

When I peel off the Post-it note, I find a second message.

Open it.

I can't hold back my grin when I spot his password hint written at the bottom of his message.

He's older than me and a lot taller, but I will always be the best-looking Howell.

With shaky hands, I type "Laken" into the password box of River's tablet. My heart rattles against my chest when it opens on the notes app.

Nicole,
It's my fault. Laken did it for me.
Please don't hate him because he loves me.
He loves you, too. Maybe even more than me. He just has a hard time showing it since our mother didn't teach him how

to love like he taught me. She forgot to tell him that the people you love aren't meant to hurt you the most.

Laken has never hurt or yelled at me. He is the best big brother I could ever ask for. He taught me how to ride a bike and promised when he got a car, he'd teach me how to drive too.

Then he went away to keep the promise he made to me when our mother left.

I begged him to come back, and after a long time, he finally did. But now they're trying to take him away again.

I can't let that happen. He is my brother, and families are meant to look out for each other.

Please don't be upset I left.

Laken will take care of me. He always has.

Rivadlfkjaijier.

He must have gotten interrupted because a string of letters ends his note like he had to store his tablet away in a hurry.

"Oh, River…"

As my guilt doubles, a message pops up on the screen of River's tablet.

EMILY:
Thank you for the update, River. We recently spoke to Nicole, and she does seem better today, but are you okay? Your voice sounded a little croaky in your last video. I hope you're not getting sick. Em xx

When I click on Emily's message to open it, I learn how River kept them updated on my heartache's progress. He took video blogs. In almost every video, I'm sleeping, but a handful see me begrudgingly eating some of the food wheeled into my room each day.

A broad smile creases the corners of my eyes when River gives a running commentary of my every move in a video that saw me gulping down unsweetened coffee since I was too lazy to go into the kitchen to fetch sugar. "She's like a bear with a sore head, forced from hibernation by the very people wanting to hunt her."

I realize Emily wasn't the only one he was communicating with when I scroll down his contacts list. My parents were given daily vlogs, and he's been in contact with Petra for longer than I've been heartbroken.

They talk about the weather, flowers, and rainy rooftop concerts while exchanging a handful of pictures. Laken and I feature in most of them.

It's weird looking at our dynamic from the outside in. Almost surreal. He seems completely different from the man his criminal record depicts.

He's humble and sweet, even occasionally shy.

And the adoration he expresses when looking at his brother can't be denied.

He'd do anything for River.

Anything at all.

As words River wrote circle through my weary head, a shadow fills the door of his room.

"What are you doing in here, Nicole?" Knox asks, his tone suspicious.

"River left," I reply while shaking his tablet.

"What?" I can't tell if his voice is shocked or relieved. "Are you sure he's gone? He might have just popped out to grab some sarsaparilla. He's notorious for wandering off when hungry."

"He hasn't gone out for a soda. He left me a note."

"Where is it?"

His eyes stop darting in all directions when I shake the tablet for a second time. Then he snatches it from my grasp so fast he almost cracks the screen.

"It's fucking locked," he mutters before tossing it onto the bed. Too impatient to acknowledge I couldn't have read his note without the passcode, he asks, "What did it say?"

The unexpected fear in his voice has me speaking slowly. "That families are meant to have each other's backs and that Laken needs his help."

"Is that where you think he's gone? To find Laken?"

Nodding, I stray my eyes to the phone book that announces River's investigative skills.

"All right." Knox takes a moment to think before he checks the time on his watch. It is flashier than Laken's but just as old. "I'll send someone to"—he reads the circled hotel name—"Dusty Sky Inn to pick him up."

"You don't think we should go? He sounded pretty determined to stay away in his letter." *And heartbroken,* but I keep that to myself.

I balk when he highlights my word. "*We?*" He doesn't give me a chance to respond. "No, *we* don't have time to galivant across LA. Things are progressing too quickly for that." He bands his arm around my shoulders and guides me down the hallway. "You have an interview to conduct and a live performance to give." He chuckles like the situation isn't as dire as it is. "And I have a fuck ton of records to sell."

When I'm shoved into my room to change out of my stained skirt, I spin to face him, disgusted he's placing record sales above River's safety. "Knox—"

"I'll bring him home, Nicole. I promise you, by the end of tonight, he'll be standing across from you, sorry he ever left."

My trust is low, but since my faith in myself is even lower, I bob my head like it isn't screaming at me to stop being so blind.

32
LAKEN

"Samson. S-A-M—"

The clerk from the umpteenth hotel I've called this evening cuts me off. "There's no guest of that name at our hotel."

I wet my lips before testing the friendliness of her tone with another name. I tried River's before Knox's, so there's only one name left on my list. "What about Nicole Reed? Is she a guest?"

"Nicole Reed…" Just her saying Nicole's name sends my heart into a frenzy. It thuds as wildly as it did this morning when Dallas pulled one of the hotel's town cars in front of me and demanded I get in.

I was seconds from being trampled.

"Reed? Did you say Nicole Reed?" the clerk double-checks.

"Uh-huh. R-E-E-D."

"I know how it's spelled." Her tone is no longer friendly. It is clipped and stern. "What did you say your name was again?"

"I didn't—"

"Listen here, you little rat-breath punk. Even if Nicole were at our hotel, I wouldn't tell you she was here. She deserves a—"

I hang up before she can rip me a new asshole like almost everyone I've encountered today. Dallas saved my hide this morning at Nicole's original hotel, but he said I was on my own when I tried to enter the studio Nicole was meant to record at today.

I got as far as the lobby before they tossed me out.

The security guard at the restaurant on the itinerary I memorized was kind enough to batter my ego in the alleyway siding the pricy establishment. It saved my shame from being broadcast across the internet.

My endeavor to find Nicole has been recorded, uploaded, and shared millions of times. Although I'd rather not be mocked by strangers, some good came of my public humiliation. It proves Knox's claim that Nicole requested a restraining order was false.

A handful of LA's finest added to the vault of evidence of my desperation.

After breathing out the worry that hasn't stopped circling in my stomach, I run my finger down the outdated phone book of the two-star hotel I paid for in cash after pawning my father's watch. I've called all the five-star hotels, so I shift my focus to the ones ranked half a star lower.

"Rot in hell!"

I pull the hotel's phone from my ear in just enough time. The clerk's phone must be corded like the one I'm using because the clang it makes when she returns it to its receiver is deafening.

Needing to take a breather before I snap, I move to the window of my room to peer out at the stars.

"Stars don't exist in the sky in LA," I murmur to myself when the only twinkling of lights are junkies melting their stash.

The motel clerk took one look at my arm before issuing a stern warning. "No shooting up in your room. If it can't wait until you're no longer staying at my fine establishment, do it in the alley."

"I'm not a junkie," I replied.

He scoffed at me before showing me my room and explaining how the square televisions don't have built-in antennas, so if I want to watch something, I need to move the rabbit-shaped antennas on the top to the desired setting.

I've been too busy to watch anything, but I realize how stupid that was of me when my eyes lock with a television in the room across from me. It is playing an interview of the woman I've spent the past twelve-plus hours searching for.

"Come on," I plead to the television in my room when it doesn't turn on, even with my pressing the remote button on repeat.

I whack its side and check the batteries are in properly before I recall the check-in saying the remote is for the built-in DVD player.

When my tug on a knob switches on the ancient contraption, I mentally fist bump the air. The picture is grainy, but the sound is clear.

After inching back so I can peer out the window, I squint until I spot the program emblem of the show my neighbor is watching. I stab my finger into the channel button on repeat until I reach my desired channel, then adjust the antenna to make sure Nicole's face presents as unblemished as it does in real life.

I step back when the flecks of blue in her eyes can't be missed. She looks good. Tired, but Bonnie has concealed that well.

"It's been quite a week for you this week, hasn't it, Nicole?"

Nicole shyly smiles before nodding. "You could say that."

"Multiple one-on-one interviews with the who's who of the entertainment industry. Numerous viral hits on YouTube and TikTok, and album sales that would make any music exec's eyes flash dollar signs," the host reads off a card in front of her. "You must be proud."

"I should be," Nicole replies. "It's more than I ever thought possible, but—"

The talk show host cuts her off. "But you've had a handful of downfalls as well." She slices Nicole's confidence in half when she brings up the video that almost ended her career before it truly started. "We're assuming this was a joke gone wrong. You surely knew the public wasn't ready for that." She laughs before shifting her focus to what I assume is the production crew. "We will *never* be ready for that disaster."

"That performance was never meant to be released," Nicole stammers out, her tone as low as her shoulders. "It was recorded without the permission of the label and myself."

"Do you think he uploaded it?" The host's voice couldn't be more ear-piercing.

"He?" Nicole asks as her eyes dance between the host's, her confusion unmissable.

"Your stalker." It dawns on me that this is the first time Nicole has faced the ruse Knox commenced to keep us apart when the host instructs her production assistant to hand Nicole the newspaper Knox showed me this morning. "He's a handsome chap. Aren't all the psychos?"

Since her question is directed to the at-home audience instead of Nicole, Nicole doesn't answer. She continues reading the article that slanders my family's name alongside hers, her focus only shifting when the host announces, "The YouTube accounts are under different names, but perhaps his new account was so you wouldn't know he almost ended your career before fixing it."

"I'm sorry, I don't understand what you're saying."

The lady pats Nicole's hand like she has air for brains. "I'll explain during the commercial break." She locks her eyes with the camera. "We'll be right back with delicious recipes for the upcoming pumpkin spice season and a live performance from our very own pumpernickel. See you soon."

When I throw the remote at her head, pissed she insulted Nicole on air by comparing her to a dense loaf of bread, the power of my hit knocks the antenna to the ground.

I curse my short temper to hell when I notice an antenna ear on the floor. It's snapped clean off.

Not eager to miss Nicole's performance, I snatch up the broken antenna and head for the twenty-four-hour reception desk. A hairdryer won't fix my fuckup this time around.

Halfway there, I'm stopped in my tracks by a dark figure standing under the awning. He's wearing a black sweatshirt, black pants, and black sneakers, but no amount of darkness can conceal the humbleness of his soul.

"River..."

When he lifts his downcast head, tears burn my eyes.

He's crying hard and drenched like he walked in the rain for miles.

"How did you get here?" I ask while yanking off my coat to cover his shuddering shoulders.

His sniffles are the worst they've been all week when he confirms my suspicion. "I walked." He drags his hand under his runny nose. "I didn't have any money for a taxi, and the men at the hotel work for Knox." He locks his drenched eyes with mine. "He said it would help you. That's why I gave it to him. He said it would make Nicole love you more." He bangs his head with his fist. "I fucked up, Laken. I'm so sorry."

"It's not your fault. You—"

"I broke everything. I fucked up." He tears at his hair, his anguish too firm for him not to self-harm before he once again hits himself. "Now Nicole doesn't want to hug me. She hates me."

Clumps of his hair fall to the ground when I band my arms around him and pull him to my chest. He fights against me and pleads for me to let him go, but just like he wouldn't let me do anything that would have seen me taken away from him again for another nine years, I hold on tight until his tears have soaked my shirt with more than rain, and his begs for forgiveness no longer ring in my ears.

33
NICOLE

"It isn't just Laken's name you're slandering, Knox!"

When my roar startles one of the production crew dismantling the set in the living room, I almost back down. I hate airing my dirty laundry for the world to see, but this time, I hang it in front of living, breathing witnesses. "You took it too far!"

The story of Laken being the driver of the car my sister died in could have been left out of the media spotlight. My live performances were already making waves, so we didn't need the sympathy vote. However, Knox still drafted multiple press releases on the very subject I wanted to keep out of the public eye.

He put not just my hurt out for the world to see but my family's as well.

"I wasn't asked a single question about Rise Up or songwriting today during my interview. Every single question either focused on my 'alleged' stalker or my sister's death." I whack him in the chest when my anger becomes too prominent to ignore. "They even went as far as visiting Colette's gravesite to get footage for an upcoming segment. That's beyond disrespectful. I've never been more disgusted."

Nothing I say gets through to him. He stands at the side of the almost-back-to-normal living room, looking smug as he rides the gravy train to the station.

"And what about River? Did you consider him at all while dragging his family's name through the mud?"

"His brother is a murderer." He laughs like he said something funny. "His name can't get more stained."

"Last time I checked, the dangerous operation of a motor vehicle that results in a death is not murder!"

I don't blame the men surrounding us for throwing the electrical equipment into their travel cases with no concern of breakages.

I want off this train too and this is my life.

Knox doesn't wait for them to leave before reminding me of the cruel words that left my mouth three nights ago. "*You* called him a murderer. *You* accused him of killing your sister."

"I was upset and confused. I didn't know what I was saying."

Am I really defending him?

Am I taking the side of the man who left my sister to die alone?

I shake off my thoughts for a better time. Today needs to be about Colette. "It doesn't matter what I said. I'm appalled you're making my family suffer through Colette's loss all over again for a couple of extra album sales. It makes me sick to my stomach that you're trying to profit from this. So much so, I'm considering pulling the album's release."

I swear steam billows out of his ears as he snatches up my arm. "What the fuck did you say?"

As his nails pierce my skin, I say, "Let go of me. You're hurting me."

When my plea falls on deaf ears, I look at the men still lingering in the living room, soundlessly seeking their assistance. I realize they're paid by Knox when they pay no heed to the cruelty of his hold. They don't come to my defense at all. They continue packing away their equipment like they're the only people in the suite.

Even scared, I yank out of Knox's hold before assuring him my family's pain will never be used for financial gain. "I won't let you do this, Knox. Death isn't a gimmick for profit."

When he throws his head back and laughs as if I couldn't be more wrong, I glare at him before storming into my room. He might think his contract is ironclad, but I have news for him.

I wanted to do this off my own back, but that doesn't mean I was stupid enough to sign a contract without having a lawyer look at it first.

"Regan ripped Knox Records' original contract to shreds before drafting a fairer and more balanced proposal." I crank my neck back to Knox before giving him one of the many narrowed glares he hit me with when he used Apollo to outvote me on concepts for my album. "If you didn't read it before signing it, that's a 'you' problem."

My anger augments when my scan of the dresser in my room has me failing to locate my phone. That's where I left it after speaking with Jenni and Emily. I placed it on top of my songbook—my missing songbook.

"Where is it?" I ask, my fury high. "Where is my stuff?"

"I don't know what you're talking about." For someone who lies for a living, Knox is horrendously bad at it. "I didn't take your shit, Nicole," he murmurs when I barge past him to storm into his office slash bedroom to search for my belongings. "I put it away for safekeeping." He looks as smug as a pig in mud while rubbing his hands together. "That book will sell for a fortune in a few years."

"It's not for sale. It will *never* be for sale."

He butts his shoulder on the doorjamb when I march to his desk and throw open the drawers. His laid-back response exposes I'm searching in the wrong area, but my anger is too perverse to see sense. That songbook is the only tangible thing I have left from Colette. The rest are memories.

Memories I wish weren't so strong when I pull a copy of Laken's record from Knox's soft leather briefcase in the bottom drawer of his desk. It isn't solely the sheet of paper Knox handed me three nights ago. It includes details of Laken's plea and his handwritten confession.

It even includes photographs of the crash scene.

Even though I shouldn't look, it is the equivalent of a train wreck.

I can't tear my eyes away.

The damage is mainly confined to the passenger side of the car. The driver's side took hardly any of the impact. The fender has a deep scrape, and the side mirror has been knocked off, but the damage is so minute that the fancy silver jaguar on the middle of the hood looks as new as the day it was driven off the showroom floor.

Jaguar? How could Laken afford to drive a Jaguar? His watch is an antique, but he has no clue of its worth.

"What the fuck are you seeing?" Knox asks when he spots my expression. He pushes off the doorframe and enters deeper into his office. "There's nothing in there but his confession." He drags his hand under his nose, a telltale sign he's struggling to keep a rational head. He did it multiple times during a lengthy recording session previously. "They checked. They said they scoured every inch of it. It should only tell you what you already know." His eyes adopt a wild, fierce look. "Laken *killed* your sister. He *murdered* her because he'd rather waste years behind bars than raise the kid she was trying to pin on him."

He hasn't just undone his entire campaign that he was clueless about my sister's accident until his PI dug up information on Laken. He's wholly obliterated it.

No one knew Colette was pregnant. It was kept hidden because it didn't benefit her case. The DA said it could have hindered it, so with my family's reputation in our local church on the line and my father's realization nothing would bring his daughter back, he agreed that sealing the records of the case was best for all involved.

The only people who know Colette was pregnant are her direct family... *and the man she went to tell the night she died.*

Between sobs, she told Petra that her meetup with the baby's father hadn't gone to plan and that he suggested she get an abortion.

She told Petra she couldn't do that, that she'd raise her baby with or without the father's help.

The crash occurred not long after that.

"Oh my god. It wasn't an accident."

It dawns on me that I said my statement out loud when Knox replies to it. "That's what I'm trying to tell you. Laken killed her. He veered his car off the road when she refused to get an abortion."

"But why would he do that? He's taken care of his brother since he was a child. That proves he isn't the type to bounce on his obligations. He isn't you." I intake a sharp breath when my final sentence rings through my head on repeat. *He isn't you.*

As theories flood my head, I flick through the arrest document like a madman, my hunt undeterred by Knox attempting to rip it from my hands.

I find what I'm seeking a short time later. The registration papers for the Jaguar.

"You were the registered owner." I stumble back when shocking truth after shocking truth pummels into me. "That's what he meant when he said he defrauded the government. He lied… for you."

"It wasn't for me," Knox denies, his tone not as harsh as anticipated. My heart squeezes with guilt when he admits, "It was for River." His laugh is off. "My father only had to make out he'd held back Child Services a handful of times, and Laken was willing to do anything to ensure he continued to have his support until he turned eighteen. He wasn't eager to sign up for time behind bars, though. It took a lot of weaselly tactics to get him over the line, but we eventually got there. Probably helped that he thought he'd only get six months." I hate the pride in his eyes when he locks them with mine and says, "It's a shame your sister wasn't as put off by the church's possible shame as your parents. Petra told the DA that Colette was pregnant. Her recent miscarriage saw her throwing the book at Laken."

My reply is stern enough to break through his husky chuckles. "You son of a bitch. You won't get away with this."

His teeth gleam as brightly as the moon breaking through the storm clouds when he says, "I already have. And you're not wrong. My mother is a bitch. But don't worry, she'll get her dues not long after you and Laken get yours."

I race to beat him to the door when he turns for it.

I'm about to step past him when a wildly flung fist sends me flying backward. I skid across the polished floorboards of his office, my slide only ending when I crash into his desk without enough force to keep me down until he exits his office and locks the door behind him.

34
LAKEN

When a smell unlike anything I've ever smelt lingers in my nose, I peer down at River, who's still huddled into my chest, watching the moon slowly break through the clouds.

Aware he's been busted, he murmurs, "I'm sorry. I get gassy when nervous."

I pray for a strong gust to blow away the stench before replying, "There's no need to be nervous... and you can't solely blame nerves for that." He laughs when I say, "That smells like you ate one too many tacos and washed it down with a bottle of fish sauce."

With how long it took to calm him down, I'm so grateful for the laughter that chops up his reply. "I might have had a couple of tacos last night." He tilts his head back, putting his big eyes on full display. "Bonnie wanted to make sure I was eating. She bought me some food." He blinks several times before confessing, "I might have also eaten the leftover scrambled eggs you made for the crew when Nicole got sick."

"Now the smell makes sense." With the mood a lot lighter than it was an hour ago, it takes me longer than I care to admit before it dawns on me what he said. "You ate *my* scrambled eggs?"

"Uh-huh," he replies, nodding. "They're always so much better than the hotel's because you use real butter."

I love his compliment, but it isn't the time to gloat. "How did you eat my eggs, River? Did you take them with you when you checked out of the hotel?"

He scoots forward before twisting his torso to face me. "We didn't leave the hotel."

"We?" I know who he's referencing. The admiration in his eyes tells me everything I need to know. I just want him to spell it out for me.

"Nicole and me." I realize I have a lot of damage to fix when his tone drops as he confesses, "And Knox. He's still there too."

"At the hotel we checked into when we first arrived in LA?"

He nods again. "Knox told Nicole that she was safe from you. That he had men on every floor."

"And in the lobby," I mutter when I recall Dallas telling me they'd checked out days ago.

I'm such a fucking idiot.

"No!" River shouts, his gas loud and proud this time around as he pulls me back down. "This is why I'm nervous. He will hurt you if you try to take Nicole away from him. He told me he would. That's why I had to leave her. I left her with him."

I grab his fist before he can whack his head again and bring it down to my face. "Look at me." When he shifts his wet eyes in any direction but mine, I repeat, "Look at me, River!" His eyes are drenched and full of panic. "The decision I made ten years ago was wrong. I took the cheat's route. I know that now." I wipe at his tears while saying, "And that's why I know I can't do it again. Leaving this to Nicole, forcing her to fix *my* decision, is the cheat's way out. It isn't fair to expect Nicole to live with my mistakes... Just like it wasn't for you ten years ago. I'm sorry that I made the wrong choice, River. I'm sorry I hurt you instead of protecting you like I promised, but this is my chance to make things right. This is *our* chance to make things right."

"He... He... He..."

"Can't hurt us anymore if we don't let him. I promise I will *never* let him hurt you again, River."

With how badly my decision hurt him, my word should mean nothing to him.

But for some reason, he believes me.

35
NICOLE

I'm unsure how long I spend at Knox's office door, banging on it before I shuffle back to his desk. It could be an hour. It could be ten minutes. Time isn't easy to tell when you don't have a single device at your disposal.

I searched Knox's office high and low since he left. The only thing I discovered was more evidence of his evil ways.

Laken didn't steal my song as pledged. I found its crumpled remains in the bottom of Knox's briefcase. It was just below the note Laken had written to say he had to run an urgent errand and for me not to leave the bed until he returned with coffee.

Knox played us from the start.

I'm just lost as to why.

Why go after my family? It makes no sense. If anything, my family should have been hunting him. We probably would have if we didn't believe the perpetrator was behind bars.

God, the system failed both Colette and Laken. Laken should never have had to worry about River's guardianship any more than the DA shouldn't have squashed Colette's voice for a quick plea. The system is meant to be on the victim's side. It's meant to be their voice.

I startle when an unexpected knock hits Knox's office door.

"Laken," I blurt out before racing for the door.

I stop partway there when a mocking laugh trills under it. "Not yet, but I'm sure it won't be too much longer. He seemed so eager when I let him go; I knew it wouldn't take him long to track you down. I just failed to factor his snitching brother into the mix."

"Why are you doing this, Knox? Why torment the people who look up to you? River—"

"Steals *everyone's* attention. Even my mother's." It dawns on me how he's spent our time apart when the slosh of a bottle he raises to his lips can't be missed. After a hefty gulp, he continues. "She happily left me with nothing but set River up with a trust fund big enough to start a record label."

Reading between the lines, I say, "A record label you're running into the ground."

His laugh is downright creepy this time around. "Statistics will prove you wrong. After every musician's death, sales skyrocket. Some sell more albums in the afterlife than when they're alive." He almost sounds sincere when he murmurs, "I hadn't planned to take this route. Originally, I just wanted to keep Laken around in case I needed another scapegoat, but then you started listening to *him* and taking *his* advice. So I had to mix things up."

He guzzles down enough alcohol to make my stomach churn before he continues. "Tell me you've never rushed to buy a physical copy of an album when you've heard of an artist's untimely demise, and I'll call you a liar." His plan becomes even more apparent when he adds, "Sales will quadruple on any record when an upcoming music starlet is killed by her deranged stalker at the start of what should have been her illustrious career. He just needs to get here so I can frame him for your murder before making it seem as if he turned the gun on himself." I hate everything about him when he says with a laugh, "If his sidekick comes with him, he'll either be an innocent bystander of a tragic obsession or return to cleaning my toilets. I'm not bothered either way."

"Your plan has more holes than a sieve. I've only known Laken a week. He won't risk his brother's life for someone he's only known for a week."

He sees straight through my lie. I understand why. There's no pussyfooting around feelings when you've read the lyrics I wrote the night I met Laken.

I was instantly smitten, and they expose that.

"Then I guess my guy outside the Dusty Sky Inn was mistaken when he told me they left five minutes ago." I hear him shrug. "Guess we're only minutes away from finding out which direction they went."

Too frustrated not to lash out, I throw anything I can get ahold of in the direction of his chortling tone. His desk. His chair. The pricy curtains hiding the fire exit stairs from anyone scared of heights. They're all tossed in his direction until the moon bouncing off the steel grates of the fire escape captures my attention.

That's my way out.

My ticket to freedom.

That's access to a voice that can warn Laken of the imminent danger he's racing toward.

I just need to overcome my fear enough to step onto the ledge.

I need to be brave.

"Step onto the railing," I say to myself, my voice a mix of Jack's and Laken's. "No peeking."

"I'm not," I reply, confident I'm too scared to look down.

This building is taller than the one in Ravenshoe, and the steelwork is flimsier.

I couldn't look down even if I wanted to.

"It's one floor," I assure myself when fear takes hold. "One floor, and you're free."

I consider chickening out, but the roar of the crowd my hotel hasn't been without the past week leaves me no choice. They haven't spotted me scaling the edge of a building built long before Ravenshoe was founded. They're screaming obscenities at the man they believe is my stalker, warning him to stay away.

Laken has arrived, which means he's eighty-seven floors from disaster.

Confident this is the right thing to do, I climb the rickety ladder as if it is part of the swing set in Noah and Emily's backyard. I race up like a monkey climbing a tree before I hook my leg over the ledge of the rooftop and drag myself to safety.

After the quickest pause to catch my breath, I sprint for the sound equipment the road crew left after today's performance. They said they'd be back in the a.m. to dismantle it.

Once all the switches are at the right setting, I grab the microphone and press my lips to the fluffy material keeping the static charge at a minimum.

In my fear, I almost make a costly mistake. I was seconds from screaming for help. But mercifully, before I make a mistake I could never take back, I remember that Knox is only one floor below me, so my fate is already decided, but Laken could still be freed of this madness.

He could still escape.

So, instead of using my voice to announce Knox's insanity to the world, I use it to free a man of the burden he should have never had.

I give Laken back his voice.

The first line of my impromptu performance is rickety, but I push through my nerves before reminding myself the best songs are the ones that come directly from the heart.

"Even though it had only been a week,
I should have given you the chance to speak.
I was scared and frightened and unsure who to trust.
But that burden didn't belong on your shoulders, Laken,
and I'm so very sorry I stuffed up.
You gave me back my voice as I was about to give up.
Picked me up when I was certain I'd run out of luck.

In under a second, you had me believing it was more than fate.
That saw us meeting on that rooftop where I thought you'd taken your date.
You're not the man your false criminal record makes you out to be.
Not close to the menace Knox will forever be.
You're honest and truthful and everything he's not.
Because you didn't just teach your brother how to love.
You made him everything Knox is not.
He's the reason you need to walk away.
To take back the power that tried to lead you astray.
Only then will he understand the pain he forced on you that day.
Only then will he face the consequences of the
crime he chose to undertake at Johnston Bay.
That's why I'm on my knees, begging you to walk away...
Because although he needs to be punished,
my heart won't survive the outcome if you choose to stay."

I realize I closed my eyes partway through my performance when a clap startles them open. Knox is standing in front of the ladder I scaled to reach the rooftop.

He should look pissed—I ruined his plan—but for some reason, he looks smug.

I learn why when he says, "Your lawyer was good, but even she forgot to remove the first refusal rights of your contract. That means I get first dibs for any song you write, whether on your death bed or before what the media will claim was your unfortunate demise when your guilt became too much." He screws up his face like vomit scorched the back of his throat. "It was a little dramatic, but when fans learn it was written only minutes before your suicide, they'll gobble it up."

With a gun he pulls from the back of his trousers, he gestures for me to join him near the ledge.

"No." My reply isn't as confident as I hoped, but Knox still hears it.

The fury that lines his face announces this, not to mention his shouted words. "I wasn't fucking asking! Come. *Here.*"

"No." That's closer to what I'm aiming for. Stern and determined. "You've already gotten away with murder once. I won't let you do it again." The anger on his face is unlike anything I've ever seen when I ask, "Or should I say twice since you killed your own child?"

"That whore's bastard had nothing to do with me!"

His gun flings to the rooftop door when a familiar voice says, "You're a liar, Knox." Laken raises his hands before lifting his shirt to show Knox he's unarmed. It lessens Knox's shakes, but only by a smidge. "But that isn't your fault. You learned from the best." He flashes his eyes to me for the quickest second to make sure I'm okay before he slowly approaches a shaky Knox. "What did he tell you that night, Knox? That she was going to ruin your family? That you'd have to share your inheritance with a child he didn't want?" I realize there's more to this story than I realized when Laken says, "Let me guess, he even blamed her for the demise of his marriage."

Knox's reply is spat from his mouth like venom. "She knew he was married. She knowingly fucked a married man."

"Then why was she upset when she showed up unannounced the night of your eighteenth? Why did she cry when she saw the family portraits adorning the walls?" When his questions remain unanswered, he asks one only Knox can answer. "Why did you offer to drive her home when you knew she was pregnant with your father's kid?"

"Because he said it was my responsibility. If I didn't want my trust dwindled to nothing, I had to help him." His priorities are undoubtedly skewed when he mutters, "He was going to take it all away. Every last cent. I had to do as asked." Knox locks his watering eyes with me. "She was going to ruin everything." He stops, screws his nose up, then starts again. "She *did* ruin everything. My mother took us to the cleaners. She left us nothing."

The gun rattles as rigidly as Knox's breaths when Laken discloses, "Your mother has been missing for over a year."

"Because she's living it up with one hundred million dollars."

"Her bank account hasn't been touched by her either." When Knox stares at Laken like there's no way he could know that, Laken breathes heavily out of his nose. "Toilet cleaning wasn't River's sole chore. He also had to collect the mail. During a heavy storm, the envelopes were soaked and disintegrated in his hands. He tried to save the documents inside with a hairdryer. They were statements from your parents' joint bank account. The only card using the substantial funds the prior three months was in your father's name."

"No! He said she took it all. That she wiped us clean. She only left money for River."

"The money in River's account is the money I sent him, Knox." Laken works his jaw side to side before correcting, "The money that *was* in River's account was the money I sent him."

Even with the truth blatantly obvious, Knox still tries to deny it. "No. My father wouldn't do this to me. He loves me. That's why he left me the task of running my car off the road. He knew I'd do it for him. That I'd take care of his whore and her baby. I killed them for him!" His voice reaches an ear-piercing level at the end of his statement, meaning the microphone I left on has no issues picking up his confession. It broadcasts his crime for the world to hear.

After yanking out the cable responsible for his suddenly white face, Knox points his gun at my head while projecting his voice at Laken. "You think you're so fucking smart, but you forget you can't manipulate the master. By the time help arrives, you'll both be dead, and I'll deliver a sob story about how you forced me to confess to a crime I didn't commit seconds after forcing her to sing the words you wrote while on a three-day bender." He tosses my songbook onto the ground. It falls open on a page that shows Laken's handwriting has been traced on repeat.

"Are you sure about that?"

When Knox's eyes shoot to Laken, who is pulling up the hem of his trousers to show his ankle is without the tracking accessory it's been wearing the past week, Laken uses the distraction to his advantage.

He races for me so fast the grunt he releases when he pushes off his feet almost drowns out the noise of a bullet being dislodged from a gun.

With one of his hands protecting the back of my head and the other bracing to take the impact of our fall, Laken tackles me to the ground just as the rooftop is filled with shouting voices and clomping feet.

"Get down!"

"Place your hands behind your back."

"Stay down!"

I have no choice but to follow the federal officers' directive. Laken is pinning me to the ground with his body—his *lifelessly* still body.

"Laken?"

It takes everything I have to push him off me, and when I do, my world is ripped from beneath my feet for the third time in my life. He's been shot, and the entrance wound is puddling blood around his frozen and rapidly whitening frame.

"Help me!" I scream while rolling Laken onto his stomach to compress his wound. "It's not my blood," I assure the brunette, who falls to her knees beside me two seconds later. "He's been shot. He's bleeding." My voice croaks when I add, "He wasn't meant to be here. He was supposed to walk away."

I repeat my mantra over and over again as they load Laken onto a gurney and race him toward an awaiting ambulance. Then I repeat it even more when the last man who should be offering me comfort wraps me up with one of his famously warm hugs.

"He wasn't meant to be here. He was supposed to walk away."

EPILOGUE
NICOLE

Nerves take flight in my stomach when I walk onto the stage at the annual Country Music Awards in Nashville's Bridgestone Arena. The mood is subdued. I'm not surprised. It always is when I perform this song. It was the number-one hit on my first album. It is titled: "It Should Have Been Him."

As I stand behind a microphone, the scene reminds me so much of the ending of *A Star is Born*. I can see the tears in the audience's eyes, and I haven't even started singing yet.

That is how much this song moves people.

That's how much it moves me.

After wetting my lips to loosen them up, I soundlessly signal to the stage crew that I'm ready.

I've performed this song hundreds of times since it was written, but there won't be a single time the opening line doesn't come out croaky.

> *It should have been him...*
> *Breaking down and shattering into pieces....*
> *He stole you just as the magic was starting to begin...*
> *And now I'm skeptical about letting anyone else in...*
> *I don't want to ever forget...*
> *all the precious moments we shared...*
> *The love, the laughter, the feelings...*
> *The memories we'll never get...*
> *He took the best parts of you...*

And twisted them to make you out to be the villain…
Before he broke my heart in two…
and made me doubt every word we'd written.
But I'll never forget…
all the precious moments we shared…
The love, the laughter, the feelings…
The memories we'll never get…
Your flame is too bright to be missed…
It burns inside of me…
And is the only reason I exist.
It is your name that will be
forever whispered by my lips…
I'll never forget…
all the precious moments we shared…
The love, the laughter, the feelings…
The memories I'll never regret…
You gave me my voice, my spirit, my fight…
All I want is for you to hold
me for one more night…
You were my light…
the most precious part of my life…
and the sole reason I've continued to fight.

I take a moment to relish the crowd's applause before I open my eyes and direct them to the third row back from the stage. The members of Rise Up are far from country artists, but they're here, waiting to see if I'll receive an award again this year because they will forever support me as I will them.

After blowing them an air kiss to thank them for their unwavering support, I apologize to the production assistant vying to get me off the stage so the stage crew can set up the next performance, before I hotfoot it through the thick stage curtains. The award everyone is waiting on is minutes from being announced.

I'm barely two feet away from the curtains when the vultures of the media circle me. Their interests haven't waned in the slightest over the past eighteen months. They've watched me stumble, then documented my resurrection with just as much footage.

"Nicole, is it true Rise Up showed up tonight to dispel claims Marcus is set to marry this weekend?"

When a camera is shoved in my face, I politely push it back before replying with the standard, "No comment."

"Nicole, what do you think your chances are of another Artist of the Year award?"

I dodge the blinding lights hindering my vision while answering, "If you'd let me back to my seat, time will soon tell."

I give up on my endeavor when another question is flung at me: "Nicole, are you less confident because the shy girls are always shoved to the back of the pack?"

"Shy? My ass. There isn't a shy bone in her entire body." My heart beats in an irregular pattern when the paparazzi part like the Red Sea until they expose the face of the man denying their insinuation that I'm shy. "Believe me, I've inspected every single inch."

Laken smiles boastfully when he spots the heat creeping up my neck before he uses the walkway the paps created to join me in the wings of the stage.

The bullet that zipped through his body and narrowly missed several vital organs doesn't impede the sexiness of his swagger in the slightest. It barely kept him in the hospital. He discharged himself on day three so he could return to Ravenshoe with me to attend a meeting with the current DA, who reopened my sister's case since the last one did such a terrible job.

Knox survived the rooftop raid, and although he foolishly believed double jeopardy would come into play, he forgot one crucial part of his live confession.

He admitted to killing my unborn niece or nephew.

There are laws against that in my home state—laws the newly appointed DA of Ravenshoe used to ensure justice was served to the right people this time around.

Although Knox's confession assisted with his arrest, his days were already short. It is rare for cocaine addicts to keep secrets, so when Knox got too comfortable with Candy, he started spilling secrets that weren't his to share.

He told her how an accident at Johnston Bay was actually a double homicide, and hinted that the man who went away for it was up for parole.

With Candy's help, Ravenshoe PD put two and two together. They reopened Colette's case before assigning a special division from their department to investigate Knox's drug-inspired insinuations.

They thought he was falsifying claims to add credit to his story that he was related to the mafia kingpin Candy worked for, but when they arrived at our hotel looking for Laken, and Knox gave them the runaround, true suspicion formed.

Knox thought sending them away would stop them from accessing Laken's DNA, but he underestimated Isabelle and Ryan's determination when it comes to justice for the innocent.

The blood they illegally took from Laken the day of my impromptu performance proved he wasn't the father of Colette's baby, but even they were shocked by the turn of events that unraveled after the federal officers stormed the rooftop.

They were there to arrest Laken.

And they begrudgingly did exactly that an hour after we landed in Ravenshoe.

Laken pled guilty to a crime he didn't commit. Although the charges he admitted to the second time around were lower than the ones Knox and his father were about to face, there are legal ramifications when you lie to law enforcement officers.

The time Laken had served behind bars mercifully meant his newest conviction was more a formality than anything. His record was adjusted, and he tried to move on with his life, unaware *any* criminal record would hamper his ability to have River's guardianship in his name.

He fought the courts for weeks, his victory only awarded when I put my name on the guardianship order he was endeavoring to get approved.

"Are you sure you want to do this, Nicole?" he asked that day, his shock blatantly obvious. "This means you'll be stuck with me for eternity. Where River goes, I go. We're a package deal."

I nodded without pause for thought. "As sure as I've ever been."

It hasn't exactly been smooth sailing since then. We had an album to produce to ensure I could return the funds Knox obliterated from River's trust when he paid off Laken's mother, and the eyes of the world were on us.

We should have fallen flat on our faces.

Thankfully, creative minds feed off tension. In weeks, I had a songbook filled with pressure-cooker moments, and my relationship with Laken became unbreakable.

He didn't mock my ideas or tell me they weren't sellable while producing my album. He encouraged my growth as an artist and let my voice be heard with a wide range of genres.

My favorite genre is country pop. Almost every song I've released in the past year has risen to the top of the country music charts. But the song I performed tonight, the one I wrote about my sister, doesn't slot into one genre. It's a ballad—a symphony. A true example of love like the thumb Laken tracks across my cheeks to make sure they're dry.

I always get teary-eyed when performing "It Should Have Been Him."

"Are you okay?" Laken asks once he's confident my cheeks are streak-free.

After twisting my lips, I sheepishly nod. "I think so."

"Only think?" He guides me back to my seat, his walk not stalled by the paparazzi, who have learned the past eighteen months that they either move out of the way or Laken will force them to. He still sees himself as my bodyguard even with his title being officially upgraded to music executive. "What's on your mind?"

In a dead-serious tone, I reply, "Frank and beans."

Laken's swallow is audible, but he remains quiet.

"And how many paparazzi I'll need to bribe to keep them off the front pages of every gossip magazine in the country."

When my elbow lands in his stomach, his boyish laugh does wild things to my insides. "Why am I getting blamed for this?" He continues talking before I can tell him that part of the guardianship order should include him not letting his little brother leave the house in skintight leather pants. "It's your fault."

"My fault? How is it my fault?" I lower my voice when we reach the audience eagerly awaiting the Artist of the Year announcement.

An award is the last thing on my mind when Laken tugs me back before he crowds me against the outer wall of the stage. He doesn't kiss me or make me want to pretend the bleachers aren't packed with the who's who of the music world. He just stares into my eyes until my brain turns to mush before he whispers, "Because he thinks my frank and beans were what attracted you to me."

I could point out all his other finer points.

I could stroke his ego like the announcement of my name for Artist of the Year for the second year in a row does mine.

But instead, I cock a brow and say, "Only thinks?"

The End!
If you enjoyed this book, please consider leaving a review.
Facebook: facebook.com/authorshandi
Instagram: instagram.com/authorshandi
Email: authorshandi@gmail.com
Reader's Group: bit.ly/ShandiBookBabes
Website: authorshandi.com
Newsletter: https://www.subscribepage.com/AuthorShandi

ALSO BY SHANDI BOYES

Denotes Standalone Books

Perception Series

Saving Noah *

Fighting Jacob*

Taming Nick*

Redeeming Slater*

Saving Emily

Wrapped Up with Rise Up

Protecting Nicole *

Enigma

Enigma

Unraveling an Enigma

Enigma The Mystery Unmasked

Enigma: The Final Chapter

Beneath The Secrets

Beneath The Sheets

Spy Thy Neighbor *

The Opposite Effect *

I Married a Mob Boss *

Second Shot *

The Way We Are

The Way We Were

Sugar and Spice *

Lady In Waiting

Man in Queue

Couple on Hold

Enigma: The Wedding

Silent Vigilante

Hushed Guardian

Quiet Protector

Enigma: An Isaac Retelling

Twisted Lies *

Bound Series

Chains

Links

Bound

Restrain

The Misfits *

Nanny Dispute *

Russian Mob Chronicles

Nikolai: A Mafia Prince Romance

Nikolai: Taking Back What's Mine

Nikolai: What's Left of Me

Nikolai: Mine to Protect

Asher: My Russian Revenge *

Nikolai: Through the Devil's Eyes

Trey *

The Italian Cartel

Dimitri

Roxanne

Reign

Mafia Ties (Novella)

Maddox

Demi

Ox

Rocco *

Clover *

Smith *

RomCom Standalones

Just Playin' *

Ain't Happenin' *

The Drop Zone *

Very Unlikely *

False Start *

Short Stories - Newsletter Downloads

Christmas Trio *

Falling For A Stranger *

One Night Only Series

Hotshot Boss *

Hotshot Neighbor *

The Bobrov Bratva Series

Wicked Intentions *

Sinful Intentions *

Devious Intentions *

Deadly Intentions *

Coming Soon

Nanny Dispute *

Protecting Nicole (December 26) *

Made in United States
Troutdale, OR
02/14/2024